the impossibility of us

KATY UPPERMAN

the impossibility of us

Swoon Reads | New York

A SWOON READS BOOK

An imprint of Feiwel and Friends and Macmillan Publishing Group, LLC

175 Fifth Avenue, New York, NY 10010

THE IMPOSSIBILITY OF US. Copyright © 2018 by Katy Upperman. All rights reserved.

Printed in the United States of America.

Our books may be purchased in bulk for promotional, educational, or business use.

Please contact your local bookseller or the Macmillan Corporate and Premium Sales

Department at (800) 221-7945 ext. 5442 or by e-mail at

MacmillanSpecialMarkets@macmillan.com.

Library of Congress Cataloging-in-Publication Data is available.

ISBN 978-1-250-12799-0 (hardcover) / ISBN 978-1-250-12800-3 (ebook)

Book design by Rebecca Syracuse

First edition, 2018

1 3 5 7 9 10 8 6 4 2

swoonreads.com

Matt . . .
thank you for the idea,
and everything else.

Don't worry that your life is turning upside down.

How do you know that the side you are used to is better than the one to come?

—Rumi

elise

On May 1, a week after my seventeenth birthday, my mother makes an announcement that sends my world spinning.

"We're leaving San Francisco," she says while we sit in the breakfast nook of our Pacific Heights condo, the home in which I've lived for the last fifteen years. She splashes cream into her coffee, then eyes me, charily, over the top of her reading glasses. My jaw might as well be resting on the tabletop. She winces, then a slew of words comes rushing out of her mouth. "Oh, Elise. Before you get upset, let me explain."

"I don't need you to explain," I say, my voice lifting in both volume and pitch. Because I'm already upset—I'm *extremely* upset. "We can't leave San Francisco. Junior year's almost done, and next year—next year's my senior year!"

"I know. And I understand—I do. But, Lissy . . . Audrey and Janie. They need us."

Audrey, my sister-in-law, and Janie, her three-year-old daughter. The list of things I wouldn't do for them is very short.

"Audrey would never ask for help," Mom goes on. "She's too strong.

Too proud. But let me tell you: Single parenthood's not easy. Work and school and Janie . . . She's got so much on her plate, and I miss her. I miss them both, so much."

My icy heart thaws, just a little. "I miss them, too."

"They're only a couple of hours south," she reminds me, spreading cream cheese over her bagel, then mine. Cleverly, she's stretching out the quiet, allowing time for the space behind my ribs to continue warming with sympathy. After another few moments, she says, "Of course you can come back to visit, to see your Pacific Heights friends. And after your senior year, you'll be back in the city anyway, at the San Francisco Art Institute."

Her declarations are flawed at best. Yes, Audrey and Janie live a few hours south, in a tiny coastal village called Cypress Beach, but they might as well be on Saturn—that's how different their town is from my city. Also, my mom knows good and well that I don't have much in the way of Pacific Heights friends; I did a superb job of isolating myself three years ago, after my big brother died. And anyway, I haven't even applied to the San Francisco Art Institute yet, let alone gotten in. What if I don't? What if I never make it back to this city I love?

None of that matters, though. Nor do my absolutely opposing feelings on the subject of changing high schools a year before graduation.

If Audrey and Janie need us in Cypress Beach, we have to go.

I sigh, a resigned sound, and bite into my bagel.

It tastes like cream-cheese-slathered cardboard.

———

During the next couple of weeks, Mom advertises our condo as available for sublet, collects a mountain of empty boxes from the neighborhood grocery store, and begins to fill them with our earthly treasures. I finish my junior year in a haze of packing paper and Bubble Wrap, dreading the day we're slated to leave.

I love my sister-in-law and niece with astonishing intensity, but I do *not* want to move.

I was born in Manhattan, but we left when I was two, immediately after the terrorist attacks of September 11. My dad was (and still is) a workaholic, so consumed by his finance career he was apparently immune to the rising fear that seized New York City after the Twin Towers fell. Mom was not. But they were married and we were a family, so we made the cross-country move as a quartet: Dad, Mom, Nick, and me. Turns out, my dad isn't a fan of the West Coast. He bailed on California (and us) after less than a year.

For me, San Francisco has always been home. It's the city where my brother and I spent countless hours exploring steeply pitched streets, and where I mastered the fundamentals of photography. I conquered public transportation here and came to appreciate the quiet beauty of art museums and to crave soup served in crusty sourdough bowls. I had my first kiss in Lafayette Park.

San Francisco is the city of my heart.

As far as I know, Cypress Beach doesn't have public transportation. It doesn't have art museums. It doesn't have high-rises, or all-night Thai restaurants, or Fisherman's Wharf and its rich chowder, ladled into warm, hollowed-out bread. It doesn't have bustle and midnight sirens and air scented like exhaust and garlic and, sometimes, sewage. It certainly doesn't have memories of Nick.

But Cypress Beach has Audrey and Janie, and so it will have Mom and me.

We roll out of town the day after school lets out.

elise

Aside from the predictable mundaneness of driving down the California coast, house hunting, and unpacking, the last several weeks can only be described as a loneliness-infused shit storm. Without verbalizing an objection or complaint (this move isn't about me—that's been made perfectly clear—so why bother?), I've plummeted through the first three stages of uproot-induced grief (denial, anger, bargaining) and bottomed out at depression, where I'm currently wallowing like a duck in a waning pond.

In an effort to catapult me into that final, glorious, *elusive* phase of acceptance, my mom let me pick paint for my new bedroom—any color on the spectrum. She was less than pleased with my chosen shade, Obsidian, which rolled onto the walls and ceiling like thick tar. Though the silent protest felt good initially, sitting in my deep-space bedroom now isn't doing much to improve my bleak mood.

Here's the thing: Cypress Beach repels teenagers the way citronella repels mosquitoes. After a month, I've made one acquaintance, Iris Higgins, who lives in the cottage next door to ours and is half a century beyond my age bracket. She's into gardening—like, obsessively into gardening—and she's bananas, in a good way.

My mom worries. She wants me to make friends before school starts (in a month and a half... *God*). She's been begging me to attend the New Student Orientation at Cypress Valley High, scheduled for a few weeks from now, and she's constantly dropping not-so-subtle hints about my needing to spend more time in town, at the coffee shop or the one-screen movie theater or the library, because those are places cool kids hang out, apparently.

Two weeks ago, in a last-ditch effort if ever there was one, she surprised me with a corkscrew-haired mess of a pup who gallops around our cottage on feet she's yet to grow into and chews table legs like they're made of rawhide.

Her name is Bambi, and I love her.

She's the reason I'm out now, at the crack of dawn, trudging down the dog-friendly beach that runs parallel to our dog-friendly town, holding a slobber-soaked tennis ball between two fingers. She's tearing around up ahead, a honey-colored ball of fluff, scaring seagulls with her ferocious *woof, woof!*

"Bambi!"

She skids to a halt, kicking up sand, swishing her tail like it's a whip. She looks at me with big cocoa eyes, trusting and adoring and expectant. I chuck her ball into the waves, exactly as she wants, and she leaps after it, crashing into the cold water like it's her job—which I guess it is. She's a goldendoodle, a golden retriever crossed with a standard poodle, a designer dog my mom undoubtedly paid too much for because the newest member of the Parker clan had to be hypoallergenic. Bambi has *hair*, not *fur*, because my niece, Janie, inherited allergies from her mama. Janie's the one who branded my dog with her name, actually, a nod to the clumsy Disney deer.

She springs out of the Pacific, neon ball clamped between her jaws, and dashes at me, sailing over mounds of slippery, stinky kelp that have washed onto the beach with the tide. She pulls to a halt just short of my shins, dropping her disgusting ball at my feet. She shakes, a slo-mo, full-body convulsion, and I scramble to block my camera from the drops of water that go flying. I should be annoyed—I'm wet now, and the morning is gray and windy, not exactly summer-balmy—but it's impossible to be frustrated with Bambi. She is at all times oblivi-ously joyful.

I bend to scratch her wet head, and she paws the sand with an ungainly puppy paw. "Again?" I ask in the falsetto I reserve for her and Janie.

We go through the motions another dozen times. Me, hurling the drool-drenched ball into the surf. Bambi, chasing and swimming and splashing, coming to me time and again to seek a pat and another throw.

We've got the beach pretty much to ourselves. Central California doesn't get much of a summer—not on the coast, anyway. We're lucky if the fog burns off in time to catch the sunset. Thanks to so many years spent in San Francisco, I'm used to the dreariness, but somehow it was more tolerable there, haze hovering over asphalt and structures of steel and glass. Here, where building code dictates no property should rise above three stories, the constant mist feels thick and oppressive, like a damp wool blanket.

Bambi and I walk farther down the stretch of sand, playing our endless game. As much as I hate getting up early, and as much as I dislike living in tiny Cypress Beach, I've come to look forward to these mornings with my new dog. So much so, I bring my Nikon to photograph the waves and the gulls and her. It's risky, what with her shake-off showers, but worth it. I'm snapping yet another picture, Bambi bouncing over a knoll, when movement up ahead catches my attention.

I lower my camera, letting it hang from the woven strap around my neck. Absently, I toss the tennis ball, not so far this time, because I'm watching a tall figure move down the beach. He's a ways south, but I can tell he's somewhere near my age—a small miracle in this town.

He's wearing dark track pants and a hooded sweatshirt, and his hair's black, standing out in sharp contrast to the pale sand.

He strides into the surf, fully clothed.

The air is cool and crisp, and the ocean is *frigid*. He's up to his knees when a white-capped wave breaks hard against his middle, driving him back a few steps. I expect him to wade out, back to the beach, but he presses forward, undeterred, immersing his lower half completely. He uses his hands against the surging breakers like he thinks he can control them, like he's unaware of the water's absolute power.

I'm no fearmonger—that's more in keeping with my mom's personality—but the Pacific's scary along this strip of the coast. I've seen surfers in dry suits, but unless you've got a board, this isn't a swimming beach. Thanks to the California Current, the water's bitter cold and the undertows are unreal. There are sharks, too. Big ones, which normally feed on harbor seals and sea lions, but are probably ravenous for breakfast at the moment and would likely settle for a nice big bite of boy.

"Hey!" I call as he moves farther into the swells. Stupid, because there's no way he can hear me over the wind and the waves.

What he's doing . . . It's *so* unsafe.

Without a second thought, I take off in his direction, clutching my camera so it doesn't knock against my chest. Bambi chases me, nipping at my heels.

He's up to his shoulders when I reach the dragging footsteps he left in the sand. I watch him jump as waves distend, then advance beyond him in a race for the beach. His head bobs the way Bambi's ball does after landing in the surf. If he goes any deeper, he could be sucked out to sea.

"Hey!" I scream again, waving my arms.

He doesn't hear me, or doesn't want to, because he pushes off and paddles farther out.

He's an adrenaline-seeking dumbass, or he's suicidal.

I keep my eyes on his dark hair and peel off my sweatshirt, trying not to strangle myself with my camera's strap in the process. I toss it into the sand and take half a second to wrap my Nikon in its fabric, praying my beloved camera doesn't get stolen or lost to an aggressive wave.

Then I bolt into the ocean.

elise

i lose my breath immediately.

The water is millions of sharp pins sinking into my flesh. The breakers are powerful, but I battle them, keeping my eyes trained on the boy. Distantly, I hear Bambi's distressed barking. I spare a quick glance over my shoulder as I slog through the deepening water; she's still on the shore, hopping around. Silly dog will follow her ball into the water, but not me.

Again, I shout at the boy.

Again, no response.

Death wish, I think. And then: *Me, too.*

By the time I reach him, a good thirty yards offshore, I'm numb. My teeth are chattering and I'm not calling out anymore because my tongue's immovable. Treading to keep my head above water, I make a grab for his shoulder. He wrenches his head around and I realize, too late, that I've startled him. He jerks out of my grip.

"I'm trying to help you!" My voice is scratchy and my throat feels raked over.

He shakes his head. *No.*

"You can't be out here—it's dangerous!"

As if to illustrate my point, a rogue wave crashes over our heads. The current yanks me deeper . . . deeper . . . deeper. I'm blinded by salt water and so disoriented my arms flail outward. My hands grapple for something solid, something to help me right myself. I'm panicking— I'm a millisecond from opening my mouth to a deep breath of cold water—but then my feet touch the seafloor. My toes curl into the murky sand. I bend my knees and shove off.

My head breaks the surface and I gasp for air. I'm choking, coughing, sputtering, and my eyes sting. I blink to clear the salt from them, and then I'm searching, kicking to keep my head above water.

He's . . . nowhere.

I whip around, terrified I've lost him, this stranger I never had in the first place.

My heart turns over when his head surfaces to my left and just out of reach. I lunge for his sleeve, and my fingers close around a handful of cotton. I yank him close, then grab for his submerged hand. It wraps around mine. He uses his other to swipe water from his face, retching and hacking, pulling in air.

"We have to get back to the beach!"

He looks at me, confused and afraid and *lost*. His raven hair is plastered to his forehead, and his skin is olive, clear with the exception of a few days of dark stubble. His eyes are arresting, fiery amber, contrary to his darkness. He appears . . . not Californian. Maybe not American. God, what if he doesn't speak English?

I gesture to the beach, treading hard to keep my head from slipping beneath the waves. "Safe-ty," I holler, enunciating the syllables in a way that might be offensive, whether he's foreign or not.

He nods, still clinging to my hand.

I force my tired legs to kick, towing him along with me. He's kicking, too, but our progress is frustratingly slow. I try not to think about rip currents and sharks. I try not to think about hypothermia. I try not to think about the stranger who's hanging on to my hand—who he is or where he came from or what the hell he was thinking when he traipsed into the ocean.

I try not to think about how I nearly drowned attempting to help him.

I focus on Bambi, running back and forth where the waves kiss the beach, woofing and howling and carrying on. When I'm shallow enough to put my feet down and tug my hand free of the boy's, she comes paddling out to swim happy circles around me. As soon as I'm clear of the surf, she takes off, jaunting down the beach, probably in search of her ball now that I'm available to throw it again.

I drag myself to the place where I left my camera and sweatshirt. My muscles are weak and my mouth tastes brackish. Years ago, my brother dumped table salt in my apple juice, just to see how I'd react; I threw up, which is exactly what I want to do now. I'm tired deep in my bones, and residually horrified. I've never been so close to dying.

How would Mom get by without me?

I shake off a torrent of sadness and turn to look for Bambi, to call her back so we can go home, where I'll shower off the salt and crawl into bed, where I'll sleep the day away beneath my soft patchwork quilt.

When I wake, this morning will be a distant memory.

I turn to find Bambi, but instead I find the boy—the idiot boy who wandered into the ocean fully clothed. He's an arm's length away, towering over me, water dripping from his coal-black hair, wildfire eyes searching my face.

I look at him, and I can't look away.

MATI

She is beautiful like shattered glass—
sharp, asymmetrical, unique.

She is soaked in seawater,
and smells of salt.
She is shades of pomegranate and peach.
She struggles to breathe,
as if the air is mud-thick,
too viscous to inhale.

I know the feeling.

She is exhausted, because of me.
My swim-gone-wrong.
My naiveté, my foolishness.

She falls, falls, falls to the ground,
nestling into the sand like a seashell.

She peers up at me,
eyes hard, expression hostile.
She wants me to go.

Instead, I sink down to sit beside her.

"What the hell's wrong with you?" she rasps.
"You could have drowned!"

She could have drowned,
and I would have been responsible.

She wrings the ocean from her long ponytail,
then pulls her shirt, drenched and transparent,
from where it clings.
I am tired and I am troubled,
but I am mesmerized by her movements—
I am mesmerized by *her*.

She glares, flagrant, and I shrink into myself.
I avert my gaze; my face sizzles with shame.

A dog bounds over—her dog.
It is discordantly cheerful,
covered in wet, wheat-colored curls.
It licks salty water from her face.
She gives its head an amiable pat,
while scowling at me.

Finally, she snaps, "You're welcome."

As if I have thanked her.

I should. I should say *some*thing.
Instead, I shiver against harsh wind,
and commit her features to memory.

She is a heart-shaped mouth.
She is slick caramel hair.
She is bottomless brown eyes.

Even in anger, she is dazzling.

elise

i throw my sweatshirt over my wet tank top (my white, see-through, no-wonder-he's-staring, thank-God-I'm-wearing-a-sports-bra tank top), clip Bambi's leash to her collar, shoulder my camera, and literally pound sand.

He never says a word.

At home, I give Bambi a once-over with an old beach towel, then stand in the shower under a blast of hot water until my skin's no longer gooseflesh. I throw on jeans and a T-shirt that bears a growling tiger, my old high school's mascot, then twist my hair into a knot at the crown of my head. Racked by a lingering chill, I shuffle into the kitchen for coffee. My mom's made a pot, a vanilla blend that's still steaming. I retrieve my favorite mug from the cupboard, a lumpy, oversize atrocity my brother spun in his high school pottery class. I pour coffee and sweeten it before wrapping my cold hands around the warm ceramic.

"Elise?" Mom, from down the hall.

I make my way to the tiny space that branches off her bedroom, the one she insists on referring to as her *library* because she's pretentious that way. She's not a writer or even an author—she's a *novelist*. Our dog is a *companion*. The many multicolored book spines that line her shelves are a *mélange*.

She's sitting at her desk, a refinished secretary littered with file folders and pens and research materials. She writes pantie-melting romances set on the western frontier and, bizarre as it sounds, she's a household name within her literary niche. Over her desk there's a wall-spanning collage of her book jackets, matted and framed, images of ladies with barrel-curled hair and bustled dresses posing with rugged men who've lost their shirts but managed to retain their cowboy hats. She hung those jackets the night we moved in, inspiration for her latest manuscript, one she sold on proposal, the first in more than three years.

"How was your walk?" she asks, swiveling around to face me.

"Eventful." I sink into the overstuffed reading chair that occupies one corner of the room and smile at the sight of Bambi, passed out on her flannel doggy pillow.

"How so?"

I sip coffee, gauging how much I can divulge without instigating an anxiety attack. "There was this guy at the beach. He went into the water."

Mom's brow crinkles. "He was swimming?"

"I guess? He was wearing his clothes, which was weird. The surf was crazy. He might've gotten into trouble if I hadn't . . ."

Her eyes have gone Frisbee wide. "If you hadn't *what*?"

I fidget. I swallow more coffee. In a minuscule voice I say, "If I hadn't helped him."

"Elise Parker, tell me you didn't go into the ocean."

"I didn't go into the ocean," I say obediently.

She glances at Bambi, who raises her head as if to counter with, *Oh, she did.*

Mom looks back at me. "You're a terrible liar."

"But I'm a good swimmer." It's true. The summer before I went into third grade, Nick and I spent hours at the pool in our neighborhood, where he taught me the crawl stroke, how to dive, and how to tread water. I'm practically a mermaid.

"Doesn't matter. Nobody's a good swimmer in those currents. Who was this guy?"

"No idea. I didn't stay to chat. He was . . . odd."

She pushes her reading glasses up her nose. "Maybe I should walk Bambi with you from now on."

"I'm fine, Mom. Besides, mornings are your writing time." It was the move to Cypress Beach that reignited her fire. She's not only writing in the mornings; she's been working all day, well into the night, sometimes. Now that she's under contract again, she seems almost happy. "And anyway, you've been bugging me to get out and meet new people. That's what I did."

"Still, you shouldn't be wandering around on your own."

"Please. *Cypress Beach: Where Old, Rich People Come to Die.* That slogan's carved into the welcome sign—surprised you didn't notice when we cruised past. Besides, I've got my vicious guard dog to keep me safe."

Mom heaves a sigh, but her mouth turns up in a slight smile. "Promise you'll stay on the beach and out of the water?"

"But what if my life's calling is to save foolish people who wander into the ocean?"

She meets my gaze, solemn now. "What if you get hurt? What if . . . ?"

What if I die? Like my brother.

"I can't do it again, Lissy," she says, her voice soft, quavering a little. "Losing Nick is the worst I've been through. If something happened to you . . ."

"I know," I say, and I do. Nick died at twenty, tragically young. I was fourteen. Janie, his daughter, was a wrinkly-faced newborn; he'd only seen pictures of her, sent as email attachments by Audrey. My mom isn't over his death—I'm not sure any of us ever will be—though she's doing better. She adores Janie, and she's gathered Audrey neatly into the Parker family fold. But she still worries. She still what-ifs.

"Please stay out of the water, Elise."

"I will." To seal my promise, I lean forward, passing her my half-full mug.

She sips, then, thankfully, changes the subject. "What are you up to later?"

"Hanging out with my slew of friends, obviously."

She frowns. She looks tired and older. I feel bad for making her worry.

"And by friends," I amend, "I mean Janie and Audrey. We're going to the park on Raspberry Street. Want to come?"

"Can't," she says, glowering at her computer. The first draft of her book is due to her editor in a month and a half, just before I start my senior year at (terrifyingly unfamiliar) Cypress Valley High. "Rain check?"

I push up out of my chair. "Definitely. I've got photos to edit until then. I'll fix us lunch before I go, okay?"

"Thanks, Lissy." She moves to hand me my coffee mug.

"Keep it," I tell her. "You're on a deadline."

elise

The park on Raspberry Street is straight out of any fanciful kid's dreams. It's a huge wooden castle, with slides and turrets and a drawbridge that swings creakily anytime someone runs across it. Janie is in heaven.

She's dressed in pink: tutu, hoodie, miniature cowgirl boots, with a glittery bow pinning her wispy hair off her face. She's the cutest—blue eyes, blond hair, perpetually golden skin—one of those kids who could be in commercials, if her equally beautiful mama was into all that.

Audrey sits on one of the benches surrounding the playground, reading from a thick textbook. She's working on an early-childhood development degree, though with everything else she's got going on, it's taking her forever. She spends a few nights a week waitressing for big tips at Camembert, one of Cypress Beach's fanciest restaurants (my mom and I have been sharing babysitting duties since we moved here), and weekday mornings, she works at the local preschool (where Janie tags along and scores a free education). Every so often, she glances up to watch her little girl take a trip down the coiled slide.

While Janie plays, I snap a million pictures. Normally, I choose inanimate objects as subjects—architecture, the seashore, and cemeteries, lately—but my niece and my dog are exceptions. Their jubilation is inspiring.

Janie scampers into the grass surrounding the playground. I follow, but at a distance, because I like to see where her imagination takes her. I snap a few shots as she stoops, teetering in her boots, to pluck a dandelion from the lawn. She examines its head, gone to seed, running a finger over the white fluff. She turns to me, holding it out. "Look, Auntie."

I lower my camera and crouch down beside her. "These are seeds," I say, pointing. "When the wind blows, they scatter. They make new flowers wherever they land." I almost say *new weeds* but catch myself. Janie doesn't see weeds; she sees beauty and believes in magic. "Do you know what your daddy and I used to do with these?"

She shakes her head, wide-eyed. She loves when I tell her stories about Nick.

"We'd pretend to be the wind. We'd take big breaths, then blow the seeds. But the best part is, we'd make wishes every time. Then, when the seeds made new flowers, our wishes would come true."

"Really?"

"Yep. Want to try?"

She nods earnestly.

"Think of a wish—something really good." I glance over at her mama and drop my voice, as if I've got a special secret. "Like, maybe you could wish for cookies. When I was little, I almost always wished for cookies."

"Daddy, too?"

I have no idea what Nick wished for. I never asked, and I'll never get to.

I swallow around the stone of regret wedged in my throat. "Yep. Daddy, too."

"Okay," she says. "You blow the seeds, too, Auntie."

We scatter dandelion fluff like gusts of wind, setting countless seeds to the breeze. We make a lot of wishes.

After, we head to the bakery for drinks and cookies. Janie gives me a conspiratorial look as we walk through the glass doors, and I wink.

Van Dough's sits in the center of town, surrounded by galleries and boutiques and touristy T-shirt shops. Cypress Beach is one of those off-the-beaten-path vacation spots frequented by Californians seeking a break from the bustle of big-city life. Though I'd never been here prior to the move, I'd formed a vague impression of its lifestyle: a charming town where the privileged flock to piss away enormous disposable incomes. It'd never occurred to me that there were actual residents in Cypress Beach, people who live in the delightful cottages and work in the restaurants and specialty shops. People with average incomes, who stroll the sidewalks year-round, like Audrey and Janie, and now, Mom and me.

Aud and I order iced teas and almond madeleines, and Janie picks a huge shortbread cookie with pink icing and sugar sprinkles. We sit on high stools at the counter that runs the length of the storefront widow, Janie in the middle, attacking her cookie.

"Unpacked yet?" Audrey asks me, breaking her madeleine in two.

"Mostly. My mom got sick of the boxes in my room and took pity on me." In fact, she unpacked everything but my vintage camera collection, which I lovingly arranged on the shelves built into the nooks on either side of my window.

"Please tell me you repainted your walls." Aud shudders. "*Obsidian.* Only you, Elise."

"What? I am a sunny person."

"Maybe, but you're also into expression, and you make snap decisions, and you like to prove your point in really passive-aggressive ways."

"I do not!" But I do, sometimes. I'm sour about the move, but I'd never complain to my mom or my sister-in-law, so I chose black paint to demonstrate my spite. Joke's on me, though, because I'm the one who's stuck suffering. "I picked Obsidian because I thought it'd make my bedroom seem like a darkroom."

"But you process all your stuff digitally." She sips her tea, raising a graceful pinky. She's blond and blue-eyed, like Janie, and she's got this cool, effortlessly boho style: flowy floral dresses or bell-bottomed jeans and tunics, always with silver jewelry. She never wears makeup because *bare is best*—she actually said that to me once, while watching me coat my lashes in mascara. "You should've picked yellow or aqua," she says, like she's studying to be an interior designer instead of a teacher.

"Or pink," Janie says through a mouthful of cookie.

Audrey nods. "Pink would've been perfect. Janie and I can help you repaint, if you want."

"No thanks. The black suits me fine. In fact, I think it offsets my sunniness."

Aud rolls her eyes.

I'm not ready to admit I was wrong about Obsidian, though I wouldn't mind spending the time repainting with them. Audrey and Janie have lived in Cypress Beach for the last year and a half, after a move that caught my mom and me completely by surprise. Aud grew up in the city like my brother and me; she and Nick met their freshman year of high school and were instant sweethearts. Even back then, when I was nine-ten-eleven, I recognized how in love they were. How they complemented each other.

As soon as they graduated, they announced their engagement. Audrey's always-apathetic parents shrugged the pending nuptials off, but my mom threw a fit. It wasn't that she didn't love Aud—she just wanted more for Nick. Degree, career, savings account, and *then* marriage. He wasn't having it, though. They argued even after the City Hall wedding, disagreements that escalated quickly and seemed infinite. Nick was eighteen, jobless and skill-less, and Aud was waiting tables at a dingy cafe in Nob Hill. They were living in his bedroom. My mom cried the day he enlisted in the army, her long-dormant fears regarding Islamic extremists reawakening.

After basic and skills training, Nick was assigned to a civil affairs brigade at Fort Bragg, and he and Audrey moved to North Carolina. They were nineteen, and she was pregnant almost immediately. A few months later, Nick deployed to Afghanistan. Aud was a mess, isolated and emotional and hormonal, and thanks in part to my alarmist mother, she was also *terrified*.

It was like she knew—like she sensed she'd never see him again.

Just before Nick's remains were interred at Sacramento Valley National Cemetery, Audrey and baby Janie returned to San Francisco. They stayed with Mom and me, in my brother's bedroom. But it was too hard, Aud explained when she broke the news that she and Janie were leaving the city—leaving *us*. She wanted a fresh start. She wanted to live in a place that wasn't saturated with memories of Nick, where every park, every street corner, every landmark wasn't a kick to the gut.

"Cypress Beach," she said. She and Nick had visited for a weekend after they were married, a sort of mini-honeymoon. "It's special, but it's not San Francisco. I think Janie and I could be happy there."

They've made a life for themselves and I'm glad, but at the same time, I wish my brother could be a part of it. It doesn't seem fair that Audrey and Janie—and now Mom and me—get to live in this lovely seaside community when he can't. Our world, no matter how beautiful, no matter how fulfilling, will forever feel off-kilter because Nicky was taken from it.

"How's your mom settling in?" Audrey asks now.

"Good, I think. She says the ocean air's doing wonders for her creativity."

"We're so glad you guys came. I know the timing's not ideal for you with school and everything, but having you here . . . It's like having a piece of Nick back."

I shrug. "I got a dog out of the deal, so there's that."

Aud shakes her head, biting her lip to hide a smile. "You can never be serious, can you?"

"Sure I can." I make a churlish face and tickle Janie. She giggles and squirms, scattering cookie crumbs over her tutu, flaunting the dimple she inherited from my brother. I help her brush the crumbs from her lap before movement out the window catches my eye, and all the merriment's knocked clean out of me.

The boy from the beach.

The tall, dark boy I hauled from the ocean a few hours ago, walking down the sidewalk in jeans and a burgundy T-shirt. His hair's dry now, short on the sides, longer on top, and his eyes reflect the sun's light as he speaks to the woman he's with. She's old enough to be his mother, wearing loose-fitting khaki pants and an indigo blouse, her hair tucked under a silky scarf. They're carrying two grocery bags apiece.

It's difficult to tear my attention from the boy's angular face, his graceful gait, his scrupulous half smile. His presence tugs at me, like there's an invisible thread spanning the space between us. The same thread that kept me from turning my back when he walked into the waves this morning.

"What are you staring at?" Audrey asks. She leans forward to follow my gaze, then groans with unmistakable disgust—*ugghhh*. I turn away from the strangers outside to focus on my sister-in-law. Her eyes hurl daggers through the window, and she's crumbling her madeleine to pieces.

"You okay?" I ask.

She looks resentful, jarringly so, but she shakes it off like it's nothing—like I don't know exactly what she's thinking about the tawny-skinned boy and his scarfed companion.

"I'm fine," she says. She kisses the top of Janie's head, as if the contact tethers her to the here and now.

When I look out the window again, the boy and the woman have disappeared.

MATI

The people of Cypress Beach stare.
Like they are curious.
Like my parents and I unnerve them.
Like we are doing something wrong.
They stare like they are wishing us away.

I hate their stares.

It is worst when I go out with Mama,
because she does not pass.
A silken hijab, blue or pink or soft green,
hides her hair and proclaims her *other*.

I am other, too.

The girl from the beach thought so.
Her expression roared loud as the rolling waves. . . .
Stupid boy, battling the sea with his hands.

Stupid boy, swimming alone in biting water.
Stupid boy, clamming up when questioned.

I'll wither if I ever see her again.
I'll wither if I *never* see her again.

Mama prefers that I escort her to the market.
The staring gets to her, as it gets to me,
and my presence makes it easier for her to bear.
I am her eldest son and since my father is ill,
it is up to me to look after her.

I walk the sidewalks
of Cypress Beach with her,
swallowing my complaints,
and smothering my quarrels.
I wear invisible blinders to block
countless pairs of probing eyes.

But today, we encounter more than stares.
After passing the bakery
and a gallery displaying paint-splattered canvases,
a slur catapults through the air,
striking Mama and me.
Her eyes widen with fear;
I want to sink into the sidewalk.

I know better than to engage,
though I cannot help but turn
when the deep voice adds,
"Go home, hajjis! You're not welcome here!"

I flinch, my vision blurring with rage
as I look at evil incarnate.

He is a large man,
leaning casually against a brick facade.
He wears work boots with jeans,
and a vest crowded with pockets.
Copper hair, flint eyes, menacing smile.

He is foolish.
He uses the word *hajji* as a slight,
though it is a title of respect
given to Muslims who have lived long enough
to make a pilgrimage to Mecca.
His ignorance is almost as offensive as his bigotry.

I open my mouth to enlighten him,
but Mama nudges me—
a reminder of where we are,
and *who* we are.

"You got somethin' to say?" the man taunts,
raising his arms in invitation.

"Matihullah," Mama says,
shifting her bags to grip my elbow.
She drags me forward, away from the threat.
"Home! We must go home."

My heart thrashes against my ribs as I follow,
listening to the man's unrelenting jeers,
clenching my hands into useless fists.

I hate him,
but I hate myself more.

It reeks of weakness,
allowing prejudice to affect me,
to *hurt* me.
But sometimes . . .
Sometimes I wish I were anywhere but here.

elise

Bambi is up at dawn. She wakes me with slobbery kisses.

I roll out of bed, then throw on a pair of leggings and a baggy sweatshirt, one my brother sent me after he and Audrey moved to Fort Bragg, leaving me behind for what would not be the first time. It's black with a crest of blue, yellow, and white, set off by a red lightning bolt. His unit's motto—*Advise, Support, Stabilize*—is embroidered below. I sport it so often it's pilling and faded. Last year I had to mend a hole along the right sleeve's seam. I'm not sure what I'll do when it's too old to pass as wearable.

Bambi bounces around while I brush my teeth and twist my long hair into a knot, her claws clicking against the hardwood. I leave the house sans camera, and she seems pleased that I've got nothing to slow me down. In the front yard, I clip her leash to her collar and hold her tennis ball out so she can clamp it between her jaws; she likes to carry it all the way to the beach. We're heading down the cobblestone path when our salt-and-pepper-haired neighbor, Iris, approaches the waist-high box hedge that separates her yard from ours.

"If it isn't my dear Elise," she says. "And Bambi, too!"

Bambi turns an excited circle, grinning around her ball. She loves Iris, and Iris loves her—almost as much as she loves her garden, which encompasses her entire yard, front and back. I appreciate her green thumb because sometimes, when my window's cracked and the wind whirls just right, my room smells of gardenia and lilac and rose. She's outside all the time, pruning, planting, weeding, and eavesdropping on neighborhood goings-on.

"Morning, Iris."

She holds up her hands, a pair of garden clippers in one, and a basket full of periwinkle hydrangeas in the other. "Seems I've got more blooms than I know what to do with. I can tie a bundle for your mother, if you think she'd like them."

"She would. Her library could use some cheering up."

"Has she locked herself in there again? Someone should remind her that soil and sunshine are good for the soul." She adjusts her knitted cardigan and casts a disparaging glance at our yard, which, generously put, is overgrown.

"I'll tell her, but do you know what she'll say? 'I'm on a deadline, Elise.'"

"We're all on a deadline. Every day's a step toward extinction. Why not make the best of our time?"

"Exactly. Why else would I be up before the birds, on my way to the beach?"

"You're better for it. So is that darling pup of yours." Bambi wags her tail as if she understands. Iris puckers her lips and blows my dog a gale of kisses before saying, "I've got to get back to work. I've got company arriving today."

"Oh yeah? Family?"

"My grandson, Ryan. He lives in Dallas, but he's coming to spend the rest of the summer with me. It's been nearly a year since I last saw him. He's a good boy, headed to Texas A&M this fall."

"Impressive," I say sincerely. I've had my sights on the San

Francisco Art Institute for years, but everything I've heard about Texas A&M has been positive. "Maybe I'll have a chance to meet him."

"I bet you will. He'll be excited when I tell him a pretty girl lives next door."

"Oh, Iris. Don't go getting his hopes up."

We come spinning out of nothingness,

scattering stars like dust.

—Rumi

elise

The beach is deserted.

Just like yesterday, the sky is thick with clouds, the air cool but humid. Bambi chases her ball ecstatically. She's got beach amnesia—for her, every morning is new and remarkable.

We play fetch long enough for the clouds to dissipate into tendrils of fog, and then other beachgoers begin to intrude on our solitude. Bambi makes all kinds of friends, human and canine, and I do my best to connect with the old people who stop to chat. Part of me wishes we would've moved to Cypress Valley, the town just east of Cypress Beach. It's ten miles from the ocean, but it's where the high school's located, and where the bulk of the teenage population lives, according to Audrey, anyway. But she and Janie are here and it would've been counterproductive to settle more than a few minutes' walk from their cottage.

Bambi starts to slow as we reach the end of the beach, walled off by an outcropping of jagged rocks that jut into the sky. There's a set of wooden stairs just before the rocks, as there are sporadically down the length of the shore. I can put on Bambi's leash and take them up to town for a walk through the neighborhoods of Cypress Beach, or I can backtrack the way we came, to the stairs that are a few blocks from home. I'm debating, sand or sidewalk, when I see him—the boy from yesterday.

He's wearing a sweatshirt with the hood pulled over his head, and his hands are crammed into its kangaroo pocket. He's got on workout pants again, lightweight and loose, and he's trotting down the stairs I was considering—*was*, because now they're a no-go.

I spin away from him, hoping he doesn't spot me. Doesn't recognize me. Though Bambi's splashing around in the nearby surf, and she's memorable. I pat my leg, hoping she'll come running. She looks up at me, then beyond, to the stairs the boy has descended. Her ears perk and her tail wags and—damn it!—she darts toward him, barking jovially.

As much as I love my dog, I'm kind of wishing she'd vanish into a puff of smoke.

I take a breath, summon some *cojones*, and call her back. "Bambi! Come 'ere, girl!"

She might as well be deaf. She leaps, barreling into the boy, leaving two sandy paw prints on the front of his sweatshirt.

Oh God.

I chase after her, shouting her name as she jumps on him again and again. He keeps turning away, trying to block the brunt of her assault, but she thinks he's playing and now she's even more fired up. He's saying something to her, a jumble of aggravated-sounding words set aloft in the wind.

As I get closer, though, I realize he's not aggravated—he's *laughing*. He's pushing her away, but cheerfully. And she's eating it up.

"*Bambi*," I say sharply. She picks up on my exasperation and, finally, scuffles over to where I stand. I clip on her leash and snap, "*Sit*."

She does, right beside me, like the good dog she *usually* is.

I look up at the boy. He's covered in sand, and his hood has slipped down, revealing the whole of his face and his thick sable hair. He's not laughing anymore, but he looks intrigued, which is a lot like how I'm feeling. This is the third time I've seen him in twenty-four hours and that seems significant somehow.

But then I recall the woman he was with yesterday—his mother, I suspect—and the way she wore a scarf over her hair, a clue I've refused to let myself ruminate on until now. She's Muslim, which means he's likely Muslim, which makes me think of my brother—*miss* my brother. Sadness like I haven't felt in months bubbles up my throat, until I'm forced to swallow it back, blinking a haze of gloominess from my vision.

"Sorry about my dog," I mumble, still not sure he understands English.

He must not because, once again, he's quiet. *Where is he from?* I wonder, and then: *How long has he been in the States? How long will he be in the States?* Where yesterday his silence fueled my swim-induced frustration, today I feel awkward and a little anxious.

I should go.

I hurry past him, headed for the stairs. I'm all but dragging Bambi, who's clearly disappointed about leaving her new buddy.

I'm halfway up the steps when he calls, "Wait!"

I'm so surprised to hear him speak, I freeze.

Behind me, his footfalls ascend the stairs. I sense him pulling to a stop a few below the one where I stand and pivot so his face isn't level with my butt. Before I can stop her, Bambi lunges, dragging me down a step. I yank on her leash and, through clenched teeth, say, "*Heel.*"

She sits with her front paws on the step below the one her rear lands on.

"Your dog seems nice."

I eye him, wary. "Really? She just jumped all over you."

"I have survived worse."

"You *do* speak English," I blurt, and then I'm cringing at how unintentionally impolite my words sound. I attempt to clarify. "I mean, you didn't talk yesterday—not at all."

He tightens his jaw, watching me a moment before his expression relaxes. "I was . . . struck dumb. And maybe a little embarrassed."

"What the hell were you doing in the water?"

He winces. It's almost imperceptible, but I'm so abruptly aware of him, I catch it. "I needed to clear my head. Impulsivity got the better of me, but I *can* swim."

"Can you? Because that was . . ."

Pitiful. Dangerous. Stupid.

All the above.

He looks out over the water, slate and spirited. "I have experience with pools and lakes and rivers," he says, low, emphatic, hypnotic. He speaks precisely, with a lilting accent I can't place. "But the ocean and its waves are new to me. I didn't realize they could be so powerful."

"But you were wearing your clothes."

He shrugs, chagrined.

How does it feel to act so spontaneously? To ignore risk? Consequence? I wonder how old he is—now that I'm up close, I'm thinking he's a year or two older than me. His face has the chiseled quality of a man's, but there's something innocent about his eyes—a vulnerability.

"You learned your lesson? No more impromptu swims?"

The corners of his mouth rise, a tiny smile I read as assent.

"Are you new to town?" I ask, to keep the conversation afloat.

"I've been here nearly a year, but I am finding it . . . hard to adjust."

His candor surprises me. So does the sudden sense of camaraderie that's replaced my earlier anxiety. "Me, too. Though I've only been here a few weeks."

He peers at me, then murmurs something, *kaishta*, I think. I have no idea what the word means, and I don't have a chance to ask before he says, "What's your name?"

"Elise."

"I'm Mati." His accent makes the syllables sound like *pitter-patter* raindrops: *Mati*. Gentle, genial, a name that clashes with his ruggedness, his solemnness. He climbs up a step and leans forward to pat my dog. "And who is this?"

"Bambi."

The slight curve of his mouth pulls into a genuine smile. "Like the little deer?"

"Yep. My three-year-old niece named her. Watch a lot of Disney movies, do you?"

"Among others. They help me with my English. *Bambi* might be a secret favorite, though."

And I'm grinning, just like that.

My dog lets out an impatient whine, and Mati gestures up the stairs, toward town. "Do you need to go?"

"Oh—yeah." And then I just turn away, like the freak show I apparently am, and start up the stairs. No goodbye, not even a parting glance. Bambi trots after me, snuffling my legs like, *What the heck are you doing?*

"Elise?"

My heart cartwheels as I turn to the sound of his voice.

He's regarding me with an expression like indecision, like he's not ready to say goodbye but knows he probably should. His eyes are spectacular—gilded, almost luminous. "I'll be here tomorrow. Look for me." And then, with uncertainty, "Yes?"

I wait a moment before responding, reluctant to sound too eager, though my answer requires zero deliberation. "Yes."

MATI

Devout Muslims pray five times a day.

In the early morning,
I pray before the sun crests the horizon.
I pray midday, too,
when noon has passed its pinnacle.
I pray in the afternoon,
hours before darkness,
and at twilight,
while the sky is lavender and sunless.
I pray at night,
under a dusting of stars.

Prayer is like a song:
melody, refrain, concentrated rhythm.
A recitation of verses from the Quran,
a chorus of voices praising Allah.

Prayers are like dances, too.
I stand, making my intent known.
I bow, a glorification of Allah.
I prostrate, touching my forehead to the ground.
I sit, turning my face to the left, and to the right.

In America, we pray at our cottage,
in a sparse, tidy room.
Baba, Mama, and I
visited local mosques a few times,
but the trips were too taxing for Baba.
He is too sick, too weak,
to go anywhere but the hospital.
So we kneel on woven rugs,
privately,
facing the Grand Mosque in the city of Mecca,
as all Muslims do.

I pray to honor Allah, to instill Him in my heart.
I pray to give Him thanks, and ask for His guidance.
I pray to demonstrate submission.
I pray to fortify my faith because
sometimes
I ponder Islamic teachings,
as I ponder other enigmas,
like the moon's dusty surface,
and the sea's sandy floor.

I want to know more—
I want to understand.
I want to exist,
comforted and fulfilled
by my faith.

So I pray, five times a day.

elise

The next morning, I find Mati sitting in the sand not far from where we had our spontaneous swim. He stands when he sees Bambi and me, and his face breaks into a sunrise smile, casting light over the beach.

Bambi greets him first, but only because she's willing to run at him without inhibition. I trudge behind, laughing as she leaps onto him. He stoops down to pet her head, which is quite possibly the most adorable thing I've ever seen. She noses her ball, which she's dropped at his feet. He picks it up—either not noticing or not caring about the drool—and launches it. I'm close enough now to hear him laugh as she scampers after it.

"Your arm's better than mine," I say. "You've got yourself a friend for life."

He wipes what I suspect is slobber on the leg of his pants. "She's a good friend to have."

"Truth. She's my bestie."

His brows knit together. "Bestie?"

"Best friend. I haven't met anyone my age here, with the exception of you, maybe, so Bambi's my confidant as well as my beach pal." I don't mention that my friend situation was iffy even before I came to Cypress Beach, lest he think I'm some sort of antisocial loser. I match the sincerity of his grin with one of my own. "It's nice to see you."

"Likewise. Are you starting your walk now, or finishing?"

"We're about done." I point to the staircase I usually use. "That's the way I head home."

"Me, too."

I sense his unwillingness to put me on the spot, which is unfounded. He's an opportunity to converse with someone born in the same decade as me—like I'd pass that up. "Let's head toward town," I say, tossing him a bone.

He nods, then pushes his hands into the pocket of his sweatshirt, light blue today, free of labels and graphics. I call my dog, and the three of us walk up the stairs. At the top, I secure Bambi's leash and lead her to a spigot near a crop of picnic tables. She knows the drill and sits down to wait while I turn the faucet on. As soon as a stream of fresh water gushes out, she's up and lapping.

"She's a good dog," Mati says.

"Almost always," I say, recalling the way she's repeatedly assaulted him. "Do you have a dog?"

"No. My mama doesn't care for animals."

"Oh. Your mother . . . Is she expecting you home soon?"

His shoulders lift in a shrug. "My parents are used to my disappearing."

I'm tempted to needle him with questions—why does he disappear? where does he go? what makes his parents unconcerned?—but I don't want to push him away by prying. Instead, I gesture to a picnic table. "Want to sit?"

He nods, turning toward the tables, letting the light catch his face. It's a good face, strong but refined, with a sharp, stubbly jaw, a square chin, and pronounced cheekbones. His terra-cotta gaze is warm and super expressive, worthy of endless photographs.

He empties his pockets before sitting down on the wooden bench, making a little pile of his belongings on the table. I take inventory as I claim the spot across from him: house key on a simple carabiner, slim trifold wallet, blue ballpoint pen, composition notebook—small, about the size of my hand. I notice he's not carrying a phone, strange, because even though I'm not on the receiving end of a deluge of calls, mine's like an extension of my body. "No phone?"

"Oh—I left it at the cottage. It's basic, prepaid, in case of an emergency." He says *emergency* unflaggingly, like it's a distinct possibility rather than an abstract occurrence, and my head swims with conjecture.

I point at the little notebook in front of him. "What's that for?"

He touches its worn cover. "I write."

"Write what?"

He gives me a ghost of a smile, like I amuse him, but he's not ready for me to know as much. "Notes about America and the places I've been. Things I want to remember. Things I want to do. Things I feel."

"A journal," I supply, wondering if he knows the word. "Something I have zero patience for. I take photographs of the places and people I want to remember. I want to be a photojournalist. I want to travel the world, taking pictures of *every*thing."

He nods, as if mine is a perfectly achievable dream. "Are you in school now?"

I wrinkle my nose. "One more year of high school before I escape to college—before I start my *real* education." Under the table, I cross my fingers and ask, "Will you be joining me at Cypress Valley High come August?"

He shakes his head. "I finished my schooling before I came to America last year."

"I wish I could've finished before we moved here. Senior year, and I won't know anyone."

Flipping his pen over his knuckles, he asks, "Why did you come to Cypress Beach?"

"My sister-in-law and niece moved here last year, and it was horrible, missing them all the time. So my mom and I left San Francisco to join them. Now we get to see them all the time."

"What about your father?"

"He lives in New York City. I hardly ever talk to him, let alone see him." I expect Mati to follow up with a question about Janie's father—my brother—but he doesn't; he appears suddenly lost in thought. To fill the silence, I ask, "Why did you come to Cypress Beach?"

He glances up at the cloud cover, his expression pensive. "My baba—my father—is ill. Medical care in America is the best."

Now I feel like a jerk, being all flippant about my relatively benign dad while his is sick enough to travel what I suspect is a lengthy distance for care. "What's wrong with him?"

"Cancer." His voice ripples with sadness so stark, so profound, my own throat tightens. He touches his ribs, just below his heart. "His lungs. He was granted a medical visa to come for treatment, and now he's part of an experimental therapy."

"And you came to take care of him?"

"My mama came to take care of him. I came to take care of her. It isn't safe for her to travel alone, to wander the streets of an unfamiliar city—an unfamiliar *country*—by herself."

"God. I'm so sorry your father's sick."

He shrugs. "He has always been fond of cigarettes. Many people in my country smoke."

His country . . . Lebanon? Kuwait? Pakistan? Based on looks alone, he could be Greek, but if he's Muslim, then it's more likely he's Middle Eastern or South Asian.

"Mati." It's the first time I've used his name aloud, and the shape it makes of my mouth, the taste it leaves on my tongue . . . a little thrill shoots through me. "Where are you from?"

He waits a beat, like he can sense the significance of his answer. He waits, and my palms go clammy with sudden anticipation.

Then, softly, he says, "Kabul. Afghanistan."

elise

i need to stand, to move, but my bones have gone as soft as boiled noodles. I surge upward anyway, off the bench, away from the table, and nearly fall on my ass. My chest heaves like I'm having a panic attack.

I might be.

Kabul.

Afghanistan.

Nick.

Shit.

I'm walking, moving, away, away, away, hauling my dog along with me.

I hear Mati say my name, once, and then he just . . . lets me go.

I break into a run—a *run*. Bambi, who must understand that something's wrong, assists by towing me toward our cottage like a sled dog. I don't realize I'm crying, messily, irrationally, until I push through the gate that leads into our yard and see Iris standing on her porch. She's with a blond guy who's wearing a short-sleeved plaid button-down and a pair of glasses with thick black frames.

They stare.

I drag my sweatshirt sleeve across my cheeks, but fresh tears swiftly replace the ones I've wiped away. I can't even pinpoint why I'm so upset. It's not Mati; I'm not afraid of him. He didn't *do* anything. It's my brother—it must be. Memories of his death and the weeks that followed, resurfacing thanks to the mention of Afghanistan.

Nick's constant, permanent absence, raw and aching as it was three years ago.

"Elise," Iris says, stepping up to the hedge. "Are you okay, sweetie?"

"Yeah—yes. Of course."

Bambi whine-howls discontentedly.

"You're upset."

"Really, I'm fine."

She glances dubiously at her companion—the grandson she mentioned the other day? He gives her an uneasy shrug. She leans over the hedge to examine Bambi's sandy paws. "Did you come from the beach?"

My eyes feel swollen, my face chafed. I'm desperate to be inside, but I feel like I can't bail without explanation; they're gawking at me like I just fell out of the sky. I clear my throat. "I did," I say, only just realizing that Bambi left her tennis ball under the picnic table. This, ridiculously, brings another rush of tears.

"Did somebody bother you?" Iris asks.

"No—nothing like that."

"You're sure? Maybe you shouldn't go alone. You can't be too careful."

I force a smile and inch toward our front door. "You sound like my mom. I'm sure she's waiting for me, so I'm just going to head in—"

"But you haven't met my grandson!"

God. Could there be a worse time?

"Maybe later, Gram," the blond says, giving Iris a pointed nudge.

"Nonsense. I've told Elise all about you. Come say hello!"

Ryan. She dropped his name yesterday. He's cute—of course he is. We stand at the hedge, awkwardly shaking hands over its top.

"Nice to meet you," he says. Another accent: his, a Texan's lazy drawl.

"You, too." My cheeks burn hot thanks to my run and my cry and my mortification. "Hope you have fun in Cypress Beach."

"I'm sure I will."

"Maybe you can show him around," Iris says to me.

"Gram, don't put her on the spot," Ryan says with a flustered chuckle. "She's probably busy."

"No she's not," Iris says. "All she does is spend time with her dog."

Wow. Yeah, I guess I do. Until today. For a few minutes this morning, I had what might've been a new friend. Now, loneliness floods my heart, hollowing it into a deep, dark pit. Because not only is Mati from Afghanistan, the country where my brother was killed, but he'll likely be heading back soon.

Channeling energy into a friendship with him . . . It's absurd.

I sigh and sniffle and wipe my eyes and, because civility demands it, tell Ryan, "Yeah, I could show you around." Bambi barks and turns a circle. "Not now, obviously," I add, waving a hand at my rolled-out-of-bed, stood-in-a-wind-tunnel appearance. "But sometime, maybe."

Ryan gives his glasses a nudge. "Yeah? That'd be really cool."

He grins. He has nice teeth, straight and even and white. His hair is trimmed neatly, his face is round, and his eyes, framed by his hipster glasses, are placid blue. He's very handsome, but from an artistic standpoint, a little generic. He wouldn't be as interesting to photograph as Mati, whose bone structure is sharper, whose lips are fuller, whose eyes glint like they're embedded with slivers of gold.

Mati, from Afghanistan.

In the back of my mind, in a cavern where good sense is currently cowering, I know he isn't responsible for my brother's death—of course he isn't. But what if he has friends who fight with the Taliban? What if he has relatives who are linked to al-Qaeda? On the flip side of that same coin, though, it's entirely possible that he and his family belong to the group of Afghans who help American soldiers—the farmers and shopkeepers and *mullahs* Nicky used to write about in his letters.

Based only on our few brief conversations, I peg Mati as someone who'd choose ally over adversary.

And yet, I ran from him.

Bambi barks again, agitated, like, *I want breakfast already!*

"We'll figure something out," I tell Ryan, mostly so his Gram will leave it alone.

And then I make a beeline for the front door.

When I'm finally inside, I take to my room, for once reveling in its gloominess. I finish my cry in private, clutching the sweatshirt my brother gave me to my chest.

MATI

Home is a rented cottage.

A spongy sofa,
a mattress with coiled springs.
Polished appliances,
and counters of gleaming stone.
A dining table moved to the garage,
cushions dotting the floor like lily pads in a pond.

"Home is what we make it," Mama says.

Cypress Beach is everything Kabul is not.
Green, lush, serene.
The air smells of eucalyptus and the sea.
The streets are meticulously plotted,
and the cottages carefully maintained.
The restaurants are lively,
but none sell kebabs or naan.

The shops peddle expensive wares,
but there is not a street vendor in sight.
The people here are sleek:
hair, jewelry, shoes, smiles.
Cypress Beach shines.

There is no destruction.
No signs of fatigue or failure.
There is no dust or debris.
No evidence of wars past.
It is as if history has elapsed this place.

I used to wonder if Allah
created Cypress Beach in *Jannah*'s likeness,
beautiful, peaceful, perfect.

But now I know better:
this town is not without flaws.
I have glimpsed its grit,
and experienced its hostility.

I sit on the porch of our cottage,
where the air is clean and clear,
where disease does not hover
like stagnant smoke.

I write . . .

Words about her.
Words *to* her.

Because even though she left,
without explanation or farewell,
I believe she is the key
to unlocking Cypress Beach's magic.

elise

i 'm wading out of my pity party by dinnertime, when Audrey and Janie are due to come over with Chinese takeout.

When the doorbell chimes, Mom abandons her library for the first time all day. The focus she's devoted to her cowboy-in-lust manuscript has worked to my advantage. She has no idea I came home from the beach upset, no idea I spent all day in my dungeon room, editing photographs, perusing back issues of *National Geographic*, and napping with Bambi, all in an effort to distract myself from wounds reopened.

Janie joins me on the sofa for an episode of *Mickey Mouse Clubhouse* while her mama and mine pore over the calendar tacked to the inside of our pantry door. On it are Mom's do-not-disturb writing blocks and Aud's shifts at Camembert, plus random appointments and commitments any of the four of us might have, like the New Student Orientation my mom's been hassling me about. We had a similar calendar in San Francisco during the time Audrey and Janie lived with us—it was the schedule that governed our lives. I have a very vivid memory of my mom pulling it off the wall, bending it in half, and shoving it deep into the trash can, choking on sobs, the day Aud and Janie moved to Cypress Beach.

Here we are, together again.

"Turn up Mickey, Auntie," Janie says as I weave braids into her corn-silk hair.

I oblige and stamp a kiss onto her rosy cheek. "You're my favorite. Did you know that?"

"You're my favorite, too," she says.

I wrap a pink elastic around a final braid, then circle my arms around her. We watch Mickey and his gang use an assortment of Mouseketools to solve an inane mystery, but I keep hearing Mati's rain-shower voice, two words spoken over and over—*Kabul, Afghanistan*—pronounced with intuitive apprehension. I fled the beach stunned, drowning in memories of the time surrounding Nick's deployment and death, but now, in hindsight, I'm not surprised. Deep down I knew, somehow, that a friendship with Mati was too good to be true.

"Auntie?" Janie's looking up at me, her little mouth drawn with worry. *Mickey Mouse Clubhouse* is over, and I've been staring at a commercial advertising a juicer.

"Sorry, girlie," I tell her. "Let's go tell Nana and your mama that we're ready to eat."

Dinner is a quiet affair. Audrey's tired. Mom's got glassy eyes, which means she's got her mind wrapped around her manuscript. And I'm deep-down miserable now that all the ways I miss my brother have been dredged up and splayed out.

I'm picking apart an egg roll when Mom pipes up. "Iris stopped by today," she says in a singsong tone that implores, *Ask me why*.

"Why?" I oblige, swallowing a sigh.

"To bring more hydrangeas. And . . . Her grandson was with her."

Audrey's face lights up. "She came by Camembert with him last night. They had dinner together. He's right around your age, Elise, and he's cute."

"Very cute," my mom says discerningly.

I raise a reproachful eyebrow. "Mom. Don't be creepy. I met him this morning. His name's Ryan, he's a year older than me, and he lives in Texas, so a relationship, unfortunately, isn't in the cards."

"Who needs a relationship?" Audrey says. "You guys can have"—she clears her throat theatrically—"*fun*. All-summer-long, no-strings-attached fun. But be safe. Nobody wants you to have this guy's baby."

My mom blanches, though I'm not sure why; when Audrey and Nick were my age, they had a lot of—*ahem*—fun, mostly behind his locked bedroom door, and they weren't very quiet about it, either. Maybe this is one of those instances that's *different with daughters*, an expression I've heard an annoying number of times in my seventeen years.

Mom reaches over to squeeze my hand, shooting a glower in Audrey's direction. "I think it'd be wonderful for you to get to know him, Lissy. Iris and her garden probably aren't his idea of a dream summer vacation."

The sigh I tried to suppress earlier works its way out. "I already told him I'd show him around," I say, meaning to end the conversation. But Mom and Audrey jump on this tidbit like Bambi on a Milk Bone.

"A new friend!" Mom says.

"A match made in heaven!" Aud says.

"Oh my God," I say.

"Dessert?" Janie says.

"Dessert's a good idea." I grab for the bag of fortune cookies in the middle of the table and pass them around, glad to be done with talk of Ryan. Poor guy—he'd probably be mortified to know he's the topic of conversation around the Parker dinner table.

Audrey cracks open her cookie and reads from its skinny slip of white paper. "'You will conquer obstacles to find success.'" She snorts, throwing her hair over her shoulder. "Obstacles . . . That's an understatement. Jocelyn, what's yours say?"

Mom pulls her reading glasses from the nest of her hair, perching them on her nose. "'You have a deep interest in all that is artistic.'"

"Nana is a writer," Janie says. "Isn't that like being artistic?"

"Yep," I say. "It's the perfect fortune for her."

"Read mine, Auntie," Janie says, pushing her slip of paper into my hand.

I clear my throat. " 'Everyone agrees. You are the best.' Aww, that's a fact, girlie."

"A statement of truth," Audrey says, smiling. "Okay, Lissy, you're up."

I pluck my fortune from the crumbles of my cookie and read: " 'A very attractive stranger has a message for you.' "

I should've read it to myself first—I should have *only* read it to myself because, God . . .

Really?

"A very attractive stranger," Audrey says gleefully. "Iris's grandson! I wonder what his message could be?"

Conversation continues, mostly about Ryan and how *very attractive* he is, which is so silly. None of us knows anything about him. And truthfully, he couldn't be further from my thoughts.

The moment I read my fortune—*attractive, stranger, message*—I thought of Mati.

elise

After Aud and Janie leave, I take a bath, soaking until my fingers prune. Then I bury myself between my sheets. I try to think happy thoughts—not about how my parents used to argue on the phone at night, when my mom thought my brother and I were sleeping, and not about how news of Nick's death came after a night as long as this one, a vehement knock that changed everything.

Instead, I picture Ryan, blue eyes hemmed in by the dark frames of his glasses. I try to get excited about the wide-open possibility his arrival promises and I feel . . . nothing at all. I think of Mati, and how his presence fills me with curiosity and exuberance and a strange sort of nostalgia. Then I remember that he's from Afghanistan—that he'll almost certainly *return* to Afghanistan—and all that hope-anticipation-optimism disappears like a sandcastle overtaken by a wave.

Very late, when the world outside my window is quiet, I drift off.

In the morning, after a fitful sleep that leaves me groggy, Bambi and I are running behind. She's wound up—she probably has to pee—and she's the very opposite of patient as I throw a baggy sweater over a pair of leggings. My hair goes up in its usual twist and we're out the door to the tune of a distracted, "Have fun and stay safe," shouted from Mom's library.

I nearly lose my footing as I step onto the porch; for once the sun is out, and it's blinding. I debate going back for sunglasses, but Bambi's turning excited circles and I don't have the heart to crush her fragile doggy spirit by holding us up any longer. "All right, girl, let's go," I say, holding out a new tennis ball.

We're headed down the cobblestones when Ryan's head pops up from behind the box hedge. I jump back, slapping a hand over my racing heart.

"Oh, sorry!" He pulls off a pair of gardening gloves and grins. "Didn't mean to scare you."

"It's okay. You surprised me, is all."

Bambi drops her ball to yelp about the delay.

Ryan turns his smile on her. His fair hair's smartly combed, and he's wearing a Texas-y plaid button-down. Combined with his glasses, it's a cool look. "Where're y'all off to?"

"The beach. Bambi fetches and I walk."

"Sounds fun."

He's casting *you should invite me* vibes like the sun's casting warmth, so I oblige, waving a hand westward, toward the Pacific. "Do you want to come along?"

He eyes his gardening gloves. "Forgo the weed-pulling? Man, I don't know...."

Bambi barks, picks up her ball, then drops it on the path to bark again.

He laughs. "Oh, all right. You've convinced me."

The three of us make quick work of the walk, and when we reach the beach, we find it crowded. It's Independence Day, the reason for the influx of tourists, but that doesn't stop Bambi and me from doing our beach thing. I chuck her tennis ball and she retrieves, terrifying seagulls with her throaty barks. When Ryan takes a turn throwing, I allow myself a quick scan of the busy sand, wondering if Mati will appear. *Hoping* Mati will appear, because after yesterday, I have a wrong to right.

He's nowhere to be seen.

Disheartened, I return my focus to Ryan, because he seems like the sort of person I need in my life right now: cheerful and easygoing. He tells me about his family (mom, dad, twelve-year-old twin sisters), Texas A&M (coolest school in the Lone Star State), and his ex, Jordan, who broke up with him the night they graduated from high school (yikes—real nice).

"That's so shitty," I say, giving Bambi's ball another toss. Ryan's clearly bummed about the split, but he still smiles, like, all the time.

"Isn't it? So what if we're going to schools in different cities? We'll both be in Texas. We could've made it work."

"Sure," I say. "Long distance love ain't no thang."

He laughs. "Is that experience talking?"

"More like sarcasm. I was sort of seeing someone in San Francisco, this guy named Kurt, but I ended it the day my mom told me we were moving. It's not like we were going to get married, so what was the point?" I weigh my words and realize I might be talking out of my ass. I mean, Kurt and I spent more time making out in his parked Camry than we spent bonding. Maybe Ryan's relationship with Jordan was the real deal—I wouldn't know love if it slapped me across the face. "Wait, sorry, do you want to marry Jordan?"

"Not anymore," he says, "but I'm not entirely over it, in case you haven't noticed. I wouldn't normally go on about my ex while walking the beach with a cool girl. It's just . . . I thought Jordan was special." He lets go of a sigh so big, his shoulders slump.

I reach over to squeeze his arm. "Aww, I'm sorry you're broken-hearted."

"Eh, I'll be okay," he says, shucking his sadness. "And anyway, what about you? Sorry if I'm overstepping, but you were crying yesterday. You brokenhearted, too?"

"Oh . . . that. Rough morning."

"Today seems better, though."

"Yeah. It's the Fourth of July. And the sun's out—a rare delight."

"Plus you have me for company." He grins, and I can't help but smile back.

By the time we've made it to the stairs, I've laughed more than I have since we moved to Cypress Beach, and Bambi's paws are dragging through the sand. I'm about to tell Ryan he's welcome to tag along next time we walk, but as we reach the top of the steps, my attention's drawn to the grove of picnic tables where I sat with Mati yesterday.

Today, I'm living an alternate reality with an alternate boy, and it's a little disorienting. I turn on the spigot to let Bambi drink and end up spraying my feet with water.

Ryan chases my stare to where it lingers on the tables. "Did you want to sit?"

"No, thanks." I fasten Bambi's leash to her collar and say, "I should get home."

We move down the gravel path, but I can't resist a last look over my shoulder. My gaze lands on the table Mati and I shared and . . . There's something sitting on top of it. A bit of folded paper pinned down by an egg-size stone, planted purposefully.

My fingertips go tingly. That piece of paper, that *message* . . . It's meant for me.

I stop, giving Bambi's leash a little tug so she'll heel. I make a show of patting my leggings' nonexistent pockets through the knit of my long sweater. "Oh no," I say. "I must've dropped my lip balm."

Ryan turns around. "Do you have more at home?"

"Yeah, but this one's my favorite. I'm going to check to see if I dropped it on the stairs."

"I'll help you look."

"No, that's okay. Go on ahead."

"But—"

"Seriously. I'll be two minutes behind you." I give him an

encouraging nod, praying he'll cooperate. I can't unfold that piece of paper with his peeking over my shoulder.

"You're sure?" He knows something's up—lip balm? who cares?—but it appears he might let me get away with my weirdness if I give him a gentle nudge.

I paste on a smile. "I'm sure. This was fun, though. Let me know if you want to walk with us again."

"Yeah. See y'all later." And then he turns and lopes away.

I feel a momentary pang of guilt as I hurry to the stairs. I've dismissed him, though he's done nothing wrong. I'd like to make a friend my age, yet I just treated a super nice guy like he's litter ripe for tossing.

Still, I don't go after him.

I fake a quick search of the stairs (just in case Ryan doubles back), then hurry to the picnic tables. Bambi follows, mystified but up for adventure. My heart's racing as I lift the stone and toss it aside. Clutching the message, I sink onto the wooden bench, praying it's from Mati, hoping I've been granted a second chance, and then, carefully, I unfold the paper.

MATI

I said the wrong thing.
I must have,
because your manner changed,
and my heart stumbled.

I would take it back if I could,
but I wonder if it is
the quintessence of
me
which upsets you.
That . . . I cannot take back.

Last night I dreamt of you.
Your eyes like the moon,
a glimmer of light in a sea of dark.
Your mouth like a rosebud,
speaking candidly, dreamily,

of loneliness and aspiration.
I woke up remembering you.

I like the way you smile,
as if with your whole self.
I like the timbre of your voice,
the confident soprano of your words.
I like your courage,
the way you fearlessly
return danger's black gaze.

But there are things I do not like....

The shape your shoulders make,
when they bow with sorrow.
The sad shuffle of your feet,
when they carry you away.
And the way my heart misses
a girl it hardly knows.

That morning,
on the beach with you,
I unfurled like a kite's long tail.
I unfurled,
and I caught the wind.

elise

*h*e wrote to me.

He wrote *about* me.

I keep thinking of him. Last night, while watching fireworks at the beach with Mom, Audrey, and Janie. Today, while hanging out in the yard with Bambi. And tonight, as I walk to Aud's for dinner.

Mom's stuck on a climactic scene in which her story's hero must race on horseback to an abandoned mine, where his heroine is being held by brutes who demand gold in exchange for her safe return. Mom's better left alone when she's in book mode, so Aud offered to feed me. She fixes grilled cheese and tomato soup; she may work in a restaurant known for its fine food, but she's culinarily inept. We eat on the living room sofa while Janie sits in a miniature chair pulled up to the coffee table, surrounded by toys.

I like Audrey and Janie's cottage much more than the one Mom and I share. The walls here are a soft honey color, the sofa is overstuffed and upholstered in sage twill, and the TV is mounted over a repurposed library catalog cabinet. There are framed black-and-white photographs everywhere, mostly my work, mostly images of Janie, plus a few of Audrey and Nick when they were in high school, and a few from the day they were married, eating frosted cupcakes, grinning like they're in on a secret the rest of the world would be lucky to know.

While my mom pays rent on our cottage, Audrey owns hers free and clear. Turns out there's a big payout to army spouses whose soldiers are killed in action, plus, Nick took out a hefty life insurance policy before he enlisted. A long time passed before Aud touched that money—it sat in a savings account collecting pennies of interest the whole time she and Janie lived with Mom and me—but when her heart had scabbed over enough for her to face the windfall without anxiety attacks, she put a chunk of it aside for Janie and spent what was left on their home. I only know this because I am, for all intents and purposes, Aud's closest friend.

When we're done with dinner and the kitchen's mostly tidy, I put Janie to bed so Audrey can study. We go through her elaborate bedtime routine (bath, teeth, song, books, music box, night-light), and then I pepper her face with kisses and flip off the lamp. When I return to the living room, I find Aud with her nose in a textbook.

"You're not leaving, are you?" she asks, barely glancing up from the note she's scribbling across a cluttered sheet of paper.

"I'll hang out if you want."

"Sure, but give me thirty to finish this study guide, okay?"

While I wait, I use her laptop to check my email. It's spam, plus a notice from Cypress Valley High, reminding me, again, of the New Student Orientation.

God, *no*.

I sign out of my account and think of how lucky Mati is to be finished with school, free to live his life as he pleases. After his father's treatments are over, he'll probably head back to his country and . . . what? What do Afghan boys do when their schooling is done? There's not a lot of industry in Afghanistan, as far as I know, and I can't imagine commerce is anything to write home about. Maybe he'll farm parched fields in a rural village. Or, maybe he'll marry and reign like a lord. Or, he could join the Taliban and attack American soldiers—many of whom, like my brother, were deployed to Afghanistan to help.

But, *no*. Those are stereotypes propagated by surface-level journalism. With a jolt of shame, I realize that when it comes to Afghanistan, I don't know anything *but* stereotypes.

I give Audrey a quick glance—she's still wrapped up in her schoolwork—then type *Afghanistan* into an online search engine. A zillion links pop up, everything from war histories to harems, health care to housing. I dig deeper, scanning articles on poetry and proverbs, Islamic holidays, and popular Afghan cuisine—rice and soup, kebabs and lavash. I'm horrified to discover that the national infant mortality rate is dismal, and the literacy rate isn't much better. I peruse paragraphs about the country's complex tribal systems, the end of its monarchy, and the toll of the Soviet War. I learn about the subsequent civil war, the inception of the Taliban, made up in large part of Soviet War orphans, and the ongoing war in Afghanistan.

Since Nick's death, I've pictured the arid South Asian country where he gasped for his last breath in monochrome shades of sinister and severe, but now, suddenly, Afghanistan is lit up in Technicolor. I'm not sure if my prejudice was ingrained in me by my mother, who's feared Muslims since the Twin Towers fell—doubly after my brother was killed—or if I've chosen narrow-mindedness because it's easier than acknowledging how utterly complex this world is, but I am certain of this: Nick would disapprove of complacent ignorance.

Once, when I was eleven, he took me to pick up groceries while our mom was in the weeds with edits. On our way home, laden with bags of food, he paused to fish a ten-dollar bill out of his pocket. He gave it to a homeless man—a war veteran, his sign declared—who loitered regularly a few blocks from our condo. I'd never seen my brother do such a thing, and I'd definitely never witnessed my mom giving money to the less fortunate; she always insisted we cross to the other side of the street when there were homeless people on the sidewalk. When I asked Nicky why he'd given his hard-earned cash to a stranger, he said, "Because he's a person, Elise. Somebody's son. Somebody's father, maybe, and I see him. I see how we're connected, him and me, to each other, to this great big world." He bumped me affectionately as we continued to make our way home. "Don't walk through life blind, okay?"

I'm thinking about connections when Audrey snaps her book shut. "Whatcha looking at?"

I close the website I've been studying and, nonchalantly, clear the computer's search history, too. "Just a photography blog."

"How's your portfolio coming?"

I will the guilty staccato of my heart to slow; I hate lying to Aud. "Not bad. Should be ready by the time I need it for applications."

"Sticking with the death theme?"

I wrinkle my nose and set her laptop on the coffee table. "The theme is life *among* death."

She shudders. "Creepy."

She doesn't get my portfolio, and neither does my mom. I'm photographing cemeteries, yeah, but my goal is to capture the way lively subjects play off backgrounds of the grimmer variety. A black-and-orange butterfly perched atop a crumbling memorial, or a yellow pansy sprouting beside a marble headstone. Audrey and Mom think my work is morbid, but on good days, when the light's just right and I've chosen the perfect aperture, capturing a blue bird roosting in the eaves of a centuries-old mausoleum, I think it might be brilliant.

"*You're* creepy," I say, nudging her foot with my own.

She laughs. "How's the boy next door?"

"Hung up on his ex, which is fine by me."

"Lissy, with that attitude, you'll never find love."

"I don't want to find love—I want it to find me. I want it to crash into me. Knock me down. *Seize* me."

"Spoken like a true Parker." She twirls her hair between her fingers. She still wears her wedding band on her left hand, and its modest diamonds glint in the lamplight. "Your brother was a romantic, too, and we all know how obsessed your mom is with yearning and passion and devotion—fictional, of course."

"Of course." I nestle further into the couch cushions. "Audrey, how'd you know? With Nick, I mean? How'd you know it was real love?"

"It's *still* real love," she says, which makes my chest tighten. She places a hand over her heart. "I feel it here—a squeeze, a tenderness, a longing. It never goes away."

"Do you think it'd be easier if you could stop loving him?"

"No. Would it be easier for you?"

"No," I say, but my tone is unconvincing. Because honestly, sometimes I feel like a husk of a person, a milky-eyed zombie wandering a dark forest, capable only of missing my brother.

Audrey sighs, letting the curl she twisted into her hair fall to her shoulder. "Okay, maybe every once in a while, on particularly rough days, I toy with the idea of forgetting because, yeah, maybe it *would* be easier. But easier isn't always better. I don't ever want to *not* remember Nick or the way he made me feel, like I was something special—like I was *every*thing special. Besides, Janie deserves two parents who love each other, even if one's only here in spirit."

I contemplate this, wishing I were as strong as my sister-in-law. "If you could go back and start over," I say, "but with the knowledge that Nicky would die young . . . would you let yourself fall in love with him?"

She gives me a sad smile—the *saddest* smile. "A million times."

Out beyond ideas of wrongdoing and rightdoing, there is a field.

I'll meet you there.

—Rumi

elise

The following morning, Bambi and I make our walk to the beach. I've got my camera and she's got her ball, and if I had to guess, I'd say she's as eager as I am. As soon as we hear the sound of crashing waves, I sweep my surroundings for movement, a flash of color, a shock of dark hair.

I think, *Please be here.*

And then I see him, sitting at the picnic table I've started to think of as ours, writing in his notebook. Bambi's spotted him, too, and she's straining against her leash in an effort to get to him. She lets out an impatient whine, and he lifts his head, catching sight of us. His features go immediately slack, his eyes devastatingly impassive.

Indifference. It's what I deserve.

I raise my hand in a lame little wave, and it's as if a pail of warm relief splashes over him.

I feel it, too.

He stands, pockets his notebook and pen, and strides on long legs toward Bambi and me. As soon as he's in her ambush zone, she drops her ball and lets out a yowl, pulling at her leash. Mati bends to pet her head, and her tail swishes accordingly.

"Elise," he says in greeting, straightening to his full height. "Going for a walk?"

I nod because my throat is suddenly too dry for conversation.

"I thought I might see you yesterday." He watches the toe of his shoe scuff the dirt, like he's worried about how his admission will be received. "Or the day before."

I swallow, mustering some poise. "I found the note you left."

"Ah. Is that why you're looking at me like I'm dangerous?"

I smile. "Not dangerous. Unpredictable. That was ballsy, the way you left it sitting out. What if the wind had taken it?"

He gives me a long, charged look, then says, "The wind has taken me."

I stand, rootless, staring at him with a feeling not unlike reverence.

"Do you know how we say *wind* at home?"

I shake my head.

"*Baad*." His voice is low and airy, like his very breath is a breeze.

"*Baad*," I repeat. "What language is that?"

"Pashto. It is how I speak with my family."

"Do you know other languages?"

"Dari. Enough Arabic to understand the phrasing in the Quran."

"Wow. I only know English—barely, sometimes."

"Well, your actions speak loudly. You've pulled me out of surging water, made me warm with your smile, and left me sitting alone. Even when you're quiet, you say plenty."

And now I'm the one scuffing my shoe. "That looked bad the other day, I know it did. I had—" I pause, blink away the threat of tears, and try again. "I had a lot of feelings. I was kind of a mess, actually. But I shouldn't have walked away."

"It was your right."

"And it's your right to call me a blazing racist."

"Is that what you are?"

I consider his question seriously. I don't categorize or put down or judge many based on the actions of few. I don't believe myself better than anyone else. And I don't hate. Except . . . yes, I do. I *despise* the people who killed my brother, who fight and oppress, who punish with fists and stones, who launch rocket-propelled grenades at American military vehicles. But I also understand that the men who took Nicky aren't representative of all Afghans, or all Muslims.

"No," I say. "I'm not."

"What is it about me?" he asks, more curious than combative.

I wrap both hands around my dog's leash; they're shaky thanks to this deserved interrogation. "It's nothing about *you*."

"It must be. My language? My religion? My home?"

"I . . ."

"Or maybe it's something else. Something off-putting I have yet to think of."

"No," I say in a small voice, wishing I'd disintegrate, disappear into the dust beneath my feet. I am so out of my league. So void of the intelligence, the directness, the *compassion* necessary for this conversation. Nick's death stripped me of those things, at least in the way of Afghanistan and its people, which is ironic. He'd hate the way I treated Mati, no matter the reason. But I can do better—I know I can.

"I'm sorry," I tell Mati, my voice barely a whisper. "For walking away, and for how that must've made you feel."

He nods, his expression more understanding than I probably deserve.

I want to know if I'm forgiven, if we're okay, but I won't ask; forgiveness is his to grant when he's ready. Still, even though he's humored me, heard me out and accepted my apology—even though we're clearly done here—I can't bring myself to tell him goodbye, to continue my walk, to leave him behind again.

Bambi nudges my leg with her wet nose, *Are you all right?* combined with *Can we get going?* I reach down to stroke her head and she pops up out of her sit to pick up her tennis ball.

"She is ready to walk," Mati says.

"Always."

"Then you should go. We can talk another day, if you'd like."

"Or . . . you could walk with us." I second-guess the invitation as soon as it's free of my mouth. I mean, I want him to come along, but mixed signals much? The next message he leaves me will be about the wicked case of whiplash I've given him.

But he smiles. "I think I will."

We spend a long time on the beach, trekking to the end of the sand and most of the way back. There isn't a lot of talking involved. Mati seems comfortable with a morning set to mute, and I don't mind the quiet, either; it's companionable. Every once in a while, though, I'll lower my camera to glance toward him and find his lips subtly moving, like he's silently reciting, or trying to learn something by rote, or committing the beach to memory so he can write about it later. I'm charmed.

There's a fallen log, near the stairs that'll take us back to town. It's wind-ravaged, its bark worn away by ages in the elements. Mati points at it. "Should we sit?"

The wood is smooth and cool. I perch with my knees inclined toward him, and he mirrors my posture. Bambi drops onto my feet, drenching them with her sea-soaked hair. She spits her tennis ball onto her paws, sighs, and closes her eyes.

"We wore her out," Mati says.

"She likes to nap midmorning, and again after lunch. She also likes a good brushing every few days, and a full bowl of fresh water available to her at all times. She's kind of high maintenance—the opposite of me."

He scans my yoga pants, cuffs frosted with sand, my too-big sweatshirt, and the messy knot of my hair. He sounds appreciative when he says, "I think you're too focused on your camera to be high maintenance."

I am; I care more about perfecting my photographs than perfecting the way I look, and I like that about myself. I think Mati might, too, because he's still gazing into my eyes, like he can see my dreams playing out on an invisible film reel. Somehow, I'm not uncomfortable.

He says softly, "*Kaishta.*"

I recognize the word, the perfect intonation of his accent. "You said that the other day. What does it mean?"

He smiles, guilty, like he's been caught with a fistful of candy, then translates: "Beautiful."

Okay, *now* I'm uncomfortable.

But, like, wonderfully, gloriously, amazingly uncomfortable.

MATI

She looks out over the water,
face flushed.
I have flattered her,
and I will never be sorry.

She *is* beautiful,
an impossible sort of beautiful—
a mirror-still lake,
a soaring hawk,
a meadow of wildflowers.
She is fragile,
and she is valorous,
and for me, she is fleeting.

"Afghans are not evil," I tell her,
circling back to our earlier conversation.
She turns her face to mine;

I can see that she wants to hear more,
that she is open to correcting misconception.

"We live our lives charitably," I say.
"We try to be humble and kind."
I lean forward to gather a great scoop of sand.
"Hold out your hands."
She complies, dubious,
mapping me with her stare.
I pour the cool grains from my hands to hers.
I wave an open palm over the sand she holds
and say, "The people of my country."

She nods, bright-eyed.

I brace her cupped hands with one of mine.
I only mean to hold them steady,
but her soft skin makes my breath falter.
I rob a few grains from the wealth she holds.
They nest among the whorls of my fingertip.
I show them to her.
"These are Afghans who are bad," I say.
"They twist Allah's words,
and use the Quran to justify violence."

I blow the sand from my finger;
it finds the wind and sails away.
"The Taliban, al-Qaeda,
others who harbor extreme beliefs . . .
they are not true Afghans,
or faithful Muslims—
not in my eyes."

She's quiet for a long moment, reflecting.
Then, in her sweet voice she says,
"Thank you for showing me."

And I know ... she is genuine.

elise

A new day.

Mati can't come to the beach this morning; his father has a medical appointment in San Jose, an hour north. His doctors have scans to run and progress to share, and Mati's mother wants to be there, so Mati will go, too. He told me all this yesterday, after he filled my hands with sand, restructuring the framework I've regarded as truth since Nick died. We've made plans to meet later, though, at Van Dough's.

Ryan catches Bambi and me as we're headed out the gate toward the ocean. "Find your lip balm?" he asks, falling into step beside me.

"Huh?"

"The other day? You dropped it?"

"Oh . . . no. Gone forever. Figures, right?"

"Figures." He gives me a side-eye. He reeks of suspicion, though he's still ambling along next to me. I only have to wonder at what he's thinking for a moment, because he says, "Elise, if you don't want to hang out, all you have to do is say so. I swear, I'll take it like a man."

"That's not—I do want to hang out. It's just... The other day, I needed time alone and I didn't know how to say so."

"What about today? Still need time alone?"

Bambi hurls herself toward a squirrel that's crossing her path and, a millisecond later, I'm yanked after her. I recover, barely, and tuck an escaped lock of hair back into my ponytail. "I think I'm over time alone, actually."

Ryan grins. "Cool, 'cause I'm over sitting around my gram's."

Fine as I am with Ryan's company, the closer we get to the shore, the more I feel like I'm sneaking around behind Mati's back. Ridiculous because, God, he and I are *nothing*, but after yesterday, the beach feels special, like our place. Visiting with another boy—a cute, blond Texan with a broken heart in need of mending—seems wrong.

We're approaching the stairs, passing the picnic table with the tumultuous history, when I feel the phantom tingle of Mati's palm on the backs of my hands. My heart does a little flip, and then I'm spewing a stream of imprudent words in Ryan's direction: "I'm seeing someone. Talking to him. Hanging out with him... I don't know. Maybe it's not a big deal, but I don't want to give you the wrong impression."

He puts a hand on my shoulder, edging me around so we're face-to-face. I'm expecting him to be chagrined or indignant or maybe even pissed, but his eyes are lit with mirth and his mouth is turned up in an amused smile. "You think I want to be your boyfriend?"

"I—uh, that might be premature. But you're up early again, just to help me walk my dog." My face blazes as I say, "Am I reading the situation wrong?"

"Just a little. Weren't you listening the other day when I told you about Jordan?"

"Yeah, but you guys are over. I thought you were looking for someone to distract you."

He laughs, but not unkindly. Now *I'm* chagrined. Damn it—I should've kept my mouth shut. Bambi must feel my confusion, my discomfort, because she sits at my feet and lets out a long, low whine.

"Sorry," Ryan says, coughing laughter from his throat. "I thought I was clear."

"Apparently not clear enough."

"Maybe you're right. Maybe I am looking for someone to distract me. Just . . . not you."

"Wow," I say, taking a step back. "Don't soften the blow or anything."

He looks me up and down in a decidedly nonthreatening manner. "It's not personal, Elise. It's just, my tastes run toward people of the more . . . masculine variety."

In the swirling mess of my head, a lightbulb blinks on. "Wait—Jordan's a . . . ?"

"Guy."

"Oh God," I say, covering my face. "No wonder you were laughing at me."

"Not at *you*. At the situation. I mean, I thought it was pretty obvious."

"Maybe now that I'm paying attention!" I recall the way Iris spoke about him last week, before he arrived in Cypress Beach, her mention of living next door to a pretty girl, and her implication that Ryan would appreciate as much. "Wait—does your gram know?"

"Nah. My parents are cool, but Gram's old-school. She's hung up on big weddings and bigger families and white picket fences—she'd never understand."

"But you *can* have a big wedding and a bigger family and a white picket fence."

He grins. "Truth. So, we're cool? You're not worried about my trying to seduce you?"

I laugh. "We're totally cool."

elise

After my walk with Ryan, I hustle through a shower and, despite the *don't try too hard* whispers of my conscience, stumble through a blowout and a basic makeup job. Coffee at Van Dough's isn't a formal affair, but that doesn't mean I'm going to walk in looking like a slouch.

I leave Bambi on her doggy pillow in the library (Mom barely glances up from her computer to mumble a goodbye), then walk the few blocks from our cottage to town. The bakery's empty—now's the downtime between lunch and dinner—and the middle-aged woman behind the counter appears happy to have someone to serve. I tell her I'm waiting for a friend, then pick a table in the front corner, close to the window but hidden from the glances of passersby. Somehow, solitude seems judicious.

Mati walks in a few minutes late. He's wearing jeans, plus a gray T-shirt that's doing his frame all sorts of favors. His dark hair's tousled, like he's been pushing his hand through it, and he's full of apologies. His father's appointment ran over, they ended up stuck in noontime San

Jose traffic, and there was a questioning about where he was going and who he was meeting.

"What did you tell them?" I ask while we wait for my coffee and his chai.

"That I was meeting a friend in town—the truth."

The woman behind the counter peers at him as she makes our drinks. She doesn't seem so pleased to have customers anymore, and I'm puzzled—she was so nice before. When our order's ready, steaming in trough-size mugs, she clanks them onto the countertop. Liquid sloshes over the mugs' rims, but she doesn't apologize. She doesn't say anything, actually, which is weird. And annoying. But Mati pretends not to notice, so I do, too.

We take our drinks to the table I claimed earlier. It seems intimate, tiny, now that Mati and his long limbs are present. Before sitting, he empties the back pocket of his jeans: key, pen, wallet, and notebook of what I suppose are eloquent words. I'm so preoccupied by it and its secrets, we bump knees as we scoot in across from each other. I giggle nervously. He looks like I stuck him with a hot poker.

"Would your parents be upset," I ask when my laughter has died, "if they saw you now?"

He hesitates—because he doesn't want me to think negatively of his parents, or because he doesn't want to offend me, I'm not sure. He clears his throat. "My father would probably understand. He knows what it's like to be ..." He fiddles with the string of the tea bag dangling from his mug. When he glances up again, he's flushed. The sight of him discomfited is so endearing, it's hard to resist the urge to touch his hand. He starts again. "My mother would likely disapprove. She is very traditional."

As far as ... ? I want to say.

"How's your chai?" I ask instead.

He smiles. "Weak. But I'm not complaining. Ramadan recently ended and after a month of daylight fasting, weak chai in the afternoon is a treat."

Ramadan. I make a mental note to look it up later. "How was your father's appointment?"

His smile thins, though I can tell he's trying to maintain an intrepid facade. "There's been no real change. His doctors tell us the medicines take their time to work. They tell us not to be discouraged, but my baba—my *father*—was quiet during the ride back to Cypress Beach."

"I can't even imagine. I'm really sorry."

He shrugs even as worry tightens his jaw. "We've been hearing the same for months. One day, the doctor will give us good news and my father will have reason to celebrate."

"I hope so. Also, if you call him baba at home, then you should call him baba when you're with me, too."

He smiles again, appreciative. "How's your coffee?"

"It's okay. I only really like it when it's swimming with sugar."

"Sweet," he says. "*Khwazza* is the Pashto word."

"*Khwazza,*" I repeat, wishing I could say it with the elegance that's inherent to him.

"And *bura* is sugar."

"*Bura.*"

He nods proudly, like I've spoken a whole soliloquy of Pashto, not two simple words. "At home, we sometimes flavor our chai with saffron. And we often sit on the floor when we drink it. On a rug, or cushions. But not at a table like this."

I glance over my shoulder at the woman behind the counter. She's stocking the pastry case with buttery baked goods, paying no attention to us now. "We could ditch our chairs, if you want. Camp out on the floor."

"I have no desire to draw extra attention to myself."

I appraise him, trying to make sense of his remark, and his suddenly serious expression. When I can't, I ask, "Do you hate it here?"

His mouth lifts with wry amusement. "At this cafe?"

I smile—I can't help it. These peeks at his playful side are surreptitious glimpses of the person he really is; the person who I suspect is being stifled by family illness and a foreign land. "America," I clarify. "The differences?"

"I did. I still do, occasionally. Not the differences—I like learning about your culture—but the judgment. The stares. The assumptions."

"You're ready to go home," I say, an observation, not a question.

"Sometimes. And sometimes I feel rushed, like I'm hurtling toward August tenth, like there's no way I'll be ready to go when the time comes."

August 10 . . . God, just over a month from now. Five weeks—that's how long we have to get to know each other before a country halfway around the world reclaims him.

I knew it—I *knew* he was too good to be true.

Afraid my disappointment might be transparent, I look down, swirling my coffee in its mug. Across from me, Mati shifts, stretching like he's going to touch my arm. My heart trips over itself, but then he drops his hand to the table, letting his fingertips rest beside mine.

Their warmth reaches for me.

"Tell me something about you," he says, a blatant attempt at a lighter topic. He lifts his mug, inhales steam, then waits—for me to share an enlightening tidbit, I guess. When I've been quiet too long, he prompts me. "I want to hear about the pictures you take."

I break into an irrepressible grin—photography fills me with intangible joy. "I snap photos every chance I get. My dog and my niece are my most challenging subjects—they're *never* still—but their pictures are usually my favorites. I'm working on a series of cemetery images, part of a portfolio I'll use for college admissions down the road. It's a life-among-death sort of thing. My mom doesn't get it."

"Is she a photographer, too?"

"No, she's a writer. My older brother took a photography class in high school, though, and he was really into it. Back then, I wanted to do everything he did, so I'd sneak his camera out of his room and take pictures of the street in front of our condo: fire hydrants, power lines, stoops. When he figured out what I'd been doing—and that I had a pretty good eye—he bought me a camera of my own. Not a very good one, but the best he could afford. I've been hooked ever since."

"He sounds like a good brother."

My throat swells with sorrow. "He was the *best* brother."

We're quiet for a pause, watching each other over the tops of our mugs.

Mati says, "I'm afraid to ask about him."

"Because you don't want me to walk away?"

"Because I don't want you to be sad."

I look out the window; my vision's gone watery and I'll die before I cry at this table. I blink, inhaling, wheedling a thread of composure from the warm, coffee-infused air. I meet his gaze and, monotone, say, "He was killed three years ago. He was in the army, he deployed, and . . . that was it."

Mati's face changes, constricts with conjecture, followed closely by comprehension.

"I am very sorry," he says, so softly I wonder, for a moment, if I imagined his apology. But he's looking at me with intensity that makes the sights and scents and sounds of the bakery fade away. I feel his stare, physically, in the depths of me. I feel it in the way my flesh tingles and my heart skips and my cheeks warm.

He knows, and I know he knows, and somehow—some miraculous way—we've made a complete circle.

MATI

Baba: strong, vigorous, indomitable.
Deteriorate: decline, worsen, fail.

A sight no son should witness:
the systematic wasting
of the man who gifted him life.

There is . . .

nothing
worse

. . . than watching Baba's light fade.

He is warm, tolerant, selfless.
He values education over power,
and earns the respect some demand.
He is the sort of man I hope to be.

Cancer: a proliferation of poison,
a robber of dignity,
a squanderer of vitality, money, time.
A plague—multiplying, intensifying, destroying.

Worse than its symptoms?
Worse than the side-effects of its treatment—
coughing, nausea, fatigue, infection?
Worse than a head pillaged of hair?
Worse than weeks, months, *years*
spent suffering?

The knowledge that it never had to be.

Wisps of smoke
curl through my memories.
When I was young,
the acrid fumes burned my nose.
Later, cigarettes were the scent of comfort;
Baba was near.
Now, tobacco smells of regret,
of slow decline,
of encroaching death.

The new medicines are
why we came to America,
Baba, Mama, and me.
They are meant to help, to heal.
I am not sure they are doing their job.

It is possible we have traveled around the world for nothing.
Left Leila, my older sister,
under the governance of her husband,

and Aamir, my younger brother,
in the care of my crooked uncle.

It terrifies me to think ours is a journey spurred by false hope.

Death: unavoidable, undeniable, unbearable.

elise

Audrey and Janie join Mom and me for dinner. We've just finished sub sandwiches, and now we're hanging out in the living room. I'm curled up in the leather recliner with my laptop, and Janie's on the floor in front of a mountain of Barbie dolls, some hers, some mine from eons ago. My mom and Audrey share the couch with twin mugs of tea. Tonight is Aud's last night off before she works a string of closing shifts at Camembert, and she claims to be banking relaxation.

"So? What'd you do today, Lissy?" she asks, resting her feet on the coffee table.

I've spent the last half hour reading up on Ramadan (a month of ritual fasting meant to help Muslims seek nearness to and forgiveness from God), but now I give her my attention. "I walked Bambi. Worked on my portfolio. Went to Van Dough's."

Aud lights up. "With who? The boy next door?"

"His name's Ryan."

"Okay, with *Ryan*?"

"No, someone else. But I did hang out with Ryan at the beach this morning."

"Hang on," my mom interjects, holding up her hand. "You suddenly have *two* new friends? After months—*years*—of solitude?"

"God, Mom. Way to make me sound like a loser."

"Tutu, please," Janie says, handing her mama a naked Barbie and a miniature pink tutu.

"You're not a loser," Audrey says, slipping Barbie's tutu over her nonexistent hips. She passes the doll back to Janie. "Now, are you going to tell us about this mysterious second friend or not?"

I refocus on my computer, reluctant to spill about Mati. I suspect it'll take my family a while to warm to his background; between Mom's presence in New York City on September 11 and Nicky's death in Afghanistan, their firsthand experiences with Islam have been negative, and deeply impactful. I'm not sure they'll be willing to accept that when it comes to Muslims, Mati is the rule, not the exception. "All you need to know is that he's very nice," I say. "And, he bought me a coffee."

"What's his name?" they ask in unison.

I glance up and am met with a pair of inquisitive stares. Feeling double-teamed and sort of isolated all the way over here in my chair, I mumble, "Mati."

Mom lifts an eyebrow. "He'll go to school with you in the fall?"

Code for, *He's not too old for you, is he?* "He's only here through August tenth. He's visiting with his parents."

"Visiting from where?"

I could lie, easily, but lying feels like disloyalty, and I know Mati well enough now to feel shitty about betrayal by omission. "I'm going to tell you," I say, "because I like him and I want you both to like him, too. But you're going to be surprised. You might even be unhappy, at first. But just . . . think before you react, okay?"

"He's from Mars, isn't he?" Aud says with a cheeky grin.

"No. He's from Kabul."

Her smile vanishes, and her mouth gapes open like the entrance to a cave. *"What?"*

I close my eyes, praying for patience, for grace. "It's not a big deal."

"I think it is! Who the hell is this guy and *why* are you hanging out with him?"

I give a brief recount of what Mati's told me about his father, his cancer and year of experimental treatment, finishing with, "He came along to help his parents."

Audrey's eyes spark with realization. "Wait—we saw him in town last week."

"I didn't know him then."

"Why would you *want* to know him?"

"Because I don't know anyone else? Because he's nice? Because I'm allowed to choose my friends?"

My mom's been quiet, frowning and fidgeting, but now, she says, "Elise, I don't like—"

"Mom, *think*, okay?"

She sighs, a tired, shrewd, *mom* sort of sigh. "You don't know what you're getting yourself into."

"Does anyone ever? He's nothing like what you're thinking." Because she's thinking of terrorists and Aud's thinking of firefights, and they're both so, so wrong. "Mati's . . ." *smart, sweet, sincere*, ". . . different."

"I'm sure," Audrey says, emitting waves of cynicism. "All boys want you to believe they're different, but be logical. Do you have any idea how women are treated in Afghanistan?"

"Mati's not trying to dominate anyone."

"How can you be sure?" Mom says. "I've read stories about Afghan women who've been stoned, women who've gone to prison for premarital sex, women who've been lynched for *suspected* adultery. Do you want to be involved with a boy who believes in honor killings?"

"Oh my God! Mati does not believe in honor killings!"

Audrey arcs an eyebrow. "You don't know that. Does he even speak English?"

I blow out an exasperated breath. "No. We've been communicating in Pig Latin."

"English is probably the only thing you two have in common." She shudders. "Does he know about Nick?"

"He knows enough."

"Well, don't bring him around me."

"Me, neither," Mom says.

I fight the urge to pick up the Ken doll by my feet and chuck it at them. I throw glares instead, aiming first at Audrey, then my mom. "You're both being terrible. He's a *person*."

"A person who can't be trusted," Audrey says. She glances at Janie, her eyes murky with sadness. She's thinking about Nick, his death and its cause, and I don't blame her. My brother lost his life because of duplicity at the hand of the Afghan Army. I understand her wariness, and I understand that she's worried about me, but I absolutely cannot accept her assumption that Mati—that *all* Afghans—are the enemy.

"Shoes, please," Janie says, holding out Barbie and a pair of tiny high heels.

Aud lets go of whatever memory she fell into and pushes the heels onto Barbie's perpetually arched feet. Her hands are trembling and, despite my frustration concerning this conversation—concerning my family's reaction to a boy they've never even met—I feel sorry for her. Losing Nick changed her in a lot of ways; this is one.

She hands the doll back to Janie, tucking a strand of baby-fine hair behind her daughter's ear before returning her attention to me. Gravely, she says, "I think you should stay away from him."

Mom, who's staring me down like she pities me—like *I'm* the ignorant one—nods. "I agree."

Damn it—I'm so flustered. They're teaming up on me, making me doubt my judgment and my instincts, but it's the two of them—a woman who fled a city she loved instead of braving its risks, and a woman who's so hung up on her dead husband she still cries herself to sleep at night—who've got issues. They're issues rooted in fear, in grief, but that doesn't make them any less offensive.

I push out of my chair and bend to kiss Janie's cheek. "I'm going to bed. Night, girlie."

"Night, Auntie."

"You're just going to walk away?" Audrey says, halting me mid-step. "Real mature, Elise."

"You should talk," I sputter. "You're the one playing with dolls, like life's some sort of freaking fairy tale."

"Yeah. I sure got a happily ever after, didn't I?"

Mom makes a little choking sound.

Audrey touches her knee. "I'm sorry, Jocelyn. That was insensitive."

They look to me, like they're waiting for *my* apology. I stand, stunned and solitary, thinking of Nicky and that day on the sidewalk all those years ago.

Don't walk through life blind, he told me, and I'm starting to understand what he meant.

"You're wrong, both of you," I tell Mom and Audrey. "Someday you'll see."

Mom rolls her eyes, infuriatingly haughty. "I don't understand why you can't chase a nice, normal boy. A boy like Ryan."

I snort. "I'm not *chasing* anyone. Besides, Ryan's gay."

I whirl around and bolt for the safety of my room.

elise

The next morning, after we've strolled the beach, Mati offers to walk me home. "Unless you're ready to tell me goodbye," he adds, bashful.

I surrender to an irrepressible smile. "No. I'm not ready to tell you goodbye."

He holds his hand out, and time screeches to a standstill as I stare at his palm. His life line is long, deeply defined, and commalike. I'm not surprised; he's full of spirit and warmth. His love line is almost indiscernible, fading well before it reaches his index finger.

Wait—does he want to hold my hand?

"May I walk Bambi?" he says, tipping his chin toward her leash.

"Oh. *Oh.* Yeah. Of course." I pass the leash over, silently berating myself for entertaining the *possibility* of taking his hand.

We head for the Parker cottage, walking at the leisurely pace I set because I'm not in a big hurry to get home. I point out Audrey's cottage, and we detour through a few side streets, admiring yards bursting with flowers.

"My mama's fallen in love with gardening since we came here," Mati tells me.

"Mine hasn't. She hardly leaves our cottage."

"Because she's so busy writing, I bet. That was me before I met you."

I glance up at him, wondering whether he means to flatter me, or if saying lovely things is something he does inherently. The latter, I think. "Does your mom garden in Afghanistan?"

He shakes his head. "We have a courtyard with some grass and a few plants, but Kabul is not so good for growing things. It's arid and urban and very crowded."

"Have you always lived there?"

"No, I was born in Ghazni Province. My baba is *khan*—leader—of a tribe there. After Americans started coming to Afghanistan in the early 2000s, he helped launch contracting companies for the U.S. and Afghan governments, which made him more money than he ever could have imagined. We moved to Kabul so he could expand his business, and so my brother and sister and I could go to international schools."

I think about leaving bustling San Francisco for quiet Cypress Beach, what an adjustment it's been. "Was it hard, starting over in a new city?"

"Sometimes. I'll go back to Ghazni eventually, but had we never left, I probably wouldn't have learned English. I probably wouldn't have started writing. I might not have come to America, either." Our eyes meet, and it's there, unspoken, but etched into the bronze of his gaze: *I wouldn't have met you.*

I look away, pleased, and a little rattled. "Are your brother and sister still in Kabul?"

"My sister, Leila, is married. She and her husband live in Ghazni. My brother, Aamir, is in Kabul. He's still in school, so he is staying"—he pauses, his jaw tensing—"with my uncle."

"That's not good?"

He nudges Bambi away from a tree she's stopped to sniff. His voice is cool when he says, "I don't trust my uncle."

His statement holds a note of finality, but I can't let it go. "Because . . . ?"

"Because he is disgraceful. He will do anything to gain the money and power my baba earned honorably. I worry his influence will be bad for Aamir."

"Bad how?"

He sighs, like the subject drains him. "The day we met—our ocean swim? That morning, I read an email from my brother. He wrote about the people he's met since moving in with my uncle. They are not good people."

Audrey's voice echoes in my head: *I think you should stay away from him.* A shiver skitters up my spine. "What do you mean, *not good*?"

Mati starts walking again. In a clipped tone, he says, "Elise, I'd rather not talk about it."

I have to hurry to keep up with his long strides.

He stays quiet for the duration of a block, though my mind is anything but. I think in frantic circles, of the Afghans responsible for Nick's death. Of my mom's warnings, her mention of stones and prison and lynchings. Of Audrey's distrust, her *disgust.* Of my innate confidence where Mati is concerned.

I can't decide if I'm right, or if my family's right, or if right falls somewhere in the middle, in that gray area between their intolerance and my suddenly smitten heart. Is my acceptance of what Mati tells me about life in Afghanistan the same as naiveté? The same as oblivion?

No. He might be from a place known for violence, a place with a seemingly endless history of war, a place that's different from America, but I have to believe he's everything good about Afghanistan: cultured and complex, rugged and beautiful.

I have to believe we're connected, the way Nicky once talked about.

As we make our way up the sidewalk, nearer and nearer my yard, Mati's posture begins to relax, and I'm starting to feel better, calmer, once again sure of the rightness of my choices, my instincts—until Bambi recognizes our gate and gives an unexpected jerk toward it, yanking Mati forward. I reach out to grab his elbow, stopping his forward motion.

"Bambi, heel!"

She listens, sort of, because now she's an easy trot to the gate and there's slack in her leash. She waits in front of it, wagging her tail expectantly like, *Open it already.*

My fingers are still wrapped around Mati's elbow.

I snatch my hand back, but he's noticed the contact and he's staring at me, mouth open, like he's not sure who I am or how he came to be standing on the sidewalk with me.

"I'm sorry." My face is sweltering and I'm sure he notices and *why did I touch him?*

He rubs his arm, the spot my hand vacated, like the ghost of my fingerprints linger there.

"Elise," a friendly voice calls. "Hello, sweetie!"

Iris, manning her side of the hedge like a freaking sentry.

"Hey," I say. Bambi howl-barks.

"Hello, precious dog," she singsongs before eyeing Mati. "Who's this?"

"Oh, sorry," I say, opening our gate and pushing through. I worry about how my mother will react if she spots Mati in our yard, but I hold the gate open so he can follow—it'd be rude not to. I manage something resembling an introduction, praying Mom doesn't dig out of her library and glance through the window. "Anyway, Mati walked me home," I finish lamely.

"I'm happy to meet you, Iris," Mati says, his impeccable manners amplified in the presence of an old person.

"Ryan," Iris calls. "Come say hello to Elise and her friend."

She wanders across the yard to resume pruning as he emerges from the back. He's wearing a faded A&M T-shirt and a backward baseball cap, plus what I'm starting to think is a hallmark smile. "Hey, neighbor," he says, wiping soil-caked hands on his jeans. "Long time, no see."

"Yeah. Like, a whole day? You must be a master weed-puller by now."

"Something like that," he says, still grinning. His gaze shifts from me to Mati. He makes no effort to hide his curiosity. And so, I muddle through another round of introductions.

"Welcome to Cypress Beach," Mati says, his politeness waning just slightly. "How long will you be in town?"

"Through the middle of August. I head back to Texas on the tenth."

Mati tilts his head. "The tenth is when I leave for Kabul."

"No shit?" Ryan exclaims. "I've gotta say, another month in this town would be insufferable if I didn't have Elise to hang out with. And speaking of Elise," he says, swinging his attention to me. "Uh, why didn't you tell me about the MLI?"

The Military Language Institute, in Cypress Valley. It's a language school for service members. My brother considered it but decided he'd rather start his career sooner than later. All I know about the MLI is that it's open to all branches, and that students move to Cypress Valley to attend full-time, living in barracks on campus while immersing themselves in whatever language their aptitude tests and future job assignments point them toward. I remember Nick talking about the barracks and what a drawback they were; with the exception of a legit deployment, he didn't want to be anywhere Audrey wasn't.

I squint at Ryan. "Why do you care about the MLI? Planning to ditch A&M to enlist?"

"I care because it's a wealth of possibility." He gives me a frisky smile, winking all provocatively. "I'm looking for the next best thing, if you know what I mean."

"I do," I say, laughing.

I catch Mati surveying me, brow lifted in a revelatory way. Abruptly, he says, "I should go."

"Nah," Ryan says. "Hang out."

Mati shakes his head. "I need to get home." He looks at me again, questioningly, *dejectedly*, and it hits me—he thinks Ryan's into me. Or maybe he thinks I'm into Ryan?

"I'll see you out," I say, a gratuitous gesture because we're already *out*, but I need a minute alone with him.

I let Bambi off her leash to roam the yard, and then I follow Mati through the gate and onto the sidewalk. We move a few steps away from Iris's house, clear of her supersonic hearing.

"Thanks for walking me home," I say.

He pushes his hands into his pockets, his ocher eyes dull. "You're welcome." In a strained voice, he adds, "Thank you for introducing me to Ryan."

It's hard not to smile because, God, he *is* jealous. It's cute, and complimentary, and so, so unnecessary. "There's a reason he's all fired up about the MLI, you know. There are a lot of guys at that school, which is what he was referring to with his 'wealth of possibility' comment."

Mati's eyes widen. "I'm . . . surprised. He seems to like you."

"Yeah, because I'm awesome. But I assure you, he doesn't *like* me."

He gives me a smile that reads like relief. I resist attempting to analyze its implications.

"Okay," he says.

"Okay?"

"Thank you for explaining."

"Thank you for listening."

"I'll see you and Bambi tomorrow at the beach?"

Now I'm smiling, too. "We'll be there."

MATI

We take walks for the next seven days,
meeting at the beach after prayer, after sunrise.
There are no more inquiries about Ryan's motives,
or questions about my extremist-leaning uncle,
but there is talk of everything else.

She tells me about her plan
to attend the San Francisco Art Institute.
She cannot wait to return to the vibrant city.
She makes me want to travel there, too.

I learn about her vintage camera collection,
her mother's bout with writer's block,
her sister-in-law and their unwavering bond.
I learn more about her brother,
and begin to appreciate his enduring spirit.

She talks about how she loves to eat sweets,
fitting, because her voice is honeyed,
and she smells of vanilla.
She tells me she hates mushrooms:
"So gross, Mati! They taste like dirt!"

And then, she shares a story
about dandelions and her little niece.
They blow on magical blossoms,
sending seeds and wishes into the breeze.
It is my favorite of all her stories.

She makes me laugh,
and sometimes,
when she smiles,
I feel like I could cry.

Two weeks after we met,
she asks me to visit Sacramento with her.

"To see Nick," she says, watching the waves.
"I think you two should meet."

You have escaped the cage. Your wings are stretched out. Now fly.

—Rumi

elise

i haven't visited my brother since we moved.

Sacramento Valley National Cemetery is an hour-and-a-half drive from San Francisco; from Cypress Beach, it's double that. I miss its pristine lawns and curved white headstones. I miss the half-mast flag, the symmetry, the absolute silence. I miss my brother, and six hours round-trip is no excuse for staying away.

My mom hasn't been to the cemetery since Nick was buried—"It's too hard," she claims—but she agrees to let me use her car, a ten-year-old BMW that rarely leaves the garage because neither of us ever goes anywhere that's not within walking distance.

I throw a baby-doll dress, gifted to me by Audrey, over a pair of leggings and pull my hair into a high ponytail. Then I pack my camera and lenses, plus a couple of apples, several bottles of water, and a box of crackers, wave goodbye to my mom and my dog, and lock myself inside the BMW. Sitting in the driveway, I text Mati to let him know I'm on my way.

Mom has no idea I'll have company for this trip.

I cruise to the address he's given me, a cottage that, while on the opposite side of town, is similar to the one we rent—sloped roof, whimsical stone facade, paned windows. The only notable difference is the garden; Mati's front yard is bursting with flowers so bold and colorful, they rival Iris's.

He's waiting on the curb in jeans and a light jacket. There's a slouchy knit hat on his head, charcoal and trendy and sort of ridiculous, but he's rocking it. For someone so soft-spoken and humble, he exudes confidence like a high-wattage bulb radiates light.

When I pull to a stop in front of him, he hops up. "Good service," he says when he gets into the car. "How are you, Elise?"

I watch as he moves the seat back to accommodate his endless legs. If we were different—different people with different histories in a different world—I'd lean over and kiss his cheek.

"Better now," I say instead. "I like your hat."

We leave the quaint streets of Cypress Beach and cut east to pick up I-5. From there, the drive's easy. As soon as we've put the coast to our backs, the fog dissipates and the temperature climbs. Mati sheds his jacket, draping it neatly over the back of his seat, in favor of the white T-shirt he wears beneath. That's it—jeans and a white T-shirt and that slouchy hat—but oh God, I have to constantly redirect my attention to the freeway because he looks dreamy. His arms are long and sinewy, a beautiful baked color, and his shirt is fitted in this incredibly appealing way that keeps tossing my mind into the gutteriest of gutters.

I wonder if he notices me as often as I notice him.

I wonder if he finds me as enticing as I find him.

In an effort to keep my eyes on the road and my hands to myself, I pull out the apples I packed. I pass one to him, and we eat like we're ravenous (for food, not each other, *obviously*). When we're done, we toss the cores out our windows, into the scorched air.

"I'm glad you're coming with me today," I say for lack of anything savvier.

He glances back at my camera bag, nestled safely on the floor behind my seat. "I'm looking forward to seeing you work."

"Your parents are cool with you missing prayers? Hanging out with a girl?"

"Oh, totally cool," he says, and then he grins, waiting for me to acknowledge his use of slang, I think.

"Nice," I tell him. "Now we've just got to get you cursing."

He laughs. "To be honest, I only told my baba where I'm going and who I'm with."

"Your mother wouldn't be totally cool?"

He considers. "You and me out all day, alone . . . She would object."

"Why?"

"Because she follows Islamic values closely. She is also a proud Pashtun, and she wants me to settle with a Pashtun girl, a match that would benefit our family and our tribe."

"Your father—your baba—doesn't want that for you?"

"He does, eventually. His stance is less fixed. He understands that there are . . ." He clears his throat, turning to look out his window at the speed-smeared landscape as he mumbles, "Urges."

"So, wait—you've never been alone with a girl?" This, to me, is unimaginable. But then, I was raised in San Francisco, where dating and sexual experimentation have long been part of coming of age. I spent my formative years living with a mother who writes what is essentially historical smut, who barely batted an eye when my brother and his girlfriend hung out behind his closed bedroom door, so long as they *made good choices*.

Mati's grinning an arrogant grin; it looks good on him. "I've been alone with you," he points out. "But otherwise, no. Dating is not something I need to do—it's not necessary."

"So you've never . . . ?" Had sex? Rounded second base? *Kissed* a girl?

Oh my God—how is this only now occurring to me?

"The Quran says Muslims must guard their modesty. I've guarded mine."

This is troublesome—like, *very* troublesome. I've guarded my modesty, too, though it hangs by a precarious thread, its former weave diligently unraveled by Kurt, my last quasi-boyfriend. Mati's friendship is a banana split on a hot day—*perfection*—but the realization that romance is off the table sends my heart into the most terrible nosedive. Even considering his impending departure, the tentative circling we've done over the last couple of weeks was all sorts of thrilling, before, when making good on our flirtation was a possibility. To know that we *can't*—I can't kiss him or hug him or hold his hand; he'll never make a move on me—is a crushing disappointment.

"So there's no such thing as a casual Muslim?" I ask.

"Is there such a thing as a casual Christian?"

"Uh, yeah. You're looking at one."

He laughs, adjusting his hat.

"Seriously," I go on, in case he thinks I'm kidding. "I go to church with my mom on Christmas Eve, and that's it. When I was little, she read me stories from the Bible, but more for their moral lessons than their religious implications. I pray, but mostly just when I want something. I believe in a higher power, but I don't picture the traditional white-bearded God sitting among clouds, dictating our fates, moving us around like pawns. And I doubted Him—*hated* Him—when He took my brother away."

"That's understandable," Mati says charitably. His elbow comes to rest on the console that separates us, but when it brushes mine, he pulls back. Shifting in his seat, he creates a chasm between us.

I fill it with a question: "What you said about guarding your modesty . . . What if you don't?"

"Well, if there was proof of an indiscretion, that would be a punishable offense. More than that, though, I would have to live with myself knowing that I willfully defied Allah."

"But you're human. You can't be expected to be perfect."

"No, of course not. Muslims are not immune to sin—*I'm* not immune to sin. But I do my best to honor Allah. There's an Islamic concept, *niyyah*, which has to do with the intention in a person's heart. It reminds us to pray with purpose, to act with forethought. To conduct ourselves with Allah in mind. It's not always easy, but I try."

"That's because you're a good person."

He shrugs. "Thanks to the way I was raised—my family and my faith."

"And because the laws in Afghanistan are strict?"

He spends a few seconds thinking on that, then says, "Maybe. These days, the Afghan government is more lenient—more liberal-minded. But it's still establishing itself, which means it operates sluggishly. In more rural areas, especially in the south, Taliban forces are strong—" He cuts himself off, sending a remorseful glance my way. I haven't told him outright that the Taliban is to blame for my brother's death, but it's clear he's inferred. It's obvious he feels sorry for even speaking the word.

"It's okay," I say. "Learning about the *whys* . . . It's helpful."

He lifts a brow, like *You're sure?* I nod and, after a moment, he goes on. "The Taliban exacts swift justice, but seeking their help can be risky. Where the Afghan government functions under a combination of Sharia law and more democratic principles, the Taliban believes exclusively in Sharia law. Do you know what that means?"

I mentally sift through my recent readings on Afghanistan and Islam. "I remember coming across something about it—Sharia law and Pashtunwali. Is there a difference?"

"They're similar. Pashtunwali is an ethical code—principles by which Pashtuns should live their lives. It encourages loyalty, righteousness, hospitality, self-respect, and forgiveness. It also advocates for justice, and revenge for wrongdoers. It's a Pashtun's responsibility to live by the morals Pashtunwali establishes."

"Okay. That doesn't sound unreasonable."

He shrugs. "In many cases, it's not. Sharia law is a legal system practiced not just by Pashtuns, but by Muslims in many countries. It dictates behavior. Commands order. It's broad, and it can be interpreted in many different ways. It can also be severe."

My stomach clenches. "Severe, how?"

"It says theft is punishable by cutting off the right hand, for example."

I turn to gape at him. *"Seriously?"*

"And denouncing any part of the Quran is punishable by death."

"Oh my God. Mati!"

"Hey," he says, as calm as I was shrill. "I'm not telling you this to scare you, or to make you feel sorry for me, or bad about asking questions. I just want you to understand how different our worlds are. You can hate God when he disappoints you, then reclaim your conviction the next day. I . . . cannot."

"But you're so . . ." So, what? *So much like me,* is what I want to say.

"Progressive?" he supplies, his tone relaying how little stock he puts in the word. "If that's true, it's because of my baba. He's like many educated Afghan men in that he reads extensively and thinks critically. But while he is deeply faithful, he also believes there are many ways to be Muslim, and he realizes that texts can be deciphered subjectively— even religious texts. Even the Quran."

"And you agree?"

"Absolutely. I wish parts of the Quran could be different. I wish it dictated equality between men and women, and I wish mixed-gendered friendships weren't so restricted. Do I think it's absurd that I shouldn't take a walk on the beach with a girl? Take a day trip with her? Invite her to meet my parents without worry? Yes. Will I ever bend to desire or make a decision based on what I want, what *I* think is right, even if the Quran says differently?" Quietly, he answers his own question. "Probably."

Our gazes collide. It's momentary, but it initiates that familiar tug toward him. *Into* him.

I refocus on the road, my heart thudding as I think about what he's said. Selfishly, I want him to bend to desire, but I don't want to be responsible for making him violate the edicts of his faith.

"So if Muslims aren't supposed to hang out with people of the opposite gender—theoretically," I add pointedly, "how do they find the person they want to settle down with?"

"You mean marry?"

I move into the left lane to pass a crawling semi. "I guess, yeah."

"In Afghanistan, marriages are usually matches made by parents. The arrangements are carefully considered, but not always based on whether the couple is compatible, or if they will eventually fall in love. The most important factor is often what each family will gain."

"What does that mean?"

He sighs—not like he's annoyed with my questions, but like he's suddenly glum. I peek over at him and, yeah, he looks deflated. "My older sister is married to a traditionalist. He requires her to wear a burka when they're in public—something she never would have done before the marriage. We've visited them in Ghazni a few times, and it's frustrating, the way he treats her. He's not violent or even cruel, but he doesn't believe Leila should have any sort of independence. Still, the match was a smart move for my baba and for Leila's husband's baba; it was a link between tribes, one that made each stronger. The match made sense within the community, so it was done."

"Your baba doesn't care that your sister lives with a man who allows her no freedom?"

"He cares. But he has to think of the greater good. Leila's happiness had to be a sacrifice."

"That's the saddest thing I've ever heard."

"I know," Mati says quietly. "Me, too."

I drive on, feeling hollowed out and hopeless—I can't imagine how he must feel. His sister, stuck in a presumably loveless marriage to a man who's only with her because of tradition and tribal benefit. It seems so unfair—so archaic.

And then an even more disturbing realization hits me. I inhale a wobbly breath. "Mati . . . is that how marriage will be for you?"

His expression is solemn. So desperately, I want to take his hand. I want to wrap my fingers around his and squeeze until he knows he's not alone. Instead, I steal glances as he chafes his palms against the denim of his jeans, unsettlingly anxious.

Finally, he lets his head fall back on the rest. It tips in my direction, his features wilted.

"It has to be."

elise

We spend the remainder of the drive in silence. I'm lost in thought. Mati seems to be drifting in a similar haze.

His background, his culture, his religion . . . His differences make him *him*. I'm as grateful for them as I am for our chance meeting and the unexplainable draw I feel whenever he's in my vicinity. But at the same time, his differences are why he and I can never be more than passing friends. The sweeping disappointment I feel when I consider all the reasons we'll never work and the hopelessness that overcomes me when I think about his imminent departure slow my pulse enough to leave me light-headed.

It's a relief to arrive at the cemetery. I need fresh air. I need to move.

We leave the BMW in the mostly empty parking lot and make our way onto the grounds. The sky is clear, intensely blue, as it rarely is on the coast. Mati fiddles with his hat and I smooth my skirt as a breeze ripples by. I'm weirdly nervous, and I get the sense he is, too.

"Can we see my brother first?" I ask.

"Yes, please," he says, reaching over to adjust the strap of my camera bag where it's slipping from my shoulder. When it's in place, he gives me a sheepish smile and tucks his hands into his pockets, where I hope they'll stay. My heart does crazy things when they're hovering over my skin.

"It's strange having you here," I confess as we walk down a path that bisects fields of emerald grass lined with row after row of white headstones. As unvaried as the scenery is, I know the way to Nick as well as I know the beach Bambi and I walk each morning. "I usually only come with Audrey and Janie, and I came with my father, once, shortly after the funeral. That's it, though."

"What about your mother?"

"She doesn't visit. She says she prefers to remember Nicky in life, but I think the real reason is that being here hurts her too much."

Mati sits with that a moment before saying, "You've never brought a friend?"

"My friend situation is . . . unusual. I detached after my brother died. It was hard to be around people who didn't get it, and I was sad. And pissed. And kind of just . . . lost. I spent my time with Audrey and Janie, and my mom, too, when she was up for it. I know a few people in San Francisco, but they're just people from school. Nobody I'd trust with something like this," I say, sweeping my hand out over the cemetery's hallowed grounds.

"What about boyfriends? Surely you've had a few of those."

"Maybe. But no boy's ever felt important enough to bring here."

"You brought me."

"You're different," I say before thinking better of it.

"*You're* different," he says, smiling down at me.

Butterflies flap hopeful wings in my stomach. It's strange to feel happiness amid this place drenched in somber memories. Strange, but not wrong. "Nicky would've liked you," I say.

"You think so?"

"You sound surprised."

"I'm Afghan." As if that explains everything.

"Yeah, and my brother deployed with the best intentions. He was worried and he was afraid, but he wanted to make a difference because he was invested in Afghanistan and its people. He was invested in *all* people. He would've loved to have met you."

"I'm not sure if you said that because it's true or because you want me to feel good." He doesn't give me a chance to respond, to tell him that the answer to his question is *both*; he just barrels on. "Whatever the reason, though, I'm grateful to you for making me feel welcome—both here, and in America."

I pause on the path, turning to face him. A warm breeze sails by, bringing with it the scent of rich soil and fresh grass and clean boy skin. "Mati," I say. "I'm glad you're here."

His gaze slips from my eyes to my mouth and lingers, and lingers, and lingers. My skin erupts with goose bumps, though the sun is overhead, showering us with heat. If we were different—different people with different histories in a different world—he'd dip his head and kiss me, sweet and tender, mindful of our surroundings, leaving me with a hint of what might come later.

He clears his throat. "Which way, Elise?"

I sigh. I point. We walk on.

After a few minutes, we reach Nick's plot. Mati stops just before it, but I move forward, stilling only when I'm in front of the headstone. *Nicholas Parker, United States Army.* I drop to my knees as I always do, just like when I was twelve and I'd walk into his room and fall onto his futon for a dose of fraternal advice.

"Hey, Nicky," I say conversationally, like I'm talking to my big brother, not a slab of cold marble. And then I go into my usual spiel. An update on our mom. A detailed summary of Janie's latest talents, and everything I know about what Audrey's been up to. I tell him about Bambi, too, because when we were kids, he wanted a dog even more than I did.

"And this," I say, when I've finished my report, "is Mati."

He steps forward and crouches down beside me. "Hello, Nick."

His tone is so respectful, his voice so saturated with reverence, I could cry.

I fish around in the small front pocket of my camera bag and produce two pennies. I drop one into Mati's hand. "We always leave pennies," I say. "For luck, but it's also a military tradition. Visitors leave a penny to let the soldier's family know they were here. A nickel says the visitor trained with the soldier in boot camp, a dime says they served together, and a quarter means the visitor was there when the soldier died."

Mati's eyes are wide. "Have you ever found coins left by others?"

"Yep. Nicky charmed everyone he met. His funeral was packed with people from San Francisco—friends, teachers, neighbors. Plus, there were tons of soldiers. They came all the way here, mostly from Fort Bragg, which is clear across the country. That day was unbearably sad, but it was comforting, too. Since, I've seen a lot of pennies, but also a few nickels and dimes. The grounds crew clears out the coins every once in a while, especially after Memorial Day, when there are lots. I've heard the money is donated."

"That is . . . incredible."

I smile. "Right?"

We place our pennies atop the headstone. "Love you, Nicky," I say as we turn to go.

It's only after we've walked away that embarrassment occurs to me. My time with my brother is personal, and all the talking I do . . . Maybe it's weird. Maybe Mati thinks I'm nuts, leaving pennies because tradition says I should. I mean, looking in from the outside, it probably seems like nonsense—why does a dead person need luck?

But he doesn't appear to be judging. He looks content, peaceful, like there's nowhere else he'd rather be.

"Thank you for introducing me to your brother," he says when we step onto the path.

"Like I said, he'd think you're cool."

"I *am* cool." He touches his hat, peeking over at me. "Right?"

I laugh. "*So* cool."

"Now we get to photograph?"

"Now *I* get to photograph. You get to trail me like a loyal puppy."

He grins. "We should have brought Bambi for that, but today I'll happily take her place."

We cruise the grounds, slowly, quietly. I stay slightly ahead and Mati, true to his word, follows like a shadow. The sun is white-bright, posing a challenge I don't have to deal with in overcast Cypress Beach, but I get some workable shots: a shaded spiderweb spanning two headstones (still sparkling with dew), arrow-straight rows of alabaster marble markers as far as the eye can see (a few with small American flags waving serenely in front of them), and my favorite: Mati stooped down in front of a grave, touching its inscription with the tips of his fingers. His expression is a coil of pain and contemplation and admiration—God, everything I feel when I come here.

When I've drained my creative well and worn my feet tired, we sit cross-legged—side by side, but absolutely not touching—on a quiet stretch of path. We scan the raw photos on my camera's digital display. Mati is full of compliments, even when it comes to the images of him, which, now that I'm looking, are numerous. His lack of inhibition is refreshing, considering Janie's always been my only willing human subject.

"Would you mind if I tried?" he asks.

I set the Nikon to auto and show him the basics before passing it over. Immediately, he's got the lens trained on me.

"No!" I say, throwing my hands over my face.

He lowers the camera. "But I thought Americans liked to have their picture taken?"

"No photographer ever likes to have her picture taken. That's an established rule, Mati, like rain is wet and chocolate is divine. Surprised you didn't know."

"Maybe I don't care." Quickly, he raises the camera and snaps my picture. It appears on the display and, after a quick assessment, he declares it, "*Ssaaista.*"

I frown. "Dare I ask what that means?"

He's looking at my lips again, like they're the most fascinating bit of anatomy he's ever set his sights on. He shakes his head to clear whatever he was thinking (God, *what* was he thinking?) and hands my camera back.

"*Ssaaista* means pretty, Elise." He raises the corner of his mouth in a smirk. "Surprised you didn't know."

MATI

"Do you believe in love at first sight?" she asks.
She is driving us home, one hand loose on the wheel,
the other resting on the console between us.
Her attention is split between the road, and me.

"I believe in *love*," I tell her.

"Everyone believes in love."

Not everyone.
My parents care for each other.
Their marriage is one of loyalty and acceptance.
But it is a match born of profit and political gain.

My marriage will be, too.

"Do *you* believe in love at first sight?"

She glances at me,
changes lanes,
then smiles.
"I think . . . maybe?"

I smile, too.
It is always like this with her—
her emotions alter mine,
change my mood the way heat and pressure
transform carbon into diamonds.

"You don't sound certain," I tell her.

"It's hard to be certain of anything these days."
She speaks like someone who knows loss,
who has waded through swamps of sorrow.
My chest aches for her.

"I believe in soul mates," I say.

Her mouth dips into a frown.
"That concept seems . . . impossible."

I inhale, and revise my statement.
"I believe two people, two *souls*,
can know each other instantaneously,
and recognize how each longs
to spend a lifetime devoted to the other.
Like when you hear a song
and feel its lyrics profoundly,
as if they were inscribed on your heart,
and yours alone.
It's a connection that eludes explanation,

and defies logic.
It seems impossible, until it happens."

Her eyes remain on the road.
Her expression is thoughtful,
and her voice has gone soft.
"Sounds like you're speaking from experience."

Her hand, unspooled across the console,
is suddenly beneath mine.
It trembles like a trapped bird;
mine shakes like a storm-tossed leaf.

I have never done anything like this,
never known anyone like her.

I thread my fingers through hers.
"Maybe I am."

elise

*t*he next day, after a walk on the beach, after depositing Bambi in the yard, Mati and I sit on the curb in front of my cottage. He's walked me home again—this is apparently a thing we do now—and we're laying low to avoid Iris and (though I don't say so aloud) my mom.

She's treated me coolly since I got home from Sacramento just before dinner. Whatever, though. After the way she and Audrey ganged up on me, I don't care if she somehow figured out that I had company yesterday. I like Mati—I like him a lot. He makes me feel understood, and important; he makes me feel like *me*. My mom can be passive-aggressively aggravated all she wants, so long as she doesn't try to keep him and me from hanging out.

I'm thinking of our conversations in the car yesterday, about the way Mati held my hand, about inevitability, when he asks, "Are you busy tomorrow?"

"I've got my regular beach walk in the morning and I'm babysitting my niece in the evening. Otherwise, no."

He rescues a smooth, round stone from the grass behind us. "Will you join me for lunch?"

My first thought is, *Like, a date?* But, no. Mati doesn't date. He doesn't have to, because a companion will be chosen for him.

"Okay," I say, despite my reservations. "Where do you want to go?"

He rubs his thumb over the surface of his stone. He's been antsy all morning, running his hands through his hair, repeatedly chucking Bambi's ball into the surf, paging through his ever-present notebook. Like he's anxious or something.

"How about my family's cottage?" he says, like *Oh hey, this is an idea that's just now occurring to me.*

"Uh . . ."

"I promise, it is a civilized place."

"But—"

"But you're worried about my parents."

"Okay, yeah. Will they be there?"

"Yes. I told them I want to invite you."

"And they're okay with that? With me? In your house?" I thought there were rules about this—about Muslims spending time with, *befriending*, people of the opposite gender. Yet Mati wants me to sit down to lunch with him and his parents?

"My baba is. It will be nontraditional, you visiting, the four of us dining together, but he's open to the idea. Honestly, I think he's looking forward to meeting you."

"And your mother?"

He looks away, turning the stone over in his palm. "She agreed to cook."

"Huh." I hold out my hand and, wordlessly, he places the stone in it. It's retained his warmth, and I take over rolling it into a series of somersaults. I hate myself for allowing this thought to worm its way into my head, but meeting Mati's parents seems pointless, like the official commencement of *nothing*.

"Can I think about it?"

"Of course. Call me later to let me know what you decide." This is something we're doing now, too: talking on the phone. Mostly at night, after my mom and his parents have gone to sleep. Drifting off to the sound of his voice . . . It feels like a gift.

"You should know," he says, smiling, "my mama is making chicken kebabs and *pilau*." He says this as if it's an enticement, as if he assumes I'm familiar with *pilau*. He must see cluelessness in my expression though, because he adds, "Rice, cooked with meat and vegetables. A traditional dish in Afghanistan, like . . . pork chops and applesauce in America."

I laugh. "I've never in my life eaten pork chops and applesauce. Have you?"

"Elise, Muslims don't eat pork," he says fondly, like to him, my ignorance is more endearing than obnoxious. "Regardless, it sounds like a terrible combination." He pushes up off the curb. "I should go. Let me know about tomorrow?"

"I will," I say, standing, too. I should accept his invitation. It's rude, stringing him along, but I need to sort through the abundance of questions in my head: what his invitation suggests, who I am to him, who he's becoming to me, and how I'll deal with the impossibility of *us*.

I pass his stone back. He pockets it and turns toward home, but then the front door of our cottage opens and my mom pokes her head out and, for a split second, gravity is nonexistent.

"Elise? I thought I heard voices." She catches sight of Mati and her eyes narrow. "Oh."

Oh shit, is more like it.

"I'm on my way in," I say, shooting her a *go away* glower.

Instead, she makes her way down the steps and along the cobblestone path, her expression steely. My heart sinks as she pushes the gate open and approaches Mati and me. "Aren't introductions in order?" she says in a tone that's the opposite of amiable.

"Mom," I say, "this is Mati."

He towers over her, and it's satisfying to watch her crane her neck to look up at him. Awe skips across her face (who can blame her—he's strikingly handsome), followed closely by displeasure. "Jocelyn Parker," she says without inflection.

"I'm happy to meet you. Elise tells me you're a writer."

She purses her lips. "A novelist."

One of Mati's eyebrows lifts, just enough to reveal his discomfort. He pushes his hands into his pockets. "I was on my way home. I'll see you tomorrow morning, Elise?"

I nod, and he turns to go, shoulders bunched up, head hanging low. My mom's watching his retreat with her hands on her hips in this repulsively superior way that pulverizes my nerves. This isn't a game, but I'm not about to let her think she's notched a point on the mental scorecard she's apparently keeping.

"Mati," I call, just before he reaches the corner. "Hang on!"

He stops and pivots. His eyes widen with surprise when he sees me jogging toward him. I capture his gaze and hold it, thinking *don't freak out*. I stop when we're a breath apart. And then I lean into him, winding my arms around his middle, pressing my cheek to his chest.

I hear his rapidly pounding heart. I feel tension contracting his muscles, and heat soaking through his T-shirt. For a half second he's motionless, rigid, and then he just . . . *melts*. He shifts his feet and releases a soft sigh and wraps his arms around me. He holds me close, so close, squeezing me against the length of his body like he's wanted to hug me for days . . . weeks . . . lifetimes.

It lasts only a moment, but it's the *best* moment.

I ease back and tip my chin so I can see his face—he's wide-eyed, flushed. He looks traumatized. I shuffled back, stammering, "I shouldn't have—that was . . . I'm so sorry."

He reaches out, watching his hand as if it were an entity separate from the rest of him. Gently, he brushes his fingertips across my cheek. "Don't be sorry. Tomorrow morning?"

I smile. "Tomorrow morning."

He rounds the corner, and I'm left to make a dead-man-walking journey back to where my mom still stands, feet rooted to the sidewalk.

"You're making a mistake, Elise," she says, tailing me through the gate and into the yard. Bambi bounds over and gives my hand a slobbery kiss.

"You're wrong."

"I don't want you to see him again."

I whirl around, surprised and, at the same time, *not*. "When did you start telling me who I can see?"

"When you started thinking with your hormones instead of your head. Was he with you yesterday?"

"Mom—"

"He was, wasn't he? How *dare* you take him to Nicky."

God, her nerve infuriates me. "Why do you care? It's not like you ever visit him."

Her eyes flash, and her fingers flex. For an instant, I think she's going to strike me, and I take a step back. "It's blasphemous," she seethes, "the way you're inviting that boy into your life. *Our* lives. Your brother would be disappointed."

"No he wouldn't. Nicky accepted differences—*embraced* differences."

"Oh, Elise. Think of Audrey."

"Think of *me*!" It's all streaming out of me at once—the grief and the anger I've kept on lockdown over the last three years, along with the resentment I've felt since Mom insisted on moving to Cypress Beach. "It's thanks to you I'm stuck in this town," I say, pointing a finger in her face. "It's thanks to you I met Mati."

She sets her mouth in a firm line. Her arms are crossed and her shoulders are squared; she's exhaling puffs of air in quick succession, like an angry bull. She was like this after Nick died: insensitive to anyone's needs but her own, paranoid, and so distressed, *depressed*, years passed before she could write again.

She's afraid—stupidly afraid.

"I mean it," she says, callous, as if I haven't spoken at all. "I want you to stay away from him."

elise

i spend the afternoon holed up in my room, editing the photos from Sacramento.

They're good, with the exception of the one Mati snapped of me. The fault's not his; technically, the picture is fine. He framed it well, setting me slightly left of center to capture an American flag undulating on a tall flagpole in the background, and the way the afternoon light hits my face has a softening effect. Too bad my expression is all sorts of dopey.

I'm trying to figure out a way to crop myself out altogether when the doorbell chimes. Bambi barks, claws clicking against the hardwood as she does her doorbell dance. I wait, listening, hoping my monster mom will emerge from her library to answer. Lo and behold, she does. I catch a few hints of murmured conversation before she calls, "Elise!"

Her tone is saccharine-sweet, so the visitor's not Mati. I smooth my ponytail as I make my way to the foyer. There's Ryan, all smiles. Bambi's practically mauling him.

"Hey, neighbor," he says, nudging my dog away. "I need a milk-shake. Show me where to get one?"

"Um . . . ?"

"She'd love to," Mom says. Her expression asserts *be nice*. Of course she's all pleasantries with Ryan. I bet she thinks she can drag him into heterosexuality, just like she thinks she can drag me away from Mati. "There's a diner in town, The Hamlet. Their milkshakes are to-die-for. Aren't they, Elise?"

I frown. "They're average."

"Average works," Ryan says. He looks around suspiciously, like he thinks our cottage might be bugged. He whispers, "I need to get out for a while. Gram wants to teach me to knit."

I can't help but laugh.

"It's not funny," he says, bumping his glasses up his nose. "Plus . . . I met someone. Come with me, and I'll fill ya in on the details."

"Okay, yeah. I could go for a milkshake." The Hamlet and gos-sip about Ryan's love life are a thousand times better than being trapped in the cottage, stewing over how my mom acted on the side-walk earlier.

"Have fun!" she calls, waving us out the door.

When we arrive at The Hamlet, we claim seats at the end of the counter and order shakes: Oreo for Ryan, coconut for me.

"Okay," I say, swiveling in my stool as we wait for our drinks. "Let's hear about this new prospect of yours."

His smile is immediate. "His name's Xavier. We met at the library. I was trying to escape Gram, and he was studying. He's in the air force."

"Your interest in the MLI paid off, then?"

His smile turns sly. "He's a student there, studying Portuguese. They sent him right after boot camp. He's got another six months before he graduates and gets an assignment."

"So he's smart?"

"Totally. And hot. Gram met him the other night. I introduced him as a friend—which he is, but you know. Anyway, she hasn't stopped talking about how great he is."

"Does he know you're here short term?"

"Yeah, and it's cool 'cause he's short term, too." He pauses as a waitress serves our milkshakes. He thanks her, pops straws into our glasses, then takes a gigantic gulp of his shake. After wiping his mouth with a napkin, he says, "Who knows what'll happen, but for now, we're caught up in that phase where everything's new and glorious." He pokes me with his elbow, waggling his eyebrows. "You know what I mean, right?"

I swirl my straw through my shake, mixing in the whipped cream, and shrug noncommittally. "When do I get to meet this guy?"

"I'll set something up. But in the meantime—and this is the real reason I wanted you to come with me today—I have a confession." He rolls his shoulders, like whatever he's got to tell me is a big deal. I brace myself. "I heard what went down in front of your cottage this morning," he says. "Between you and Mati and your mom." He grimaces. "Brutal."

"I'd say so. Wait—were you spying?"

"Give me some credit. You know how Gram is with her windows. Always open. I just—I felt for you, you know? My mom and dad are cool now, but they haven't always been. Sucks when your parents are assholes to the person you're dating."

"Mati and I aren't dating."

He flashes me a knowing grin. "Call it what you will. Your mom was cold, and I thought it was awesome that you stood up to her. Takes balls to do that."

But have I stood up to her? I snuck Mati to Sacramento because I knew she'd object. Plus, I'm waffling about lunch with his parents, partly because sharing a meal with them makes me so nervous my palms sweat anytime I think about it, but also because my mom would freak at the idea of my visiting their cottage.

Granted, there's a whole lot of unfamiliar protocol and extraneous nonsense dictating this thing between Mati and me, but still . . . I could be more assertive.

I look Ryan in the eye and say, "You know girls don't have balls, right?"

He laughs. "Noted."

I sip my milkshake. The coconut's good. Above average, actually, though I will not be admitting as much to my mom. After weathering a wicked brain freeze, I tell Ryan, "Mati asked me to have lunch with him and his parents. I'm pretty sure my mom's head will explode if I go and she finds out."

"What's her beef, anyway?"

I give him the abridged version of Mom's past in New York, as well as my brother's deployment and resulting death. "Mati might as well have been there that night, on the wrong side of the attack. My mom acts like he's reprehensible, but he's not. He's . . ." *Amazing-extraordinary-incredible*. Because there's no one word to describe Mati. He's an intangible feeling: a force, a sense, a *purpose*.

"So? What're you gonna do?"

"I don't know. I mean, I think I want to go, but at the same time, I'm scared."

"Of your mom?"

"Sort of. And also of making a bad impression."

"Elise, Mati wouldn't have invited you if he didn't think you could hang. One of my buddies back in Texas is Muslim. His parents moved to the States from Bangladesh—nice guy. I hang out at his house sometimes and seriously, it's a lot like my house. There are a few things I had to get a handle on so I didn't come off as, like, a heathen, but it was no big deal. Want the lowdown?"

I push my milkshake back and fold my hands on the countertop. "Okay, yeah. Lay it on me."

"So I'm sure it's not a universal experience, having a meal in a Muslim home, but here's what I picked up." He ticks suggestions off on his fingers. "Show up on time, and take a gift—something small. Take

126

your shoes off in the foyer. Smile. Be gracious, but not timid. Don't swear, and don't talk about religion or politics, but compliment the food. Oh, and drink the tea. I passed at my buddy's house once, and he told me later that his mother was offended."

"That's a lot to remember," I say. A lot to screw up. And God, I swear in front of Mati all the time, plus I've grilled him about Islam *and* Afghan politics. How does he not think I'm a complete barbarian?

"Don't stress, Elise," Ryan says, squeezing my shoulder. "Just be your delightful self."

I snort, because I'm *totally* delightful. "Easier said than done. Also, if I'd known you were a savant in all things Islam, I would've treated you to your milkshake."

He grins. "Next time. And hello? This milkshake rocks. Average, my ass."

MATI

I think about girls.
Often, and without abandon.
I used to think of them in the abstract,
a mysterious,
forbidden,
segment of the population.

Now, I think about her.

Her fingers,
wandering the length of my spine.
Her ribs,
rising and falling with breath,
as they press against my chest.
Her hair,
silky and fine,
vanilla-infused,

tickling my throat.
I think about intimacy—
and not as the necessary exploit
of an arranged union.
I think about intimacy with *her*.

I will endure her mother's wrath
a thousand times
for the chance to touch her again.

Later, she calls to tell me that
she will come to our cottage for lunch.
My veins flood with
relief,
excitement,
anxiety . . .

Friendships between girls and boys
defy Islamic ideals,
but Baba is sympathetic;
he understands the Western way,
and my need to spread my wings.
More than that, though,
he recognizes that our time in America
is brief, temporary, transitory.
Being with her may be a sin,
but our expiration date is fixed.
Therefore, a shared lunch
gives him little reason for concern.

Mama, however, is contrary.
"Girls are temptation, Matihullah.
She will lead you to wrongdoing.
She will bring you shame."

No. *Secrets* bring me shame.

"Let the boy have fun while he can," Baba says.
And then he coughs,
a ferocious fit that shakes our cottage.
Mama brings water.
After he drinks, he says,
"When summer is over,
there will be no time for fun."

When summer is over,
we will know whether he will live or die.
When summer is over,
we will make the long journey back to Afghanistan.
When summer is over . . .

I will say goodbye to her.

elise

*t*his morning I met Mati at the beach in yoga pants and a tattered sweatshirt because whatever, but choosing an outfit for lunch is no joke. Shorts won't do, and most of my dresses are scant in the fabric department. Jeans seem like a safe enough option, but finding a pair that doesn't fit super-skinny or have intentionally shredded holes is a challenge.

I finally manage to dig a dark-rinsed pair from the depths of my closet, which I top with a pale pink cardigan. I weave my hair into a French braid, then pack lip gloss, my wallet, and my Canon pocket camera (just in case) into a shoulder bag.

Good enough, I hope.

I cut through town and stop by the florist, then walk on, checking my appearance in every shop window I pass. Now that I'm nearing Mati's cottage, I worry that I look all wrong. Maybe it's my reflection, warped in the windowpanes, but my jeans stretch too tight across my butt, the heels of my ankle boots appear a smidge too high, and my hair . . . Maybe I should've left it down?

I grip my just-purchased bouquet a little tighter and pick up my pace.

I knock on the door at noon—right on time. I mentally review Ryan's notes: compliments good, cursing bad; gracious good, timid bad; drinking tea good, talk of religion bad. I'm so nervous, so on-edge, I'm dizzy.

Mati swings the door open. He's wearing jeans, too, and a hoodie, dark green, zipped all the way up. He looks handsome—he looks *hot*. Of course he does. Because if I'm not thinking naughty things about him while his parents serve me rice, cooked with meat and vegetables, lunch just won't be any fun.

"I'm glad you're here," he says, moving aside so I can step into the foyer, where the scents of grilled meat and earthy spices—saffron, turmeric, paprika—waft through the air.

I indicate my appearance and, with a perfunctory cringe, whisper, "Do I look okay?"

He leans in, just a little, and whispers, "*Kaishta*."

And now I'm blushing. Perfect.

I hold up the bunch of gerber daisies I bought in town. They're vivid pink and sunny yellow, and their stems are tied with a burlap ribbon. "I brought these for your mother. Do you think they're okay?"

He nods, smiling. Cue sigh of relief.

He steps out of the foyer, toward what I assume is the living room, and I'm a half second from following when I notice his sock-clad feet and remember what Ryan said about removing my shoes. I slip off my boots, relieved to find my socks presentable. God—what if I hadn't worn socks? I'd be traipsing around in my bare feet with my Very Cherry pedicure calling attention to my toes. I glance up to see Mati watching as I line my boots neatly by the door. "Is this okay?"

He laughs. Gently. Sweetly. "*Every*thing is okay." He grasps my hand and gives it the briefest squeeze. "Please, stop worrying."

I take a deep breath. He's right—I'm freaking out. *Be gracious, but not timid.* I repeat Ryan's words like a mantra as I follow Mati into the living room.

The cottage is very tidy and sparsely decorated, though there are beautiful rugs thrown randomly across the floor. Mati's parents sit on a sofa not unlike ours, overstuffed and comfortable-looking, across the room from a dark television. His mother, who I remember seeing in town weeks ago, the day Mati and I met, holds a jacketless book. His father—and I'm despicable for even *thinking* this phrase—looks like death warmed over. He's thin and pale, and a cream-colored cap covers what I suspect is a bald scalp. He's got his head tipped to rest on the back of the sofa, and his eyes are closed. I'm pretty sure he's dozing.

"Mama, Baba," Mati says with enough volume to coax his father awake. "This is Elise. Elise, my parents, Hala and Rasoul."

Hala helps her husband stand, gripping his elbow, and I smile as Rasoul welcomes me. His English is as good as his son's, though his voice is raspier, and his accent is thicker. Hala, while cool and quiet, seems satisfied enough by the bouquet I offer. She leaves the room while Mati and I make small talk with his father, then returns a few minutes later carrying the flowers in a vase filled with water.

She waves us into the dining room, and we sit down to lunch, cross-legged on cushions placed in a circle on the dining room floor. Mati's across from me, next to his father. His mother takes the spot beside me after bringing an enormous platter from the kitchen. It's overflowing with golden rice, bits of brightly colored vegetables, and hunks of unidentifiable meat—though, I guess it's safe to assume it's not pork.

This must be *pilau.*

There are skewers of grilled chicken, too, plus flattened bread that reminds me of pita, and a bowl of what looks like diluted milk. There are flecks of green floating in it.

We sit, staring at the bounty of food, until Mati gives me a nod. "Go ahead, Elise."

Confession . . . Last night I watched videos online about Afghan dining customs. It was all very communal, the way they served and shared and consumed. In most of the clips, men ate separately from women, and utensils appeared to be optional. So now I'm thrown. Here we are, a mix of genders sitting together, and there's definitely silverware beside my plate. There's a large spoon beside the platter of *pilau*, too, which is a relief. I cannot even fathom digging in with my hand.

I take a kebab and some of the flat bread. Using the spoon, I scoop rice from the platter. Out of the corner of my eye, I see Hala watching me, hawklike. I strong-arm a rush of worry.

Mati's not shy about loading his plate. He serves his parents, too, a surprising gesture that invokes a fluttering in my chest, like the delicate beat of hummingbirds' wings.

The food is good, thank God, and I shower it with compliments, but the fact that I have no idea what animal died to provide the rice's protein is a little unsettling. Mati explains that the diluted milk concoction is *shlombay*, and is actually yogurt thinned with water. The green bits are mint and cucumber. After some persuading from Rasoul, I try a sip and, nope—not good. It's trying to be refreshing, but I'm getting saltwater-flavored-with-toothpaste vibes. It's a challenge not to shudder as I drink, but I manage because I am not about to insult these people who invited me into their home.

Still, Hala eyes me cynically, like she's just waiting for me to make a misstep. As a diversion, I think, Mati launches into a monologue about my photography in a voice that rings with pride. Rasoul picks up the thread, asking about how I got started and what kind of camera I prefer and if I'm one of those people who "snaps pictures using the tiny screen of a phone."

I laugh. "On occasion. I don't always carry an actual camera, but I have a very cute niece and sometimes I can't resist taking pictures of her, even if all that's handy is my phone."

"Elise has a dog, too," Mati says. "Bambi. She takes pictures of her as well."

Hala's face twists sourly.

"In Afghanistan, dogs that aren't strays are mostly used for work," Mati explains to me. "Things like guarding and herding." He smiles at his mother, a smile different from any I've seen him wear before; it's genteel, almost artificial. Still, it helps to unscrew her expression. "Even you might like Elise's dog, Mama. She is very friendly."

Hala gives her head a frantic shake. "Dirty."

"Oh, nonsense," Rasoul says, then hacks his way through a few violent coughs. He hasn't eaten much, I notice. "American dogs are domesticated," he says when he's recovered. "If we were staying, perhaps we could befriend Elise's."

If we were staying . . .

The hummingbirds that took up residence in my chest a few minutes ago drop into the well of my stomach, already heavy with *pilau* and *shlombay*, leaving me queasy. Ever since Mati told me about his August 10 departure, I've done my best to avoiding thinking about it. Now that I've gotten to know him—now that I've grown to care about him—it sucks especially. He has to go, and I'll be left behind.

Again.

He peers at me, eyes darkened with guilt, like he knows what I'm thinking, like it's somehow his fault that he has to leave Cypress Beach.

In a voice far stronger than I feel, I tell Rasoul, "You can visit with Bambi anytime. She loves meeting new people."

He laughs, which brings another coughing fit, leading to an entire glass of sipped water and a chest pounded into submission. After regaining control, he croaks, "I would like that."

When we've had our fill, Mati's mother clears the platters away. I offer to help, but she shushes me with a dismissive wave. Mati smiles his plastic smile, making me want to rescue him from the confines of this cottage. It's obvious he loves his parents, but it's even more obvious he's a different version of himself when he's with them.

Tea is a brief affair. Rasoul has evidently burned through his energy store; he sits quietly, sipping from his cup and—holy shit—smoking a cigarette. In the cottage. Exhaling and inhaling through a windpipe that sounds as if it's been rubbed over with coarse sandpaper. Hala's cold exterior has yet to thaw. She hasn't been outright rude—nothing like my mom yesterday—but I get the distinct impression she won't be bummed when I head out the door.

And then it's time to do just that. I thank my hosts, giving Rasoul my warmest smile because God, sick as he is, he's been so nice. Mati walks me to the foyer and watches as I slip my boots on. I straighten, blowing a stray tendril of hair from my face, and he hands me my bag.

"Thanks for having me," I say with more awkwardness than I thought myself capable. Then, unsure of how to execute a goodbye with his parents in the next room, I turn for the door.

A warm hand lands low on my back, sending tiny currents of elation zinging up my spine. The contact disappears before I've turned all the way around, but Mati's there, his expression a combination of plaintive and hopeful. He stuffs his fists into the pockets of his sweatshirt and asks, "Do you need to go home?"

I shake my head. My face is hot, a silly, instinctual response to his brief touch.

He smiles—his real smile. "Take a walk with me?"

elise

We walk to Cypress Beach's cemetery, a quaint block of land that's everything the Sacramento Valley National Cemetery isn't: haphazard, antiquated, fantastical. Of course, Nick's not here, which is a mixed bag. The loss of him doesn't loom over me, but I miss the chance to talk to him.

I've been here before, camera in hand, so the disorderly layout isn't a problem. I choose a spot in the cemetery's oldest section, specifically for it seclusion. Its headstones are weather-beaten and crumbling, and its trees are sky-high and blanketed in moss. Light filters through their highest branches, making shadows like lace. I snap a few pictures, then sit on a nearby bench, all crooked and dilapidated. Deliberately, I opt for the far side, just to see how close Mati will park himself.

He takes the other end.

"Is this weird?" I ask after a few moments of quiet.

He glances around. "What? This setting?"

"Yeah. Do you think it's gruesome that I've led you to two separate cemeteries?"

"Do *you* think it's gruesome?"

"No. But maybe that's a problem?"

He drapes an arm over the back of the bench. His hand is six inches from my shoulder. I could lean into it, if I wanted.

That would be weird.

"I suppose it could be construed as gruesome," he says, "but only by someone who doesn't know you."

I raise an eyebrow. "You know me?"

"I think so," he says, sounding suddenly unsure.

I swivel around and put my feet up on the bench's warped wooden slats, knees bent. I'm closer to his outstretched hand now, and he doesn't shift away. I wrap my cardigan more snugly around myself because it's cool beneath the tall, tall redwoods and the whispering Cypresses. "I think so, too," I say.

He looks me over, the way I've folded in on myself, and because he *does* know me, because he's always paying attention, reading my cues like the mysterious words in his little notebook, he says, "You're cold."

"No, I'm okay." I fail to quell an ill-timed shiver.

He unzips his sweatshirt, then shrugs it off. He's got a T-shirt on underneath, not enough to keep him comfortable in the shade. Still, he holds his hoodie out to me.

"Mati, no. Then you'll be cold."

"I will not." He gives his hoodie a little shake. "Go ahead."

I take it, slipping my arms into the soft cotton. I zip it all the way up, the way he wore it, and his scent engulfs me. It's so good—comforting, like being in a bathtub full of warm, rich bubbles. I'm reminded of yesterday, the hug that felt more intimate than any interaction I've ever had with a boy. The hug that felt like a promise. I relive it down to its finest detail, wrapped up in his hoodie.

"Thank you," I say.

"You're welcome," he answers.

Somehow, there's more behind our words than a borrowed sweatshirt.

"Your parents are nice," I tell him.

"Baba likes you."

"I like him, too. God, Mati, he's so sick. And he still smokes?"

"One cigarette, always after lunch. He says it's a reward for making it to another day, but I think he lacks the strength to quit completely."

"I didn't realize it was . . ." *so bad.*

"I know. Today is a good day, though, believe it or not, and his doctors say he's showing improvement."

"Do you think he really wants to meet Bambi?"

Mati nods. "I can already picture him playing with her in the yard. Most things Westerners do, he wants to try. He would probably eat pork chops and applesauce if he could."

"What about your mother?"

He grimaces. "She prefers the Afghan way. I wish she would have acted . . . differently."

"She's an amazing cook."

"But with you . . . I wish she would have been different with you."

I give a humorless laugh; I sound like a baying hound. "Yesterday my mom treated you like shit. Your mom was downright chummy in comparison."

"Your mom did not treat me like—she did not treat me badly. She was uncomfortable. It's hard to let go of conceptions we've spent years building. When I think about your brother, it makes sense that she's angry."

"Her anger is misguided. Maybe you're too understanding."

He touches the tail of my braid where it's fallen over my shoulder, rubbing the strands of my hair between his fingers. He must be preoccupied by his thoughts because when he catches himself, he snatches his hand away, glaring at it like it's got a mind of its own. His expression pulls taut and he moves to shove his fists into his sweatshirt pockets—his "I'm uncomfortable" tell—but he's not wearing his sweatshirt anymore and, oh, if I could just take his hand and tangle it with mine, all the tension and strain and yearning of this moment would disappear.

Or not. Maybe it'd be worse, like on the way home from Sacramento, when he held my hand for hours, literally. Every second I spent with my palm enveloped in his was incredible, but I was left feeling . . . not content. I dropped him off wanting more, more, *more*.

Kind of like right now.

I slip my hands into the pockets of the borrowed sweatshirt, mostly to keep from reaching for him. As his face relaxes, like there's relief in watching me perform his action, my fingers close over a firm rectangle—his notebook.

I trace its cardboard cover within the depths of the pocket, its feathered-paper edges, its coiled spine. I pull it out and let it rest on my palm, but I don't open it. It's too personal. His lockbox of secrets and wishes and dreams.

He regards it warily, as if it's sprouted sharp teeth and a pointed-dagger tail.

I let my gaze travel from where it sits on my palm, to his face. "Do you write in Pashto?"

"English, since I've been in America."

"What would you say if I asked to read something?"

One corner of his mouth quirks up, fashioning an adorably askew smile. "I would say, 'You are a very curious person.'"

This, for some reason, makes me laugh. "I like when you joke."

"I like when you make me feel light enough for jokes."

I hold his gaze and tell him what he must already know: "I like *you*."

He blinks, languid, thick lashes brushing high cheekbones. When his eyes meet mine again, they're a flurry of conflict. "Elise . . . all this . . . *us*. It's very complicated. You understand, don't you?"

"I do." I understand that his response isn't a rebuff, or a denial of his feelings. It's the opposite. He likes me, too; that's *why* it's complicated.

He glances at his notebook, still balanced on my hand, then looks at me. I see trust in his eyes, trust and affirmation and affection, and my skin prickles with heat.

He says, "You can read something, if you really want to."

"I *really* want to."

He takes the notebook and thumbs through it, his face drawn in circumspection. He flips past some pages quickly, wearing an expression like, *Oh, hell no*, and considers others more carefully. I'm wondering at the criteria he's using for this prudent selection process when, finally, he opens the notebook's pages wide and looks up at me.

"This one was for fun," he says, smiling reluctantly. "I was just . . . playing around."

He holds the notebook out to me.

MATI

Twinkle, twinkle shiny star,
set ablaze the sky so far.

In his world she lights a spark,
illuminating swathes of dark.
Her eyes, her smile, glowing bright,
twinkle, twinkle, up all night.

Waves and gulls, at the beach,
words to teach and walls to breech.
In her he has found a friend,
links to mend, bonds transcend.

Walking, wandering, toes in sand,
how he longs to take her hand.
Dandelions, foggy skies,
sights now seen through wondrous eyes.

Glinting in a night of black,
thanks to her he can't look back.
Take a breath, away they'll fly,
up above the world so high.

Twinkle, twinkle shiny star,
she has marked him like a scar.

I was dead, then alive. Weeping, then laughing.

—Rumi

elise

the day after my lunch at Mati's cottage (the day after he let me read about stars and scars and wondrous eyes, the day after I nearly swooned in the middle of a busted-up cemetery), I'm cruising out the gate with Bambi and her trusty tennis ball when Ryan intercepts me.

"You're headed to the beach, aren't you?" he says over the hedge.

"Yep."

"Perfect, because Xavier and I are about to meet up. If you're going to hang out with Mati, we can double."

I hesitate, wavering between my need to be a good friend, my wish to lay eyes on Xavier, and my selfish desire to keep Mati to myself.

"I take it your lunch with the parents went well," Ryan says with a pointed raise of his brow. "It may not have, if it weren't for me. Keep that in mind while you're trying to come up with an excuse for ditching us."

I crack a smile. "Oh, all right. You guys can tag along."

"Cool. I'll call Xavier and tell him to head for the beach."

Bambi woofs, wagging her tail at the gate. I wave an arm. "Call while we walk."

On the way, I text Mati to fill him in about Xavier, and by the time Ryan and I reach the beach, we find the two of them waiting near the top of the stairs. There's a red Wrangler parked nearby, a US Air Force sticker adhered to its rear window. Ryan was right—Xavier is good-looking. He's almost as tall as Mati, with a similar wiry build. His skin is brown, his eyes nearly black, and his smile is warm. He'd blend right in with the company of young soldiers who came to Sacramento for my brother's burial. He greets Ryan with an affectionate shoulder bump, which makes me smile. It's nice, seeing Ryan so happy.

I'm equally happy when Mati reaches out to tuck a lock of hair behind my ear. "Good morning, Elise," he says and, benign as they are, his words feel like a secret—a private exchange between the two of us.

Xavier's brought a football, which strikes me as kind of funny. Ryan's not exactly sporty, and though Nicky taught me the ins and outs of soccer, helmets and shoulder pads weren't his thing. Somehow, I can't see Mati throwing a football on the streets of Kabul.

But as soon as we hit the sand, he and Xavier are tossing the ball back and forth, the gap between them stretching wider and wider as they make their way down the beach. Ryan and I follow, taking turns throwing Bambi's tennis ball into the surf. When we reach the end of the sand, we stop to watch her frolic, chasing seagulls like she was born to do it. Ryan asks about yesterday's lunch, and Mati tells him how impressed his parents were with me, a half truth, I'm sure—I doubt Hala spent the evening singing my praises. Then I feel obligated to admit to Mati that Ryan schooled me on how not to make a fool of myself during a Muslim meal. He seems touched—that Ryan went to the trouble to tutor me, or that I bothered to learn, I'm not sure.

After our long walk back, Xavier and Mati persuade Ryan and me to play a game of catch. I'm terrible and Ryan's not much better, but Mati surprises me with his athleticism. I mean, he's tall and lean and his arms are corded with muscle, but football. It's so . . . *American.*

We pass, and pass, and pass, and then, conversationally, Ryan says, "So Jordan called yesterday."

Xavier's spiral flies wide.

Mati retrieves the ball, brushing sand from its leather. "Jordan is your . . . ?"

"Ex," Ryan says. He glances at Xavier, then quickly away. "He's having second thoughts about ending things."

"Why?" Mati asks. He tosses the ball to me, and I make a lucky catch.

"He's thinking the distance between our schools won't be so bad after all."

I throw a wobbly pass to Xavier, hoping to distract him from the awkward topic Ryan thrust upon us. He connects, but sloppily.

"How far apart will you be?" Mati asks.

"We'll both be in Texas. Couple of hours' drive."

"Oh." Mati sounds let down. I try to catch his eye, but Bambi's barreling toward him, wet and sandy, and he has to dodge her before he's bowled over.

"Miles are miles," Xavier says, throwing the ball to Ryan. "There are ways to stay in touch—if you want to." Like an oh-so-casual afterthought, he adds, "What did you tell him?"

Ryan holds the ball at his chest, looking right at Xavier. "That what we had was good, but I can see now that it's run its course."

Their shared gaze holds, and I can guess what they're both thinking: If they stay together, eventually they'll have to deal with a lot of miles.

"Have you done the long-distance thing before, Xavier?" I ask.

He shakes his head. "I don't think I'd mind, so long as I cared about the guy enough. It's all about putting effort into the intellectual stuff even when there's not much physical payoff."

"Physical payoff's not all that's important," I say.

Ryan remembers the football he's holding and lobs it to Mati. "True," he says, watching as Mati makes a neat catch. "And I bet that when there *is* physical payoff, it's better after the time apart."

"Absence makes the heart grow fonder?" I say.

Ryan winks. "Pretty much."

"I can get behind that," Xavier says. He smiles at Ryan, and Ryan grins back.

Mati spins the football on his palm. He looks subdued. "Absence makes the heart grow fonder? This is a common expression?"

"Yeah," Ryan says. "It means—"

"I understand its meaning. I'm just..."

Reconciling it with what he's feeling. Trying to decide how it applies to him and me and the teetering tower of fondness and admiration and lust (maybe that's just me?) we've been constructing over the last few weeks.

I get it—I'm trying to do the same.

After we climb the stairs, Xavier heads back to the MLI for an afternoon class, and Mati walks almost all the way home with Ryan and me. He stops a few cottages down from Iris's, an attempt to avoid another run-in with my mom, I think. He scratches Bambi behind her ears and says, "Xavier is great, Ryan. I had a good time."

I had a good time, too. But then, why do I feel so down? Why does my head feel like a wrecking ball balanced precariously on my neck? Why do my limbs drag as if they're made of concrete?

"I think we'll start imposing ourselves on all your beach walks," Ryan says.

I glare.

He laughs and musses my hair. "Gear down, Elise. I'm kidding with y'all."

Mati's watching me, rapt, like he's trying to discern the meaning of *gear down* while at the same time figure out why I'd care whether Ryan and Xavier start tagging along on our walks.

Because I want us to be alone, I think, clinging to his gaze.

He smiles, looks at the sidewalk, then bashfully back at me.

My heart... It sings.

Ryan thumps his shoulder. "We can hang out sometime, if you want. I know Elise is prettier than me, but if she's ever busy and you're bored and want to get out..."

"Okay," Mati says. "Thanks."

Ryan passes over his phone and Mati inputs his number and, my, what a trio we make. It's been so long since I've had real friends, I almost didn't register that that's what these boys have become. Standing beneath the shade of the Cypresses, breathing ocean air, laughing with the two of them, I feel warm and lucky and full of joy.

But in the next moment, my happiness blows away, letting reality spread like a chill through the chambers of my heart. In a few weeks, Mati and Ryan will leave, just like my dad left for New York, and my brother left for Afghanistan, and Audrey and Janie left for Cypress Beach.

In a few weeks, I'll be alone again.

elise

The next morning, I return from the beach to a cottage that smells of strong coffee. I check the pot in the kitchen—fresh, still hot. Nick's malformed mug is sitting out, a spoonful of sugar waiting in its bottom.

Mom must not be hating me today. Of course, I haven't said anything about Mati since our argument on the sidewalk. As far as she knows, I've listened to her oh-so-sage advice and ended my friendship with him.

I can't fathom a world in which such a thing would actually happen.

I fill my mug with coffee and head to the library, Bambi trailing behind me. Mom's working, her fingers flying over her keyboard, tap-tap-tapping out a novel that I'm sure will send many a middle-aged woman into fits of pleasure. The small TV in the corner is on, tuned to Fox News, set to mute. I fall into my regular chair, Bambi takes to her bed, and Mom saves her file.

She spins around to face me. "How's the coffee?"

"Good, thanks. How's the work?"

"Rough." She glances over her shoulder at the calendar that's tacked to the wall to the left of her desk. Her deadline looms three weeks from now, the day after Ryan and Mati leave Cypress Beach. "I think I'll make it, though."

"You will," I say, modeling supportive behavior, hoping she absorbs it.

She picks up the newspaper on her desk. "I read a frightening article this morning."

"About what?"

"Muslims. The threat they present."

I roll my eyes but resist the urge to pop out of my chair and walk out of the room. "God, Mom. We're doing this again?"

"I think you should read the article."

"Why? Mati's not a threat. Anyone who knows him understands as much." I think of the day he poured sand into my hands and explained about the Afghans, the Muslims, who live kindly, humbly. I recall the tiny pinch of sand that represented those who do not. "Muslims aren't a threat, either," I continue, "and it's dangerous to generalize." I point at Bambi, curled up on her bed, paws twitching as she dreams. "It's like saying dogs are a killer species just because they all have sharp teeth."

Mom's gaze is level, unaffected. "They're planning to target military families. Dependents of soldiers, active-duty *and* killed-in-action."

This . . . gives me pause.

Dependents.

Audrey and Janie.

I set my coffee mug on the table, my pulse ratcheting in a way that makes my grip untrustworthy. "Really?"

She waves the newspaper. "It's all here. There've been anonymous letters sent to different media outlets around the country."

I make no move to take the paper she's still holding out. I'm curious—I can't deny that I am—but I won't give her the satisfaction.

"You can't actually think Mati is involved in making violent threats. I have never in my life met a more peaceful person."

"What about his family? Their arrival in America, the timing of it all. You have to admit—it's very coincidental."

"His father is sick!"

"You don't know for sure."

Yes, I do. I met the man, saw his sallow skin, heard his ramshackle cough, smelled illness coursing through his blood. More than that, I sensed his tranquility, and was on the receiving end of his warmth. Rasoul is not an Islamic extremist.

"Elise, I know you prefer to think the best of people, and that's one of your finest qualities. But I think, in this case, your friendship with this boy is more than you're capable of managing. You don't have the perspective to see past twinkling eyes, a chiseled jaw, and a charming smile."

"Thanks, Mom. I'm happy to know you think I'm a moron who's ready and willing to tangle with a terrorist just because he's good-looking."

She stands, crosses the room, and lays the newspaper on my lap. "He's here for, what? A few more weeks? Is he so important that you're willing to create a divide within our family? Haven't we been through enough?"

"Mati has nothing to do with what we've been through. In fact, he's making it easier for me to cope. Did that ever occur to you? Audrey has Janie, and you have your work. What do I have? The camera my dead brother gave me and a graveyard of a photography portfolio."

With that, I spring from my chair and storm out of the library.

I leave my cooling coffee on the table, but I take the newspaper.

In my cavernous bedroom, I read every word of the article that's got my mom so worked up and, yes, it's scary, but I refuse to let fear color my perception of the world. Mati is *good*. If I thought for one second that he or his parents were a threat to my family, I'd cut things off immediately. I might be idealistic, but I'm not obtuse.

I think of the poem he let me read at the cemetery, how it made me want to laugh. How it made me feel cherished ...

Twinkle, twinkle shiny star, she has marked him like a scar.

I know exactly what he means.

I find a paint pen in my desk drawer, silver, and haul myself onto a chair. I have to stretch, but I can just reach my black ceiling with the tip of the pen. I draw a star, small, the size of a silver dollar. I fill it in, and then I give it a neighbor. Feeling a little like Michelangelo, I step down from the chair and gaze up, admiring my work.

Twinkle, twinkle indeed.

MATI

"I have to babysit my niece tonight," she tells me.

We are walking home from the beach,
just the two of us.
We are closer than usual,
drawn to each other
like monarchs to milkweed.
Occasionally, the dog tugs the leash she holds,
causing our shoulders to bump,
or our hands to brush.
Her touch smooths my rough edges.

Her tone is tentative when she says,
"You should come by."

"To your sister-in-law's cottage?"

"Sure. Audrey's working the late shift."

This . . . is appealing.

She talks about her niece with wonder,
as if she were the most precious jewel.
Like oxygen, Janie feeds the flame of Nick's spirit.
I would be happy to meet her.

And I will be happy
(timorous, tentative, terrified)
when Janie undoubtedly goes to sleep,
leaving me and this beautiful girl
alone in a cottage of possibility.

I stumble over a crack in the sidewalk,
a renegade root that has disturbed the pavement.
I clear my throat and bury my hands in my pockets.
"I'm not sure your sister-in-law would approve."

"It's not like we have to tell her."
She smiles and her expression,
framed by glossy caramel hair,
is alight with hope.
"Seriously, Mati. It'll be fun."

I should not go—no, I should not.

I have devoted myself
to fostering a closeness with Allah,
and I strive to be a gracious Muslim son.
But that does not mean
I am not vulnerable to misdeeds.
I have tempted sin in her proximity already,
engaging in meandering conversations,

letting my hand drift to hers,
daydreaming about her,
when I should be doing anything but.

If we are truly alone . . .

I will not make choices that honor Allah's word.

But our situation is not so simple.
The feelings she incites in me—
affection, esteem, compassion—
strengthen my spirituality.
Being with her, sometimes,
feels transcendental.

Say yes, say yes, say yes!

"Can I think about it?"

Her eyes narrow;
I have given her invitation
the same response she gave mine.

"Of course," she says, borrowing my words.
"Call me later to let me know what you decide."

elise

i don't really think he'll come to Audrey's, and I feel guilty for heaving the pressure of my invitation on his shoulders.

Why can't I leave well enough alone?

Even when the doorbell rings thirty minutes after Aud leaves for Camembert, I don't *really* think it'll be him. My mom, maybe, or the UPS man, or some random kid selling candy bars. But when I look through the peephole set in the front door, there's Mati, wearing jeans and a butter-yellow T-shirt, a hoodie slung over his arm. His hair's grown since we met and it's everywhere, sticking up in thick black tufts. He looks nervous.

Janie runs up and grabs the hem of my shirt. "Who is it, Auntie?"

I crouch next to her. "My friend. Do you mind if he hangs out with us?"

Janie's blue eyes gleam. "I don't mind. Open the door!"

I do. Mati smiles; he's unquestionably happy to see me, and the feeling's mutual. Instinct says, *Throw your arms around him.* Logic says, *Let him lead.*

He's got a hand tucked behind his back, but he reaches out with the other. I give him mine and he squeezes my palm. My heart performs a joyful dip, and all is right in the world.

"You must be Janie," he says, stooping to talk to my niece.

I rest my palm on top of her head. "Can you say hi to Mati?"

She smiles her dimpled smile and parrots, "Hi, Mati."

He brings his arm out from behind his back, revealing a puffy white dandelion, ripe for blowing. "I heard you like to make wishes."

Her face lights up. "I do! Can I make a wish now?"

"You should probably come outside. New flowers won't grow if these seeds land on the floor of your cottage. And if the flowers don't grow—"

"My wishes won't come true!"

He grins. "That's right."

I watch from the doorway as she follows him onto the lawn. He kneels in the grass so she can take the dandelion from him. She holds it carefully, blocking it from the breeze with her little hand. "I'll wish for cookies," she says. "That's what my daddy wished for when he was little like me."

Mati opens his mouth, blinks, then wordlessly closes it. I have to look away because I'm biting hard into my lip, a vain attempt to keep tears from falling.

Oh, Janie.

She closes her eyes and gives the dandelion a mighty blow. Her lids spring open again and she watches the seeds scatter with unadulterated delight. "Thank you for my wish," she says to Mati. "You should come inside now. Auntie is making noodles."

"Is she? Well, I cannot miss that."

She leads him to the door. As she passes me, she whispers, "Cookies for dessert, Auntie, because I wished for them."

I swallow around a lump that won't let me be. "You got it, girlie."

She runs inside and plops down in front of the crayons and coloring books I put out to keep her busy while I work on dinner. Mati lingers in the foyer while I close the door.

"That was sweet," I say, which sounds trite compared with his gesture.

"But I made you sad."

"No you didn't. You made me really happy."

He raises a doubtful eyebrow. "That isn't true, but I think you'll be happy when we have cookies for dessert."

I smile. "Thanks to you and your wishes. We'd be up shit creek if you hadn't come by."

He feigns shock, as if he hasn't grown accustomed to my colorful language. "Is it okay if I stay for noodles?"

For an instant, I think of Audrey and how she'd react if she knew Mati was here. She'd be pissed—I know that for sure. And then I decide I don't care, because she'd also be wrong.

I take a step toward him, curious as to whether he'll let me into his space. He does. He smells good, summery and clean, like rosemary, and heat wafts off him in waves. The pace of his breathing changes, abbreviates, like maybe I do exactly to him what he does to me.

I look up and tumble headfirst into his firelight eyes. "You can stay as long as you want."

———

We eat our noodles and because I insist, carrot sticks, and then we hang out at the table awhile, listening to Janie recite a choppy version of *Goldilocks and the Three Bears*. Apparently, she sympathizes with Goldilocks. "She was just sleepy," she says after the part where the bears chase the intruder from their cottage.

Mati counters with a story about Buzaak Chinie, a goat whose kids get eaten by a wolf, kind of like Red Riding Hood's grandmother. Buzaak Chinie takes rescue advice from an alligator, a tiger, and a lion before finally defeating the wolf and freeing her kids from its belly. Janie giggles at the silly voices Mati adopts for each character, particularly the falsetto he gives Buzaak Chinie.

After, we head out into the yard with a bag of frosted animal cookies. The twilight sky is clear, and the air shimmers with the warmth of summer. Mati and I sit under a trellis laced with climbing jasmine, breathing its sweet scent, and he tells me about how the flower originated in his part of the world, and that its fragrance reminds him of home.

Meanwhile, Janie marks up the patio with chalk, devouring her weight in cookies. "Look, Auntie," she says, pointing to her drawing. "Rainbow."

"I love it. Do you remember our rainbow song?"

"Yes." She eyes Mati shyly, and I take her hint.

"Do you want me to sing it with you?"

"Yes!"

And so we sing to the tune of "Head, Shoulders, Knees, and Toes," the song I taught her a few weeks ago: *Red, yellow, green and blue, green and blue. Red, yellow, green and blue, green and blue. Purple, orange, brown and black. Red, yellow, green and blue, green and blue.*

When we're finished, Mati claps like he's genuinely impressed. Janie curtseys.

She continues drawing, flowers and princess crowns and sunshines with googly eyes, humming our rainbow song while she works. Mati passes me the bag of animal cookies and I take a pink elephant, then go about picking sprinkles off to eat individually.

"That is . . . an odd way to eat a cookie," he says.

"I know. I like to make them last." And then, thanks to a random but perfectly timed recollection, I grin and say, "*Khwazza.*"

His eyes widen, and then he's beaming. "Have you been studying?"

"Not really. I just happen to have an excellent teacher."

"You are a flatterer." He takes a frosted camel from the bag and bites its head off.

"And you're vicious! You're like the wolf from your story!"

He looks down at the half camel in his hand. "Oops?"

I laugh. "Put it out of its misery already."

He tosses what's left of the cookie into his mouth, watching as Janie draws her version of a cat—a circle with two triangular ears on top. She gives it long, long whiskers before looking up to seek our approval.

"Well done," Mati says as I flash her a thumbs-up.

I bend my legs in close and wrap my arms around them. I rest my cheek on my knees so I can look more comfortably at my babysitting buddy. "Is Mati your full name?"

He shakes his head. "It's Matihullah. I was named after an old friend of my baba's. My sister was Janie's age when I was born and she couldn't pronounce it, so my parents shortened it to Mati."

"Matihullah." It sounds so serious. "I like it, though I think Mati suits you better."

He bumps my knee with his. Pings of electricity dance across my skin. "I think so, too."

We're motionless, watching each other, breathing in tandem.

Enchanted . . . That's the only word that comes close to encompassing how I feel—how *he* makes me feel.

His gaze slips to my mouth. He licks his lower lip, absently I think, but God, I'd trade my Nikon to know what's going on in his head. Because *kiss me, kiss me, kiss me* is bouncing around in mine and even though I know he won't—*can't*, damn it—I want him to think about it as compulsively, as *fanatically*, as I do. He'd be a good kisser, I'm certain. He's aware and deliberate by nature, but gentle and thoughtful and passionate, too. Plus, those lips . . . He'd be a prodigy—a virtuoso of the kiss.

Janie appears in front of us suddenly, like she teleported across the yard. She's covered in chalk dust and frosting. "Auntie, I'm tired."

The spell is broken.

elise

i help Janie through a bath, brush the sugar from her tiny teeth, then lie down beside her on her twin bed. I read from a book of fairy tales, whimsical stories about princesses who meet their princes and fall in love without challenge or consequence—sort of. I mean, sometimes the infatuated couples have to outsmart an angry witch or battle a fire-breathing dragon, but there's always, always, *always* a happily ever after.

Must be nice.

When Janie's eyelids grow heavy and her thumb finds its way into her mouth, I tuck her beneath her garden fairy sheets and kiss her fine hair. I flip off the overhead light in favor of the golden glow of the night-light, then wind the music box that sits atop her bookshelf. "Once Upon a Dream" . . . Nick had it shipped to Audrey the day she told him they were expecting a baby girl, a phone call that spanned North Carolina to Afghanistan, and was, as Aud tells it, spilling over with joy.

As soon as the soft tinkle of music begins, Janie snuggles into her covers and closes her eyes, like the song chosen for her by her daddy brings a special sense of comfort. I stand over her bed for a moment that stretches into many, letting my gaze trace her chubby cheeks and her sloped nose and her lips, heart-shaped, like mine and my mom's and my brother's.

He'd be so head-over-heels in love with his little girl. He'd be the best dad, too, and with very little example to speak of.

When I return to the living room, Mati's tucked into a corner of the sofa, paging through the latest issue of *US Weekly*. He drops it onto the table when he notices me, guiltily, like I caught him doing something wrong.

"You're welcome to read Aud's celebrity gossip magazines if you like," I tell him, lingering in the doorway.

"Celebrity gossip means nothing to me," he says in that windswept voice of his.

I cross the room and sit down beside him, though not too close. Despite the energy that crackles between us, I have no idea what he wants, what he's ready for, how far he's willing to go. What's happening between us, this tentative, complicated thing, is bursting with heat, but it's also being steered by his beliefs. Still, he came to a basically empty cottage to spend time with me. That's got to mean something.

"Sorry I was gone so long," I say, slipping off my shoes and tucking my feet under. "Janie's bedtime routine is intense."

"Your niece is cute," Mati says. He leans forward, bracing his elbows on his knees like he's not sure how to manage his long limbs within the confined space of the sofa. He graces me with a smile, slight, uncertain but sincere. "And you're a good auntie. She adores you."

"Sometimes I feel bad for her, being surrounded by women all the time—not that women aren't an awesome influence or anything. I just . . . I wish my brother were here to teach her how to roughhouse and shoot a BB gun and burp the alphabet—things he taught me. Temper the flow of estrogen, you know?"

Mati's brows hitch, and heat scales my neck—I doubt anyone's ever chatted him up about female sex hormones. I clear my throat in an attempt to dislodge my foot from its depths, but his smile expands and he says, with exaggerated awe, "You know how to burp the alphabet?"

"Ha-ha," I deadpan. "Careful, or I'll demonstrate."

"You teach Janie all kinds of things. That song about the colors? She wouldn't know it without you."

I shrug. "All kids learn the colors. They're a preschool staple."

"But not all kids know *badass* songs about the colors." His eyes spark with joviality—he's clearly proud of his slang-y curse.

"Very good," I say. "You keep teaching me beautiful Pashto words, and I'll make a gutter mouth of you."

"Maybe you can teach me a song about rude words."

I laugh. "There're more important things I should teach you first."

He pivots, bringing a leg up so he can face me squarely. His knee rests against my thigh, barely, but the contact feels illicit and exciting, like the zap of a live wire. My pulse kicks into high gear as my gaze rises to his, heated but somber.

We're not teasing anymore.

His voice is a breeze in the otherwise silent room. "What can you teach me, Elise?"

I let go of a shuddery breath. "What do you want to know, Mati?"

He reaches for me, slowly, cautiously. His hand, warm, roughened with callouses, lands on my arm. I look down to find that his complexion is tawny and mine's like cream, and something about the contrast speaks to me, whispers, *This is right.*

He strokes the crook of my elbow, where my skin is tissue-paper thin. His fingers draw tiny circles, trace my forearm, brush the inside of my wrist. It's innocent, his touch, and it's everything but: stirring and sensual and suggestive. My breath comes rapidly and I'm hot everywhere, tingling from the roots of my hair to the soles of my feet. I'm certain he notices because his face is cracked open like a book, inscribed with words like *satisfied* and *smug* and—I think—*longing*.

I capture his hand, the hand with the gentle, meandering fingers, and realize, mortifyingly enough, I'm shaking. I can barely look at him, barely form a coherent thought. I was never tongue-tied when I was with Kurt, never timid or on edge. I never worried about impressing him or saying the right thing. He was a kind, handsome boy, but he was just a boy.

Mati . . . Mati is more.

I raise a hand to his cheek, grazing his perpetual stubble. His eyes close and I'm relieved. The way I'm feeling, awestruck and deferential and like I'm seconds from floating away, must be so obvious.

He keeps his eyes shut as I pass my fingers along his forehead, his jaw, his lids. I run my hand through his thick hair, something I've wanted to do for eternities. I touch his lips, feather-light, solicitous, attentive, like a kiss. I feel his warm exhale.

He covers my hand with his, stilling it, pulling it down to rest on his leg. He opens his eyes. He looks at me the way he did that first day at the beach, after we slogged out of the water, winded and weary. He looks at me like he sees through me, beyond clothes and hair and flesh—like he sees *into* me.

"I know what you can teach me," he says, a rumble of thunder deep in his throat.

I incline toward him, like he's a magnet and I'm iron. "What?"

His gaze falls, then snaps back to mine. "Teach me how to kiss."

I retreat, stunned. "But you can't—"

"I can. I want to, Elise."

He's so composed, so steadfast. Meanwhile, my heart's pounding and my skin's thrumming and my head's going crazy. I want to kiss him, too—I'm *dying* to kiss him—but I wonder if I'm corrupting this boy who's pure and stalwart, unwavering in his beliefs.

I want to, Elise.

Mati isn't corruptible. Being here, being together . . . It's as much his decision as it is mine.

I bring my palms up to rest against his cheeks. I feel his apprehension, his inexperience, through the heat of his skin, like they're my own. But he's wearing a wisp of a smile and, God, he's looking at me like he longs for me—like he *aches* for me.

I push onto my knees, matching his height. "You're sure?"

"I'm sure," he whispers.

I tilt my head and slowly lean in.

MATI

Her lips feel like flower petals,
and taste like syrup—
sugar, lemon, orange blossom.
Her kiss wards off evil,
worry,
fear.

Her kiss makes me invincible.
This . . .
This is what I have missed.
This is what I have spent a lifetime without.
This, and her.

When she withdraws,
I feel cold and needy.
I want her—
more, always, forever.
She is elemental;
she is essential.

Her retreat is cursory,
a pause, a breath, a transition.

She moves over me.
She smiles.
She closes her eyes.
She kisses me again,
or I kiss her.
We kiss each other—
her, me, *us.*

This kiss is deeper.
Hotter and headier.
Hands and lips,
contented sounds.
Hips and tongues,
heavy breaths.
Hair in knots.
Legs entwined.

I could die with the ecstasy of it.

The air shifts.
Her body freezes.
Her eyes fly open,
wide and guilty.

I am disoriented,
confused,
tumbling through fog.

Why would she stop so suddenly?

And then,
from across the room,
a gasp.

elise

*W*hat the *hell*, Elise?"

I scramble off Mati, off the couch, blotting our kiss away with the back of my hand.

"Audrey!"

"Don't *Audrey* me," she says, storming into the room. She's wearing her restaurant clothes: black slacks and a white button-down. Her hair's tied back in a long pony. Her face is aflame. She looks at Mati. No, she *glares* at Mati, who's half sitting, half lying on her sofa, exactly the way I left him. He's gaping at me like, *What should I do?*

"You're home early," I say to my sister-in-law.

She ignores my mindless observation, instead thrusting a finger in Mati's direction and spitting, "What's he doing here?"

"He's . . ." I glance at Mati again and then, because he's so surprised he's petrified, I offer him my hand. He grips it and I do my best to lug his solid frame up. It'd be comical, if every single thing about this moment weren't completely screwed up. When he's standing, folded in on himself but a head taller than Audrey and me, I say, "He's my friend."

"Your *friend*? Have you lost your mind?" She's talking too loud; she's going to wake Janie. "This is my *house*, Elise. My *daughter* is down the hall. You think it's okay to bring someone like *him* here?"

I reach out to touch Mati's arm. He's trembling, and I feel, suddenly, like I'm going to burst into tears. If I'm embarrassed, he must be mortified. The way Audrey's talking about him—like he's a piece of trash I dragged in from the alley—makes my stomach roil.

"His name is Mati," I say, like an introduction might fix this.

She clenches the strap of her bag. "I don't care what his name is!"

She's being so unfair, so spiteful, so mind-bogglingly rude, I feel like I'm addressing a stranger. "Please don't judge him, Aud."

Her eyes go wide. She wrenches her bag off and flings it onto the sofa, where it lands upside down, spilling keys and coins across the cushion. "If you don't want me to judge him, don't bring him into my house. Into my *life*!"

Janie's whimpers drift into the living room.

Audrey yanks her ponytail loose and pushes her hands through her hair. "Great. Because tonight hasn't been shitty enough." She launches a look of disgust at Mati, then me. Its impact knocks the wind out of my lungs. She falls onto the couch and starts shoving things back into her bag, her hair hanging limply. She seems a thousand years older than she did when she left for her shift, tired and hopeless, and now she's sniffling and even though I hate her for the way she's treating Mati, I still want to hug her.

"I should go," he murmurs.

"Good riddance," Audrey mutters. I'm about to round on her, but then she sniffs again and I realize she's crying legitimate tears.

Shit.

I walk Mati to the door. My heart's hammering, a residual buzz from that kiss (*God, that kiss*) and from the shock of being caught, and chastised, and humiliated by the blatant ignorance of one of my favorite people.

Audrey's tears . . . they always, *always* get me.

"I'm sorry," I whisper to Mati.

He tucks a lock of hair behind my ear, then pulls the front door open. "We can talk later."

"Soon," I say, clinging to him. "I'll call you."

He nods, extracting his hand from mine with a sad, sad smile. And then he walks out, closing the door gently behind him.

I stay in the foyer for a few minutes, leaning on the wall, catching my breath. I listen to the gut-wrenching anthem of Audrey's weeping, and then the quieter ballade of her attempting to compose herself. I hear her pad down the hall, the squeaky hinges of Janie's door, the soft hum of Aud's voice as she calms her daughter.

God, I've made a mess. I should've gotten her permission before inviting Mati. Introduced them officially, first. I should've kept my hands to myself because if she'd walked in on us talking, she might not have been so shocked. And Mati . . . he left with sorrowful eyes, his shoulders stooped with distress. I'm to blame.

Audrey appears in the foyer, eyes red, cheeks flushed. "Are you leaving?" she asks, but there's no venom left in her voice. She sounds drained, like she doesn't give a shit what I do.

"If you want me to."

She shakes her head. "Come sit down."

I follow her into the living room. She sinks onto the sofa, so I do, too, into the corner Mati vacated a few minutes ago. I can feel his lingering heat. I ask, "Is Janie okay?"

Audrey nods. "Just startled. She's never woken up to yelling."

"I'm sorry. I shouldn't have had him here while you were away."

"You shouldn't have had him here at all."

"But . . . *why?*" I truly do not understand the prejudice she and my mom have against Mati. I mean, initially, maybe—I felt it, too, the sting of the word "Afghanistan," the way it intensified every terrible second that's passed since Nick died. But I got to know him, and my apprehension disappeared. Mom and Audrey don't want to see how fantastic he is. They're too scared—too narrow-minded—to care.

"Why?" Audrey asks, flabbergasted. "Because it's too damn hard!"

"It wouldn't be, if you'd give him a chance."

"I don't want to give him a chance, and you shouldn't, either. He's leaving, thank God, and then none of us will ever have to think about him again. We'll be better off."

I blink away the threat of tears. "Not me."

Audrey shakes her head. "I saw the way you were kissing him—I saw the way you looked at him, like a lovesick puppy. You don't even know him. It's awful."

"I *know* him—I know everything I need to know. It's you who's awful, you and my mom."

"Elise, Nick *died* because of those people!"

I shoot up off the sofa. Anger courses through me, making my mouth taste bitter. "Nick *never* would've treated one of my friends the way you just treated Mati. He'd be disgusted by the way you acted."

She rears back, like I've slapped her, and guilt crashes into me. "Aud—"

"No," she says, glaring up at me. "Get out of my house."

I stare at her for a moment that stretches so long and taut, it becomes unbearable. She stares right back, eyes flashing with fury. Who *is* she?

"Elise, go!"

———

I step out of Audrey's cottage, into the night.

I dial Mati, stumbling down the sidewalk.

He answers immediately. "Are you okay?"

"Yeah," I say, but my voice sounds unsteady. "Are you home?"

"No. I walked to town. I needed air."

I need air, too. And I need him, because right now, he's the only person capable of mending the gash torn through me. "Will you meet me?"

"Where?"

Not my house. I'm sure Audrey's on the phone with my mom, and I'm sure she's reporting exactly what she walked in on, which means Mom is mid-freak-out. As if on cue, my phone beeps with an incoming call.

"There's a park on Raspberry Street," I tell Mati, letting the call go to voice mail.

"The citadel made of wood?"

I smile despite myself. "If a citadel is the same as a castle, then yes. I can be there in ten."

"I can be there in five."

elise

i find him sitting on the ground in front of the deserted play structure, illuminated by the glow of the overhead streetlamps. He's hunched over his notebook, pen in hand, scribbling furiously. His face is a valley of shadows.

I approach him cautiously, conscious of the barriers we demolished earlier, before Audrey interrupted the kiss to end all kisses. My lips tingle at the memory and, distracted, I step on a twig, splitting it with a *crack*.

Mati's head jerks up. He spots me and springs up off the ground, simultaneously pushing the notebook and pen into his pocket. A moment of heedful indecision restrains us. I attempt a smile, but it's fragmented, a half-baked effort because the sight of him, all wounded and unsure, fills my eyes with tears.

He rushes toward me, reaching out to grasp my hands. "Elise," he says, "I'm sorry."

"You have nothing to be sorry for. This is my fault—all of it."

"No. I should have known better."

"Known better than what? Audrey was *terrible* to you. I'm so mad I want to pummel her. She's messed up because of what happened to my brother, and she talks without thinking, and we surprised her, and I—I hate that you had to hear that. I'm just . . . I'm so sorry."

He quiets me with a hand on my cheek. "Don't be."

My body inclines toward him because now that I know what close-to-Mati feels like, his nearness is a craving. I place my palm flat on his chest, just over his beating heart; it's impossible *not* to touch him. "Thanks for meeting me," I whisper before I get carried away.

He nods toward a nearby bench. "Should we sit?"

I consider, and then I'm struck by a stroke of genius. "Not there."

I lead him toward a set of low steps and up onto the play structure. I pick my way through the darkness, across a row of smooth planks, to the drawbridge. I stop just before, extending a foot to give the bridge a shake. "Think you can make it across?"

He raises an eyebrow. "I've never seen a park quite like this."

"Oh, come on. If Janie can do it, you can, too."

His mouth curves into a half grin. "I didn't say I couldn't do it." He edges past me, out onto the bridge. His first steps are careful, but then he acclimates to the way the bridge swings and becomes uninhibited, candidly happy, so different from his usual vigilance.

"Come on," he says, reaching for me.

I take his hand and stagger onto the swaying bridge, bumping his hip with mine as we're jostled side to side. He's laughing and I am, too, and the last hour seems distant, like *nothing* compared with the silliness that is this moment.

If Mom and Audrey could see us now.

The bridge rocks sideways, rattling on its chains, and I totter forward. Mati hooks an arm around my waist, saving me from a fall into the moat (or whatever) like a knight in shining armor. The bridge stills because we have, but his arm stays looped around me, and I surrender a breath to surprise.

"Is this okay?" he says.

This is *more* than okay. It's new, therefore thrilling, but tender and reassuring, too. My hands land on his chest and rest there like it's their rightful place. His heart strum-strum-strums through the soft cotton of his shirt, trapped beneath the corral of his rib cage. He's looking at me like he can't believe I'm here, he's here, *we're* here. He's looking at me like he adores me.

Is this okay?

I nod.

"I was disappointed tonight," he says, "because of the way your sister-in-law treated me. But do you know what was more disappointing?"

My whisper is raw and eager: "What?"

"Being interrupted. You stopped kissing me, and that kiss . . . that kiss was everything."

"I wasn't sure. I mean, it was for me, too, but . . ."

"But?"

"But you're not supposed to be kissing girls."

He leans forward, and I do, too. There's that tug again, invisible filaments stretching from my heart to his, reaching out to meet him, capture him, claim him. He's a breath away when he says, "I am only kissing *you*."

He threads his fingers into my hair and dips to press his mouth to mine. I expect tentativeness, but there is none. There's heat, and there's hunger, and there's me, yielding, reaching up to circle my arms around his neck, pressing closer, and closer, and closer, until the bridge is swinging and Mati's pulling back, smiling.

"Where were we headed when we stepped onto this bridge?"

"That way," I say, pointing to the playground's tallest turret.

"Lead the way, *shaahazadi*."

elise

*y*ou have to tell me what it means," I say, nudging him with my elbow.

"I will, when you pronounce it correctly."

I try again, though I fear I'm a lost cause. "*Shaahazadi.*"

Butchered.

He grins, shaking his head. We're leaning against the wall of the turret, shielded from the cool night air, in a cocoon of privacy. We're side by side, aligned knee-hip-shoulder as we gaze through the turret's glassless windows. The sky is blue-black and dotted with crystalline stars, not so different from the pair on my ceiling.

"You'll get it," Mati says. "Eventually."

"What if I ask really nicely? Then will you tell me what it means?"

"What would 'really nicely' sound like?"

I stretch until my mouth is a millimeter from his ear. He's gone rigid, but he makes no effort to move away. "Mati," I breathe. "Please tell me what *shaahazadi* means."

A shiver ripples through him. "You are very persuasive, princess."

It only takes me a second. "Princess! That's it, right? I totally should've guessed."

"Context clues. They're the key to decoding a new language. They're how I work out your American slang."

"I wish I was as good with words as you are. Do you carry your notebook all the time? Just in case the mood strikes?"

He laughs. "Something like that, yes."

"Is that what you want to do with your life? Write?"

He's quiet a moment, his amber eyes shrouded. He says, "Writing is not a career option."

"Writing is my mom's career."

"Things are different in Afghanistan."

"But there are universities." Several—I know, because I looked them up late one night, curious. "Mati, you could take writing classes."

"Things are different for *me*," he amends solemnly.

"What if you went to college here, in America?" I say, voicing the idea that's only recently occurred to me. We could do it; we could work if we were together. He doesn't *have* to live halfway around the world. "There are writing programs at schools all over the US and aren't there, like, student visas?"

He lets go of a hefty breath. "There are, though that doesn't change the fact that I need to return to my country."

"But . . . *why*?"

"Because, Elise. I am my baba's eldest son, which means I will be khan of our tribe one day. It is my job to take care of things at home— it is my duty."

I'm not exactly sure what he means by *duty*, but he seems reluctant to elaborate. Rather than push, rather than risk spoiling this fragment of time that feels otherwise perfect, I sit back to watch the twinkling stars. I feel a sense of solidarity with them, so far away. I have an idea of how lonely it must be, glinting forlornly in the ceaseless sky.

Only for now, I'm not alone.

I read about binary stars once: two stars that orbit the same central mass. That's what being with Mati is like. We're linked by a common gravitational pull, circling round and round while the rest of the universe closes in.

Out the window, a flash of light streaks across the sky.

"Oh my God!" I say, and at the same time, Mati says, "Did you see that?"

"Was it—?"

"A shooting star," he says. "I've never seen one before."

"I haven't, either. We have to make a wish."

"Do we?"

"Mati, yes. Superstition demands it."

He raises a cunning eyebrow. "*Aarzo.*"

I sit up straight, tapping my chin. "Hmm, context clues . . . wish? Or star?"

His smile makes our little turret glow. "Wish. Very good. Star is *stórey.*" He sits up, too, scooting around to face me. His hands land on my knees and their heat trickles through my jeans. "What will you wish for?"

"World peace."

He nods seriously and I realize, too late, that my insensitive joke was lost on him.

"Wait, I want a redo." I close my eyes for a quiet second, then say, "There. Your turn."

"You already wished? In secret?"

"That's how wishes are made. Unless you're Janie, because then you wish for cookies all the time, loud and proud."

"Then I will wish for cookies, too, an endless supply to eat every day, with you."

"After we walk Bambi?"

"Deal." He holds out his hand; I grip it and we shake, though making plans like this, plans that include the words *endless* and *with you* as part of the same thought, twists my stomach into knots. If duty says he can't consider school in the States—*life* in the States—then we have this summer, a few more weeks. Decidedly *not* endless.

We resettle ourselves against the turret wall, my hand still entwined with is. My phone buzzes; it sounds like a helicopter cutting through the silent night. I glance at the display, expecting to read MOM because it's getting late, but I see Audrey's name instead. I turn my phone off completely. She doesn't get another chance to ruin this night.

"Your mother?" Mati says as I slide my phone back into my pocket.

"Audrey."

"I bet she's calling to apologize."

"I bet she's calling to bitch about what a horrible person I am. I just—I don't want to talk about her, okay?"

"Then tell me more about your brother. Your voice does something amazing when you talk about him—it floats into the sky, like you can't contain all the love you feel for him."

"Is that weird?"

"No. It's extraordinary."

So I tell him about Nick: silly stories from our childhood (he's particularly impressed with one about how we used to surf down the staircase on my twin-sized mattress), gifts he bought me, pranks we played, trips we took with Mom (again with the surfing—Mati's fascinated by the revelation that we took lessons in Maui). I tell him about how Nick and Audrey met, their freshman year, thanks to me and a stumble on the sidewalk in front of her house. She was home alone (eternal latchkey kid) and rushed outside with handfuls of Band-Aids. She ended up sticking them all over my leg—everywhere *but* the scrape—because she was so enamored with my big brother.

"And they were together from that day on," I say.

"Until . . ."

"Well, Aud would say they're *still* together. Some days I think her devotion's impressive. Some days I think it's unhealthy."

"Her soul knows its mate," Mati says softly.

My throat swells with sadness. "I've never thought about it like that, but yeah. Maybe."

"What happened to him, Elise?"

I can talk about Nicky until I run out of oxygen, but talking about his death . . . I still get emotional. Sometimes, I still feel like weeping. "He was a civil affairs soldier," I say, giving my composure a chance to find its footing. "So he was like a middleman between the US Army and the local Afghans. The emails he sent . . . He went on and on about the people he was meeting—kids especially. He was always asking us to send packages with things he could give them: candy, school supplies, and little toys. He loved it. I missed him, but when he called he always sounded so happy, so satisfied. It was hard to be upset about his deployment when it brought him so much gratification, you know?"

Mati nods. He shifts to put an arm around me, and I nestle into his side, inhaling the fresh scent of his skin. I can see the moon through the turret window, watching us like a pale face. It's so late; I wonder whether my mom's panicking yet. I wonder whether Audrey's still sad. I wonder what Mati really thinks about what happened earlier, about being here with me now, about leaving me soon.

I toy with the zipper of his hoodie. "Do you want to hear more?"

"Only if you want to tell me."

Strangely, I do.

"My mom didn't see Nick's deployment like I did. Neither did Audrey. She was pregnant when he left, and then Janie was born six weeks early, before Nick was due to come home on leave. My mom had to fly to North Carolina to help her. The whole thing was a mess. Aud sent Nick pictures of Janie and they talked online as often as they could, but she was stressed—like, *distraught*, all the time.

"We don't know what happened the day he died—not really. We were told one of the Afghan soldiers Nick's unit was working with was playing both sides. He gave up mission intel, there was an ambush, and an RPG hit the vehicle my brother was traveling in. Three other Americans were killed in the attack. Supposedly Nick died immediately. Supposedly he didn't suffer. But we'll never be sure."

Mati presses his lips to my hair. "Photojournalism . . . What happened to your brother is why you're set on traveling the world with your camera."

I nod. "I hate that I'll never know exactly what happened. Maybe that's morbid, but the question marks are haunting. What if he *did* suffer? What if he was crying out for Audrey? For Janie, who he never even got to hold?" Tears flood my eyes now. I've never voiced these worries—I've never had the guts—and doing so brings a rush of contradictory feelings: heartache and relief, amity and embarrassment. But none of those is enough to cut me off. "The Afghan soldier who betrayed Nick's unit . . . What happened to him? It makes me crazy that I'll never know. There should've been someone there, documenting what happened."

"That will be you, someday."

I mop my face with the sleeve of my sweatshirt. "I hope so."

"I see now why your sister-in-law acted the way she did. I don't accept it, but I understand. Grief is . . . inconcealable."

And then he pulls me close, and it's exactly what I want. Exactly what I need.

———

Later, he whispers, "I know what your shooting star wish was."

I look up to find his eyes luminescent, his cheeks darkened by prickly stubble. "You do not."

"I do. You wished to stay in this turret with me forever."

His smile says he's joking, but holy shit . . . "How did you—?"

"Maybe my wish was the same."

I snort. "You wished for cookies."

"Infinite cookies, Elise. With you."

MATI

In a citadel's tallest turret,
we exist like royalty.

It is a whimsical place,
perfect for exploring.
Perfect for learning her touch,
and how she likes to be touched.

She makes little sounds—
sighs, murmurs, mewls,
kittenlike and sweet.
They unleash something in me,
and cement what I have suspected
since we met . . .
She is right.

We are right.

In our private turret,
she is never still.
Her hands roam . . .
caress . . .
excite . . .
until I am the one who can't stay quiet.

My sounds are deep and gruff.
They are words like "yes," and "please," and "more."
They are a language she understands.
She listens. She is attentive.
She lets me return the favor.

I would stay
forever
in this turret
with her
if I could.

But where she sees white, I see black.
In the vastness between us,
there are infinite variants of gray.
I cannot stay in America,
cannot stay with her,
because somewhere,
between slate and silver and charcoal,
lies the destiny I was born to live.

After the moon has journeyed
beyond the window,
I ask her if we should go.

She whispers in my ear:
"Let's stay a little longer."

I keep expecting to feel regret,
a flood of guilt
regarding the choices I have made,
and the things I have done.
It will come—I am certain,
but for now, I only feel content.

I whisper back to her:
"I am yours for the night."

elise

We stay at the park until the sky starts its gradual lightening and the day's first birds begin their song.

Mati walks me almost all the way home and offers to go the distance, but I stop him when we're a block out. My mom will be seeing red by the time I walk through the gate; there's no need to make things worse by letting her lay eyes on the perceived villain.

"I hope she isn't too angry," Mati says, sweeping my hair over my shoulder.

"Yeah. I think she'll be pretty pissed. Whatever Audrey told her would've been enough, but now that I've stayed out all night..." I grimace.

"Will you be punished?"

"What—like grounded? I don't know. My mom's style of consequence is usually more the guilt-trip variety. She'll probably go on about how I've disappointed her, and how she worried, and how if I could *just be more thoughtful*." I say all this glibly, like I'm unaffected, like the thought of walking into the cottage doesn't scare me through, but I am and it does. Of course I long for my mom's approval. Of course I want her to be proud of my choices. Of course her scathing looks and disgruntled sighs will get to me.

But not enough to keep me from Mati.

A squirrel scampers across the sidewalk and up a tree. The sky is more light than dark now, a smattering of stars rendered nearly invisible. Soon, the sun will have officially risen.

"I probably won't go to the beach this morning. I have a feeling my mom's going to want to have a conversation." By conversation, I mean fight, but I don't want Mati to worry.

Still, he frowns. "Elise, if you don't want—"

I grab his hand, quieting him. "Don't, okay? *I want.*"

He weaves his fingers through mine and stoops to meet me. Our goodbye reaffirms the conviction I found last night, and I'm smiling when he draws back. He *is* a masterful kisser.

"Call me later?"

I nod, leaning in for one more.

———

My mom is in a *rage.*

She's disheveled and unshowered. I'm not sure she's eaten since I left to babysit Janie last night. Fox News blares in the next room, and I suspect she's been up all night, glued to the TV, cataloging Islamophobic sound bites.

"How could you do this?!" she cries, smacking the kitchen table with a rumpled dish towel. Bambi's cowering beneath, her brown eyes anxious and confused. She's not used to tension between Mom and me—we never used to argue. She lets out a low whine.

"I'm sorry," I tell my mom. I *am* sorry—for ignoring her calls and for making her worry. But I'm not sorry about Mati.

"You're *sorry*? Unacceptable. I've been up all night, waiting and worrying. Have you heard about what happened in Oakland?"

I've been cocooned in a world of bliss since I stepped onto that drawbridge. An asteroid could've struck the planet and I'd be none the wiser. Of course, my mom's so melodramatic, she might be freaking out about a fender bender. "No. What?"

"A letter arrived at the VA Office. A threat against veterans, current service members, and their families. *Terrorists*. Imagine how I felt, knowing you were out with that boy, one of *them*."

I fall into a chair. "God, Mom. Mati is *not* one of them."

She waves her hand, a throwaway gesture, like, *I've heard it all before*. "I've lost a child, Elise. My firstborn. I know you can't comprehend how that feels, but I thought you knew enough to be considerate— to avoid putting me through that sort of anguish a second time."

"Are you hearing yourself? I lost Nicky, too. I'm sorry I made you worry, but Mati and his family aren't dangerous. How many times do I have to tell you?"

She makes an exasperated sound and blows right past my point. "You can't stay out all night, not with that boy—not with anybody!"

"Fine. I get it. It won't happen again."

"No, it won't. When I said I didn't want you to see him, I meant it. Look at the trouble he's caused. When Audrey told me what she walked in on last night, I just—I couldn't believe my ears." She drags a hand over her face, creased with lines of aggravation. "It would've been inappropriate no matter who the boy was, but *that boy* . . . It's as if you're bound and determined to send me to an early grave."

I roll my eyes—a splash of gasoline on her already blazing fire. "We were kissing, Mom. Don't be ridiculous."

She drops her chin to her chest; I think she's praying for serenity, or the strength to keep from whacking me with that towel that suddenly looks more like a weapon than a rectangle of linen. "Audrey suggested it was more than a kiss, and while Janie was asleep down the hall. You took advantage of her trust, and then you snuck off to stay the night with him."

"Are you kidding? This, from the woman who used to let her teenage son and his girlfriend spend time behind a locked door?" I push my hands through my snarled hair, frustration cranking my heart rate higher and higher. "God, Mom! I know you're stressed and I know you're angry, but set all that aside. How is Mati and me hanging out at the park any more scandalous than Audrey and Nick having sleepovers in your house?"

She practically growls. "Audrey and Nick were in *love*."

I blink, stunned by her nerve. What I feel for Mati is no less powerful than what Nick felt for Audrey during their early days. All that's different in my case is Mati's background, which is completely inconsequential.

I raise a challenging eyebrow. "I'll ask again: How is my situation with Mati different?"

She inhales sharply. "Don't you dare. Don't you *dare* tell me you're in love with that boy."

"I'm not going to tell you anything, because you haven't asked. You haven't asked how I feel, or what I'm going through. It's always *how could you do this to me?* Or *think of Audrey.* Or, *we're moving and you have no say-so.*" My voice is so loud, so harsh, I suspect Ryan and Iris can hear me next door. But I don't care. I've needed to say these things for a long time, and now that I've let loose, criticisms and accusations and *anger* are blasting out of me like water from a geyser. I smack my palms against the table. "What about *me*, Mom?"

Bambi low-crawls from her hiding space, creeping out of the room. My mom shakes her head, like she's trying to jiggle the last twelve hours out of her conscience. "You're proving you're not sensible enough for a mature discussion. And besides, you could have come to me. If you're so desperate for conversation, you could have approached me. Instead, you slink around with someone I've asked you to avoid. First, your trip in Sacramento, and now this. Who knows what else you're keeping from me where he's concerned."

A lot, if we're getting technical—which we aren't. She hasn't earned the right to details, a fact that's overwhelmingly disappointing. "I shouldn't have to come to you. *You're* the adult. *You're* the mother. You should be present for more than coffee brewing and takeout dinners."

She stares at me, mournful, as if I've wounded her deeply. Then her expression closes off, like invisible shutters have swung over her face, blocking out all signs of emotion. Coolly, she says, "Give me your phone."

"What?"

"You heard me. I'm taking it. That's what present mothers do—invoke consequences when their children screw up." She holds out her hand. "Give it to me."

"You cannot be serious." My phone is my link to Mati. We talk every night, and text during the day. Our time together is already limited; surely she won't sever this tie, too.

"Oh, I'm serious," she says evenly.

I yank my phone from my pocket and slam it down on her palm. "Happy?"

"Not in the least."

I push my chair back so hard its feet screech across the hardwood. It topples over, landing with a clatter. I trace Bambi's escape route but, just before I stalk out of the kitchen, I spin around, look my mother square in the face, and say, "You'll never keep me away from him."

elise

After too many hours spent tolerating Mom's cold shoulder, lamenting the loss of my phone, and scattering hundreds more silver stars across my ceiling, I leave the house with Bambi, headed for Audrey's. Upset as I still am, I want to make a gesture that might earn me her understanding.

I knock. She opens the door. She frowns. But she lets my dog and me in, which is a start.

Preschool's out for the day and the TV is on, tuned to the Disney Channel. The cottage smells of pancakes and maple syrup. My stomach gives a hungry grumble.

"Breakfast for lunch?" I ask, overcompensating in the chipper department.

Audrey shrugs. "It was easy."

"Got any leftovers?"

"Knock yourself out."

She leaves me standing in the entryway and goes to sweep Janie up and carry her to the couch. They snuggle up under a knit throw to watch Mickey and his clubhouse friends attempt to crack another case. Bambi makes herself comfortable at their feet, a panting traitor.

I slap a stack of pancakes on a plate, douse them in syrup, and inhale them while standing at the counter. I pilfer a mug of cold, left-over coffee, too, dumping in a couple of heaping spoonfuls of sugar before effectively pounding it. Thanks to my night at the park, I'm near-ing zombie status. After rinsing my plate and refilling my mug, I shuf-fle into the living room and say, "Aud, can I talk to you?"

She doesn't look away from the television. "Go ahead."

"Yeah, Auntie," Janie says. "Go ahead."

I clear my throat. "In the kitchen, maybe?"

Audrey groans and digs out from under the blanket. She plants a kiss on Janie's head before following me to the kitchen, where she crosses her arms and says, "What?"

I fold my arms, too, but while her stance is contentious, mine's about self-preservation. "I came by to tell you . . . I feel bad about last night."

"You feel bad? You're only standing in my kitchen because you're Nick's sister and I owe it to him to hear you out, but shit, Elise. *I feel bad* is not going to cut it."

"What do you want me to say?"

"Uh, you could tell me you were wrong, and that you understand why I'm upset, and that you'll never betray me like that again."

"See, I would say those things if I thought you were mad because I had a guy here while you were out. But you're pissed because of who you *think* the guy is."

"You're right. And guess what? That's my prerogative because this is *my* house and Janie's *my* daughter. What if something had happened to her? What if something happens to her tomorrow, or next week, because your *friend* knows where I live?"

"It won't," I say.

"It *could*," Audrey retorts. "The only thing about Nick's passing that's brought me any peace is knowing that he died doing something noble and good. He was out there because he chose to be, aware of the risks but willing to face them. Bringing that boy here . . . You took away my autonomy, my right to choose who comes into my house, and who meets my daughter."

"Okay," I say, my voice trembling. She's got a point—right or wrong, she gets to decide who spends time within the walls of her cottage. "I get it. I swear I do. And I'm sorry I didn't check with you before inviting him here. If I had it to do over, I would."

"And I'd say no. I will *never* be okay with him."

"But he's the gentlest person I know. He's not a threat to Janie, or you, or anyone."

She lifts her chin. "Yeah? Prove it."

I can't, of course. I know Mati is thoughtful and benevolent—I'm confident in the same way I know the sun's outside, hanging behind the thick cloud cover—but Audrey doesn't. She never will. Not if she refuses to give him a chance.

When the silence has stretched thin and it's clear I've got no veri-fiable proof, she says haughtily, "That's what I thought. Elise, it kills me to say this, but if you can't stay away from him, then you have to stay away from us."

My eyes go wide. "What's that supposed to mean?"

She shrugs, like her assertion was clear and I'm an idiot for not comprehending. "If you're going to keep seeing him, you're not welcome here. I'm sure you've seen the news by now: Military dependents have become a target. I can't risk Janie's safety."

"But what about your job? Who will watch her?"

"Your mom, I hope, and if not her, I'll hire a nanny. I'll quit if I can't find one. Anything's better than leaving you here with my daughter, knowing I can't trust you to keep your Taliban boyfriend from drop-ping by."

"He's not—" But I can't. I can't fight this same fight again, not when she's threatening me with Janie. I'm short of breath; I'm *desperate*. "She's my niece, Audrey—she's Nicky's! How could you keep her from me?"

"It's not my decision. You want to make your own choices? Make them. But you'd better be prepared to face the consequences."

"You're being so unfair. He's *nothing* like you think. He's sweet to me, and he was so good with Janie. She liked him. If only you could have seen—"

Her eyes flare with anger. "I don't want to see! I don't want to hear another word about him! I don't want to *think* about him, or his country, or what his people did to my husband. And you shouldn't, either!"

"Mama?" Janie, from the living room.

Audrey appears momentarily startled, like she forgot Janie was in the cottage. She sucks in a breath and calmly calls, "I'll be right there, baby." And then she levels me with a look so formidable, so full of revulsion, I have to shift my gaze.

"It's time for you to go," she says in a tone that leaves no room for discussion.

I slip into the living room to retrieve my dog, pausing to give Janie the tightest squeeze.

"You're going home, Auntie?"

"Yep," I say, my vision swimming. I hate this: fighting with my mom, fighting with Audrey, worrying that my time with Janie is going to be dramatically reduced. Because I can't stop seeing Mati—I just can't, no matter what Mom takes away, no matter what Aud threatens.

He's a star, throwing light and warmth into my life, and I won't give him up.

Not until I have to.

I kiss Janie's soft hair. "I love you, girlie."

"See you soon, Auntie!"

My eyes spill a waterfall of tears as Bambi and I walk out the door.

MATI

Baba's coughing wakes me.
His hacking is nothing new.
It is as if he has swallowed metal:
iron, nickel, tin, steel.
A bucketful of nuts and bolts,
rattling behind his ribs.

I should check on him,
but I am in no mood to face Mama.
She has been chilly since I
came home from the park yesterday.
Her disappointment is explicit,
though I am not sure I care.

The coughing continues.
I hear movement in the kitchen.
A slamming cupboard door,

rushing water, hurried footsteps.
Mama calls my name,
her voice tattered with worry.
"Go to the market," she says.
"Buy honey. And peppermint.
We need to calm his cough."

I push my feet into shoes,
donning yesterday's jeans and a rumpled shirt,
and do as she asks.

In Cypress Beach,
early mornings are still and peaceful.
I breeze through the market,
where I choose local honey,
thick and amber in its jar,
and a generous sprig of peppermint.
They are nature's cure
for the grating-grinding-retching
that lives in Baba's chest.

I pay, hurriedly.
Clutching my bag,
I return to the sidewalk.

I have only just passed the bakery,
and the sun is only just beginning to rise,
when I am cuffed from behind,
a wallop that pitches me forward,
tangling my feet and my wits.
My bag plummets to the ground and,
while everything else is abruptly
jumbled,
muddled,

blurred,
so clearly, I hear the honey jar
shatter on impact.

My hands break my fall,
saving my face from striking the sidewalk.
My sluggish brain registers:
my palms, scraping coarse pavement,
male voices, slicing the quiet morning,
and ire, dense as fog.

I struggle to right myself, disoriented
but determined to confront my attackers,
to fight back.
A blow finds my middle, robbing me of breath,
creating a sharp spasm of pain in my chest.
I curl in on myself,
and try to make sense of my assailants.

A foot,
in a work boot,
attached to leg,
attached to a man.

An American man.
A citizen of Cypress Beach.
Bronzed hair and freckled skin,
he is familiar;
he mocked Mama and me weeks ago,
as we walked through town.

He stands with a friend: a blonder, squatter man,
who boasts wicked eyes and a smarmy snarl.
He glares down at me,

then kicks at the sticky, broken glass
and crushed peppermint that litter the sidewalk.

Their derisiveness sends a chill down my spine.

My stomach sours as the men,
stout and steadfast, work to move me.
Off the sidewalk.
Into an alley.

Where there will be no interruptions.
Where there will be no witnesses.

My lucidity fades
like tendrils of smoke
in a turbulent sky.

elise

My mom comes into my room bright and early, dropping a flyer on the pillow next to my head. Groggy, I squint up at her. She's frowning at my blackened walls and the mural of stars I've splashed across the ceiling. Sensing that she has no plan to leave until I engage, I tunnel out from beneath my quilt and pick up the flyer. *Cypress Valley High New Student Orientation!* printed in bold letters.

I'd forgotten; it's today.

"No way," I say.

"You can't sulk in your room forever."

"I'm not sulking—I'm *sleeping*."

"I've never known you to be such a sullen teenager," she grumbles. "This is that boy's influence, isn't it?"

Here we go . . . "Mati's? No, not at all. In fact, he'd probably encourage me to go to orientation—you know, if he could get in touch with me."

"You're wasting your summer, Elise. When will you see reason? You have no future with him."

I pull my quilt up to cover my face. Muffled, I say, "You don't know that."

She yanks the blanket away, eyes flashing. "It's not as if you can marry him!"

I sit up so I can face her head-on, rather than supine. "I'm seventeen, Mom. I'm hardly planning a wedding. But for the record, I *could* marry him. It's not unheard of for a Muslim man to marry a non-Muslim woman; it's not even against the rules. Afghanistan's current president is married to a freaking Catholic. Bet you didn't know that, for all your knowledge of Islam."

She gives me a long, hard look, then says, "You're going to orientation. You need to get to know the campus. You need to get a sense of what classes are offered. And for God's sake, you need to meet new people."

"No I don't. I have Ryan. I have Mati."

"Ryan is going back to Texas in a few weeks." She makes no more mention of Mati, like avoiding his name is as good as erasing him from existence. "I've already contacted your principal to let her know you'll be there. She's looking forward to meeting you. Two o'clock this afternoon," she says, pointing at the flyer before turning and walking out of my room.

I hem and haw all morning. Orientation is the very last thing I feel like doing, mostly because I don't want my mom to have her way. And anyway, I'd rather meet up with Mati, especially considering I haven't talked to him since my phone was swiped. Our time together is dwindling and even though it's barely been twenty-four hours, I miss him.

But, as much as I hate to admit it, my mom is right: I *do* need to put some effort into making new friends. Thanks to Mati and Ryan, I know now that I want people in my life, even if my brother can't be.

God. It's settled—I'm going to orientation.

I leave the house in Mom's BMW, dressed in tattered cutoffs and my trusty *Advise, Support, Stabilize* sweatshirt; it's like a security blanket, like having a piece of Nick with me as I brave the awfulness of a new school. When I pull into the parking lot, it occurs to me that I'm likely the only attendee old enough to drive, and I'm met with the stares of dozens of confused underclassmen as I park Mom's car.

In the gym, bright-eyed freshmen (who've presumably traveled through the Cypress Valley school system together since they were kindergartners) sit in gaggles on the bleachers, prattling and laughing, effectively ignoring me. When I look at their carefree faces and glowing smiles and tidy clothes, I feel far removed.

I'm starting to wonder if I should have stayed home after all when the lights flash off and then flicker back on, quieting the crowd and officially beginning orientation.

Cypress Valley High's principal, a surprisingly young, smartly dressed blonde who introduces herself as Mrs. Cruz, speaks from a podium in the center of the polished floor. Her voice echoes through the steamy gym as she welcomes us, promising an "illuminating and formative" educational experience.

Wonderful.

She drones on, covering hallway expectations and cafeteria procedures and the progress reports that'll be emailed to our parents periodically throughout the year. She's introducing a couple of assistant principals, who appear apathetic at best, when her attention is pulled to the doors on the far side of the gym. I follow her gaze, peering across the sea of heads that occupy the bleachers. There's some sort of scuffle taking place behind one of the closed doors, in the dim hallway barely visible through the small, rectangular window. Mrs. Cruz glances questioningly at her fellow administrators, who shrug in unison.

All's quiet now, so she resumes her speech, filling a whole thirty seconds with rambling before the door flies open, slamming against the gym's cinder block wall, drawing the attention of every single person in the vast room.

Ryan steps onto the gleaming hardwood. *Ryan*, followed by Xavier. I do a double take, my mouth dropping open.

He scans oodles of teenaged faces, clearly, frantically searching, until I make sense of his arrival—he's got to be here for me, right?—and rise from my seat.

He spots me and shouts, "Elise!"

My name echoes like thunder through the silent gymnasium. I stumble down the crowded row in which I've been sitting. Befuddled stares track me as I hurry down the stairs, my heart pounding because something's wrong. Ryan wouldn't be here otherwise.

I sprint across the gym, my flip-flops slapping the glossy floor. Distantly, I hear Mrs. Cruz call, "Excuse me!" and I'm not sure if she's questioning me or admonishing me, but I ignore her, my ponytail swinging behind me as I run. I meet Ryan and Xavier at the door, grabbing their arms, pulling them into the corridor, where a man—a teacher or a security guard, I think—ushers us away from the gym.

"You're not authorized to be in the building," he says to my intruder friends.

"Yeah," Xavier says. "It's an emergency. We're leaving now."

My stomach drops out. *An emergency.* I knew it.

Xavier leads Ryan and me down the hall, away from the man and the gym and the orientation I knew I shouldn't have come to. With every footfall, I think *Mom? Audrey? Janie? Mom? Audrey? Janie?* But I can't bring myself to ask.

This can't be happening again. I can't lose someone else.

Despite my escalating alarm, I hustle to keep up with the boys' long strides and, finally, push my panic away long enough to speak. "What happened?"

We've reached the lobby. Ryan grabs my hand as we push through the doors and into the sunlight. He's towing me along, toward where Xavier's Jeep waits, parked crookedly in the fire lane. "It's Mati," he says.

"Mati?!"

Ryan squeezes my hand. "We've got to go."

I yank free of him, planting my feet on the concrete. I'm shocked and I'm confused and I'm tired of being dragged along, clueless.

"Elise," Ryan says, gently now. "We need to go to the hospital."

"Why?"

Xavier drops a hand onto my shoulder. "Because he's hurt. He needs you."

We scramble into the Jeep. Xavier drives, swift but sure. Ryan sits shotgun, fiddling with the radio. I'm in the backseat, gusts of wind riling my hair. I'm trying not to throw up.

I think: *Mati is strong and steady, smart and sweet. Bad things don't happen to good people—he's practically invincible.*

And yet . . .

Cypress Beach isn't big enough for a hospital of its own, so we're on our way to San Jose. I borrow Ryan's phone to text my mom. I tell her that orientation's done and that I'm spending the rest of the day with my friends. Then I dial Mati because I can't *not*. The line rings unceasingly, leaving me full of apprehension and fear, buzzing with the need to get to him, get to him, *get to him*.

"What happened?" I ask Ryan over the wind whistling through the Jeep's soft-top.

"He was jumped," he says. His words sound garbled, as if they're painful to speak. "It was pretty bad."

My imagination conjures a slide show of horrific snapshots: Mati attacked, Mati hurt, Mati bleeding. I blink it all away to keep from bursting into tears. "Jumped *where*?"

"Cypress Beach. Early this morning. In an alley close to Van Dough's."

"Oh God. Ryan!"

He reaches back to touch my knee. "He's gonna be okay. He called me, so he's conscious. He's gotta be well enough to operate a phone, you know?"

No, I don't know. Because I didn't get to speak to him. I couldn't, because my phone is sitting in my mom's bedroom, useless.

I hate her.

"He tried to call you first," Ryan says, another attempt at consoling me. "Then I did, too. I had to go to your cottage to figure out where you were."

"My mom took my phone away," I mumble, embarrassed. "She doesn't like Mati."

Xavier flies past a beat-up Nissan. He's crushing Highway 101. "Why not?"

I scrub my hands over my face; the last forty-eight hours feel more like forty-eight years. "She doesn't have a good reason. She refuses to give him a chance. She pins her ignorance on *those people*, the Afghans who killed my brother. Like Mati has *any*thing to do with them."

"Damn," Xavier says. "I didn't realize. I'm sorry."

Ryan gives me an optimistic smile. "She'll come around."

"No," I say, turning away to gaze out the window. "I don't think she will."

What's more? I don't care.

elise

We pull up to Sacred Heart Hospital after fifty minutes on the road.

It's a large building, white and modern, sterile and unadorned compared with the quaint coziness I've grown accustomed to in Cypress Beach. Xavier drops me off at the main entrance, after he and Ryan promise to come up in a bit. I thank them, smoothing a hand over my wind-ravaged hair as I hurry inside. I've still got Ryan's phone and I press it to my ear, trying Mati's number again as I navigate the lobby. No answer.

The fact that he's so close, yet entirely unreachable, is making me crazy.

I give his name at the reception desk, and the elderly liaison working the counter presents me with a trifold map, pointing to the wing where he's being treated, and circling his room in red ink. "Take this with you," he says, pushing the map into my hands. He raises a liver-spotted hand and points to the bay of elevators behind me. "Those are your best bet."

I hightail it to the elevators and jab the up button with an impatient finger. It illuminates like a full moon. There's a chime as the doors lurch open and then I'm inside, alone and bouncing as the lift makes a slow skyward journey. When the doors open again, the sharp scent of disinfectant floods my nose and I have to take a steadying breath to recover my balance. I step into the corridor.

My flip-flops squeak as I jog down the hallway, my heart thudding hard against my ribs. I pull to an abrupt halt when I spot Mati's name on a small whiteboard outside one of the many doors. I check the room number against the information on my map, then step up to peer through the little window.

The room is colorless, painted in shadows. It's empty but for Mati, apparently asleep, appearing uncharacteristically frail under the crisp sheet covering the lower half of his body. His eyelids look purple, almost translucent. There's a deep bruise covering the left side of his face, and his skin is puffy, swollen. My stomach rolls over; he looks *dreadful*. If it wasn't for the muffled *beep, beep, beep* of the monitors overseeing his vitals, I'd think he was—

I ease the door open, stepping silently through and, *yes*. He's here, and I'm here, and the world spins again.

I loiter close to the entryway, watching him sleep as the wall clock's second hand makes rotation after rotation. The longer I look at him, the more I hurt. His trampled form does terrible things to my chest—crushes it with matchless force, making it difficult to siphon air. I feel my hand move to my thrashing heart; I feel my knees begin to buckle. I reach for the doorjamb to keep from crumpling.

The shape of him, shrunken and defeated, the shape of his *pain* . . .

I whisper his name.

His eyes flutter open, spiderwebbed with fine vessels. They find me, and he says, "Elise."

I close the distance separating us, taking his hand gingerly in both of mine. "Are you—?"

"I'm fine." His voice is raspy and weak, those two little words requiring a lot of effort.

"But you look—"

"I'm *fine*. Especially now that you've found me."

He doesn't look fine—not even close. The bruise on his cheek is worse up close, and his lip's split, stained with a spot of dried blood. His hospital gown reveals his throat, his clavicles, his long, ocher arms, skin mottled with angry red scrapes. An IV disappears into the wrist farthest from me, its long tube trailing up to a bag of clear liquid. His breath is shallow and brings about an occasional wince and, God, I want to *kill* the person who did this to him.

"Oh, Mati . . ."

"It's just a few bruises."

"You wouldn't be here if it was just a few bruises."

His mouth lifts in a tiny, reticent smile. "A few bruises. A couple of cracked ribs. Low-grade renal trauma. See? I've learned a new English phrase since being admitted."

My frown deepens. "There's nothing funny about this."

"I know." He gazes up at me with such stark vulnerability, I can't help but rest my palm against his unmarred cheek. He leans into my touch and says, "Thank you for coming."

I don't need to be thanked—I need to know what happened. Who did this, and when, and *why*. I need to know if he fought back, if anyone helped when it was over, if he's reported the attack. I need to know how much pain he's in, and when he'll start to feel better. But right now, all that matters is comforting him.

I hover over his damaged body. "Can I . . . ?"

He gives a nod that clearly costs him. "Carefully."

I lay my head on his shoulder, and he eases his arm around me. I reach up to lace my fingers through his, wishing I had the power to mend his broken pieces. I hold his hand tightly, lashing us together until we're seamless. Until we're *us*. Because I still can't believe this happened. I still don't understand any part of how he ended up here but, God, I'm grateful he's okay.

I'm in tears suddenly, sobbing into the starchy fabric of his gown, and it's so embarrassing, putting my worry and my fear and my helplessness out there this way when he's obviously going to be all right, but then I realize he's as upset as I am, and we're such a mess, such a perfectly beautiful mess, I don't care if time screeches to a halt and we're frozen in this dreary room for eternity.

At least I'll be frozen with him.

elise

When I've cried myself out, he kisses the top of my head, a long press of his lips to my hair.

I pull back, reluctant to put space between us but worried about his ribs and his many, many bruises. There's a chair nearby and I pull it up to the bed. I sit and run a hand along his forearm, tight muscle and satin skin blemished by a myriad of scrapes. "Where are your parents?"

"Walking the corridors. They left me alone to sleep."

"And now I'm here, interrupting your rest."

He looks at me all adoringly. "You are never an interruption."

I spend a moment under his glow before broaching the unavoidable. "Mati, what happened?"

His face contorts, eyes glassy, his gaze growing distant. "I remember going to the market," he says, sort of sluggishly. "I picked up honey and peppermint because my mama asked me to. I remember hurrying because Baba was in the middle of a coughing fit and I wanted to get back to the cottage. I wasn't paying attention to my surroundings, though I should have been." He shakes his head, frustrated now.

"There were two men; they came from behind and nearly knocked me out. It's cloudy, all of it, but they worked together, the two of them against me."

My hand travels the length of his arm, a vain attempt at consoling him, at keeping my mind focused on his story, not my tumultuous emotions. "Who were they?"

"I don't know. I've seen one of them in Cypress Beach before, several weeks ago." He pauses, watching me warily. I sense that he's censoring his story, and I hate that he feels the need. "That day, he was spiteful; he threw hateful slurs at me and my mama, but Cypress Beach was busy, so he had no choice but to let me walk away. This morning, I wasn't so lucky."

I feel somehow responsible. Americans—*my* people—attacked this person they'd be lucky to know. I'm ashamed for them; I'm ashamed *of* them. "How did you get away?"

"They grew bored quickly—probably because I made little effort to fight back. After they ran off, I managed to get home. When I walked into the cottage, stooped and bleeding, my parents were horrified." He sighs, a dismal sound, then grimaces at the toll that exhale must have taken on his ribs. "They called for help, and here I am. I'm fortunate: my ribs are only cracked, and the bruising to my kidney is minimal. The doctor said I'll need to stay a night or two, then I'll return to Cypress Beach with medicine for my pain."

I'm teary again, but due more to anger than worry. There's nothing *fortunate* about what happened to him. His attackers were vicious and cowardly, and they deserve nothing but a hasty trip to hell. Taking his hand, I ask, "Where are they now?"

"I don't know. I don't care, as long as they stay far from my parents and me."

"Have you talked to the police?"

His eyes fall closed. When they open again, his expression betrays his powerlessness, and his concentrated sadness. "No, Elise. I can't."

"*Why*? What they did to you—you can't let them get away with it."

"I don't have a choice. I'm a visitor in your country, and the climate is not good for Muslims—you know that. My baba needs to finish his treatment. I can't do anything to jeopardize that."

"But if you reported what happened, told the police exactly what you just told me—"

"They would measure my account against the account of two American citizens. There's no question who they'd believe."

"But that's not fair."

"*Life* isn't fair."

"Mati, this is wrong. They deserve consequences."

"The chance of me, an Afghan with a quickly expiring visa, getting justice in America is slim. There are too many people who look at me and see a threat. Who associate my family with bombs and fire and death, with men who carry assault rifles, who pledge their undying obedience to Allah and defend their brutality with the Quran. When I say that the climate for Muslims is 'not good,' I really mean that it's dangerous—very dangerous. I can't walk into a police station and accuse two white Americans of attacking me because who knows what lies they might counter with? I cannot entangle my family with the law, not now, when Baba is as near as he's ever been to healthy. Not now, when we are so close to returning to Afghanistan."

My face is hot with rage. A rash of disjointed arguments scramble up my throat, but then Mati eases his hand out of mine and raises it to the crown of my head. He runs his palm over my hair, slowing my pulse, nudging my anger away, if only for a moment. The way he's looking at me . . . it's an appeal, a plea for understanding, and while I absolutely do *not* understand—will *never* understand how he can be so rational, so selfless, so composed in the face of gross inequality—I can appreciate how different his experience is from mine.

I've never walked in his shoes, but that doesn't mean I can't stroll beside him. That doesn't mean I can't learn from his perspective and offer support in all the ways I know how.

His hand moves to my face, his thumb brushing the arc of my

cheekbone, the curve of my jaw. "Elise, this morning . . . I was scared. I was *lost*. I made it through, back to the cottage and all the way here, thinking of you. I don't know what that means for me, for you, for us, but . . ." He trails off, his expression unguarded, simultaneously hopeful and tormented, and I see us, suddenly, as if out-of-body: his hand cupping my face, my fingers clutching his elbow, our cheeks rosy and tear-stained, our eyes wide and worshipful.

We look lovesick, just like Audrey said.

"Kiss me," he whispers.

I do, gingerly pressing my mouth to his, mindful of his split lip and bruised cheek, gentle with his battered body. I have never kissed anyone so carefully, so attentively, yet I'm as hungry for him as I've ever been. It's a good kiss, a restorative kiss, a long-overdue kiss. It lasts a fraction of a second, and a thousand lifetimes.

And then I hear muffled voices, an opening door, Ryan's amused, "Oh, oops," followed by deep chuckles.

I draw away from Mati as our friends crowd into the room, bellowing reassurances and sympathies, which Mati accepts amiably, if not wearily.

Not a minute later, Hala and Rasoul arrive. It happens so fast: She gives Ryan and Xavier inquisitive glances, and then she turns toward where I sit beside her son, my heart drowning in the pit of my stomach. Her mouth falls open as she observes my body, inclined toward Mati's, my palm, aligned with his, my face, cloaked in a passion-induced haze—like his.

"Matihullah!" she cries.

I snatch my hand away as she unleashes a string of Pashto as rapid and sharp as machine-gun blasts. Rasoul touches her shoulder, but she doesn't quiet until she's said her piece, punctuating her tirade with an arctic glare aimed right at me.

Thank God she didn't see us kissing.

Mati looks like a snared animal—cornered, fearful, humiliated. "Elise, maybe you should . . ."

He doesn't have to finish; he needs me to go. The regret saturating his voice is the same as a thousand hailstones, pelting my skin.

"Thank you for coming," Rasoul says, gracious. His hand lingers on his wife's shoulder, equal parts cautionary and reassuring, making it clear that he sees the world in loops and curves, while Hala only perceives hard lines. Because she's still looking at me like I'm depraved—like it's my fault her son was attacked.

Her judgment seeps into my flesh, making me cold with shame.

Mati watches as I back toward the door, toward where Ryan and Xavier wait, toward escape from Hala's harsh gaze.

"We'll get her home safe," Xavier says before stepping into the hallway with Ryan close behind.

I keep my shoulders back and my head high as I pass Mati's parents. They say nothing, but his curiosity and her animosity, their combined concern, overwhelming in its intensity, make me wonder if I shouldn't have come here after all.

MATI

She leaves with my heart in her hands.

Mama does not talk to me
for what remains of the day.
She listens to nurses and doctors,
and is attentive when Baba
translates words she does not know.
She purses her lips
and makes muted *tsk*ing sounds
as she puzzles over diagnoses
and prescribed treatments.
But she does not talk to me.

I wonder...
Should we return to Afghanistan early?
Should we flee America,
and the monsters who lurk

in its idyllic towns?
Because what if it had been Mama,
beaten because of her flowing hijab?
What if it had been Baba's frail body,
dragged into a dark alley?

I raise the topic aloud,
and Baba reminds me:
"Leaving America early
is the same as succumbing to fear.
Leaving America early
means prejudice has won."
I am not surprised by his response;
he is stubborn and he is righteous.
I long to be more like him.

He and Mama stay with me
until the sun ducks behind the horizon.
As they ready to leave for the cottage,
Baba promises they will return tomorrow.
Mama looks relieved to be on her way.
She is disappointed because I have sinned,
and because I have been attacked.

I am disappointed, too,
for the very same reasons.

Finally, I am alone with my pain.
While the whole of my body aches,
my chest is hurt's epicenter.
Breaths and coughs
bring lightning bolts of agony.
I am caught in a vice,

squeezed slowly,
as my ribs begin to knit back together.

To distract myself, I think of her.
She balked earlier
when I said I was fortunate,
but there is nothing truer.
It could have been worse,
there in that alley.
It could have been worse,
this year in Cypress Beach.

I met her, after all.

She is fire: bright, hot, consuming.
All the rest is smoke on a breeze.

For three more weeks,
she is mine, and I am hers.

elise

Mati makes a relatively swift recovery—I know, thanks to Ryan's updates.

He spends two more days in the hospital, where doctors monitor his injured kidney, where he's deluged with fluids and curative medicines, where he practices getting around, carefully and slowly, so his ribs will continue to heal.

He returns to his cottage three days after the assault, where he spends more time recuperating. We talk on the phone often, thanks to Ryan's generosity and a little sneaking around, though I'm still going bananas, worrying about him, lamenting the loss of my own phone, wishing I could drop by and check in on him. But I haven't forgotten the way his mother looked at me when she walked into his hospital room. I'm not sure I'll ever feel comfortable sharing space with her again.

I want Mati healthy; I want to see him, hug him, kiss him.

I want to stop thinking about how at summer's end, all I'll have left to do is miss him.

Ryan knocks on our cottage door a week after the alleyway attack. My mom answers, a rare reprieve from her library and her manuscript, and spends a few minutes chatting him up. She gives me a quick kiss on the cheek as she heads back into the cottage, which appears loving but feels manipulative. She's been super nice lately, but only because she thinks I've omitted Mati from my life, thanks to her crackerjack parenting.

I haven't talked to her about what happened last week, the thugs who pummeled him because of where he's from, how he looks, what he believes. I let her go on thinking what she wants to think, because she won't hear me. She doesn't want to.

Ryan waves me into the yard, where we sit on the cool grass close to the box hedge. I ask him about Xavier, and he goes incandescent, talking about his air force boy. "He told me Lackland Air Force Base is on his list of possible duty stations when he's done at the MLI. That's in San Antonio, which means we wouldn't be inconceivably far from each other."

I smile, happy for them, but rueful, too, because soon, Mati and I *will* be inconceivably far from each other. "You guys are going to live happily ever after," I tell him.

He gives my arm a sympathetic squeeze. "Mati's gonna be home alone this afternoon. He wants you to come by. His parents are headed to San Jose for one of his father's appointments, and if you go over after lunch, y'all should be good for a few hours."

My impulse is to resist a secret meeting. It's shameful—not being with Mati, but the *way* we have to be together. Still, time with him out-weighs my moral hesitancies. "You really think it's okay? I don't want to get him into trouble with his parents. His *mother*."

Ryan rolls his eyes. "His *mother* will never know. But I can call him and double-check."

"I'd rather call him myself, and I'd like to visit him without feeling like a sneak. I want him to come to my cottage and hang out, talk my mom's ear off like you just did. I want the world to let us be."

"Sucks, Elise. Truly. But at least you guys will have this afternoon."
He pulls out his phone and taps out a text. "I'm gonna tell him you'll
see him later."

I should be excited—this reunion is a week in the making. But that
doesn't mean we aren't rushing headlong toward inevitable separation.
I can't stop thinking about how hard it's going to be when he leaves the
United States, because thanks to days of unavoidable distance, I know
how much it sucks—how much it *hurts*—to be away from him.

I spent most of last night awake, watching for shooting stars
through my open bedroom window, trying to decide if being with Mati
is worth the worry and the stress and the feeling of pending doom that
won't let me be. His mother's reaction to us at the hospital flung seeds
of doubt through my conscience, and they're taking root. As often as I
try to weed them away, they're invasive as thistle. I'm barely speaking to my mom, I haven't seen Audrey or Janie in ages, I haven't picked
up my camera in days.

I feel *sad*. All the time.

I wonder if I should treat this last week's time apart as the beginning of our end—if I should break things off now, today, before the task
becomes unendurable.

My heart might be better off if I don't allow it to fall further
into him.

Ryan tweaks my hair. "Cheer up, okay? I'm only willing to be
the bearer of *good* news. I'll quit playing courier if you're gonna be
bummed."

I force a smile. "Consider me cheered."

He goes. I eat a quick lunch, then hustle through a shower and pack
my camera bag. I interrupt my mom's writing to tell her I'll be shooting around town.

"Hopefully, I'll be able to return your phone soon," she says as I
stand in the doorway of her library. She's staring at her computer's
giant monitor, her mind caught somewhere between Cypress Beach
and the Wild West. "Oh!" she says, swiveling in her chair to face me. "I

almost forgot: Audrey called earlier. The restaurant asked her to fill a shift tonight, and she was hoping you'd watch Janie."

My mouth pulls into a surprised smile. God, I've missed Janie. I'm practically jumping up and down at the chance to babysit. "Yeah, I can do that. No problem."

"No boys," my mom says sternly.

"You think I'm stupid enough to make the same mistake twice?"

She turns back to her computer. "Sometimes I don't know what to think, Lissy."

I leave her to her manuscript.

I once had a thousand desires.

But in my one desire to know you all else melted away.

—Rumi

elise

Mati's waiting in his front yard.

I spot him from a ways down the block, before he sees me, and study him as I make a quiet approach. He's sporting his slouchy hat, the one he wore the first time he held my hand, which makes it my favorite of all the hats in the world, and he's got his notebook propped on a fence post. He's bent over it, scribbling. As I get closer, I notice his mouth moving, silent words flowing to the page. Even from a distance, he appears buoyant, a thousand times healthier than he did at the hospital last week.

I catch his effervescence as if it were contagious.

I stop. Carefully, silently, I retrieve my Nikon. I locate him in its viewfinder, bringing him into sharp focus. I've got only one chance at this—the first photograph has to be perfect because the sound of my camera will interrupt the moment. Biting my lip, relaxing my muscles into stillness, I press the shutter release. My camera emits a soft *click-click-click* as it captures Mati in his element, all quiet contemplation and peaceful inspiration. I feel a similar rush of creation as I review the digital image—it's flawless, and not because of anything I did. It's *him*, caught spinning something from nothing. He's stunning.

When I look away from the Mati I've frozen in time to the Mati who stands twenty yards away, I find him gazing back at me. Returning my camera to its bag, I walk the rest of the way down the sidewalk. He opens the gate. I step into the yard.

"You made it," he says.

"I did."

We stand a few feet apart, on separate cobblestones that feel like rafts in a churning sea. He really does look good; he's standing straight and tall, and the bruise that marred his cheek just a week ago has faded almost entirely. I want to launch myself into his arms, but I'm worried about his ribs, and thrown by the way he's clutching his notebook, regarding me with apprehension, like we've never been alone before.

"I'm glad you're back," I tell him. "How are you feeling?"

"Much better. Glad to be away from the hospital." His gaze falls to the ground, then, shyly, returns to mine. "Will you come inside?"

"If it's okay."

He shrugs. "It is for now."

He doesn't mean anything by it—there's not a barbed bone in his body—but his words pierce me. I'm not welcome here unaccompanied—in his mother's eyes, I might not be welcome at all. I am a surreptitious social call, a cursory friend, a dirty little secret. I am *temporary*. That's all I ever can be.

You knew going in, I think. *You've known all along.*

Nothing changes in the cottage. We're quiet, circling each other, waiting to see who'll make the first move. It hasn't been like this in weeks, since we visited Nicky in Sacramento and found a semblance of comfort, and later, at Audrey's, where we fell into an intimacy that felt special and sacred. Somewhere in the space separating all that from now, the closeness, the contentment, has funneled away.

He sits on the sofa. I do, too.

"Do you want something to drink?" he asks. "Chai? Water?"

"I'm okay."

"Did you get your photo?"

"Of you? Yep. Did you write your words?"

"About you? Yep."

I smile, though his mood is serious.

"Elise . . . I'm sorry I had to be away." He reaches across the vastness between us, letting his hand rest on my knee. His skin is warm, as always. "I've wasted our time."

"You haven't wasted anything. What happened wasn't your fault and anyway, healing is more important than hanging out with some girl."

"You are not *some girl*."

"Well, I'm not *the* girl."

He flinches. "What does that mean?"

My heart is slashed down the middle, torn between sticking whatever this is out as long as possible, and saving itself from the agony of telling him goodbye later. "It means this is never going to work," I say with all the tenderness I can spare. I'm not out to hurt him, but I have to be honest. "Mati, you know we can't last. So what if we've been talking around it? In a couple of weeks, you and me . . . we're done."

He pitches forward to take my hands. His eyes, doleful, search mine, like if he looks long enough, the impossible will rearrange its pixels and become feasible. "Don't say that."

"Tell me how we can possibly survive. You, moving back to Afghanistan with no plan to return, with this *duty* you're always talking about. Me, in America, working toward a degree I need and want and won't give up. Our families, who've made no secret of their disapproval. And don't get me started on language barriers and religious complications and cultural chaos."

"But none of that—"

"Don't say it doesn't matter. It does, all of it, and it always will. Did you know I haven't seen Audrey and Janie since the day after Aud caught us in her cottage? She's letting me babysit tonight, but only because she thinks I've stopped seeing you. My mom does, too, and today, for the first time in too long, she was almost pleasant."

His grasp on my hands tightens; despite everything I've said, I'm clinging to him, too. "I'm sorry I've caused trouble for you and your family."

"But you haven't. That's my point. It's not you and it's not me—it's you and me in combination. It's *us*."

"If there is no us, everything is easy," he says, gravelly, as if the phrase scours his throat on its way out.

"Easy for everyone else." My vision goes blurry. I squeeze my eyes shut because, God, this is the worst time to cry. I need to speak with confidence. I need to appear strong.

He frees my hands so he can press his palms to the column of my neck. I suspect he can feel my pulse strumming beneath my skin, the rapid *beat-beat-beat* of desperation. "I don't care about everyone else," he says, and I believe him. "We should spend our time with people who make us happy. *You* make me happy. I want to see you as often as possible, every day."

"But—"

"But what? Elise, I don't want to be miserable before it's necessary."

I blink up at him, covering his hands with mine. I inch forward, until I can see the variations of copper and bronze and gold swirling in his eyes. "When you go, it'll be like you've disappeared. The chances of us seeing each other again . . . I just . . . I *can't*."

He draws back, making a hopeless sound deep in his throat, a combined half sigh, half groan, as if he's steeling himself to whatever course he's decided to follow. And then his eyes harden, like the blunt points I've been trying to force into his head finally fit, pegs into holes.

He gets it.

Panic washes over me and, all at once, I don't want him to get it. I want him to fight, for me, for us. I'm frantic to backpedal. "Mati—"

"Wait," he says, holding up his hand. "It's selfish of me to ask for your time when I cannot promise you anything in return. My life isn't my own, and I cannot run from my responsibilities. If you want me to keep my distance, I will. If you think walking away now is right, go, but know you're taking a piece of me with you."

I'm grasping at fragments of what he's said, turning them over, trying to understand. *I cannot promise you anything . . . I cannot run from my responsibilities.* I want his promises, all of them. I want to be his responsibility, and I want him to be mine. I want to be the reason he wakes up, the reason he smiles, the reason he *is*.

He's not selfish; I am.

But then there are his other words; words better than empty promises, because they sing the truth. *You're taking a piece of me with you.* I understand these words. I *feel* these words. It's as if he mined them from the quarry of my heart.

"I don't want to walk away," I whisper.

His eyes widen. "No?"

I shake my head. "And can we just . . . not talk about this again?"

He laughs, his whole body unwinding. "You brought it up."

"Because I can't stop thinking about how hard it's going to be later."

"Do you know what I can't stop thinking about?"

"What?"

"How good it is *now*."

He leans in and, at the same time, so do I. We meet, and we kiss, and there is nothing careful or neat or polite about it—it's the opposite of every kiss we've shared since the night we spent at the park. He winds my ponytail around one hand and grips my hip with the other, using his height to angle me back until I'm leaning against the arm of the sofa. I open my mouth to his; he tastes like bliss, like daydreams, like *home*. Winding my arms around his neck, I tug his hat off so I can play in his thick hair. I ease back further, taking him with me, until he's stretched over me, supporting his weight on his elbows. I spend a second fretting about his ribs, his comfort, but he seems pretty okay, actually, so I settle beneath him. His kisses become deeper, and mine become greedier, and it's entirely possible I will never get enough of this. Of him.

We kiss for eternities, and oh God, it's perfect. The sort of perfect I'm not likely to forget. The sort of perfect no other boy will live up to in a lifetime of kisses.

When he pulls back, he gives me a glazed-over smile. "I could get lost, kissing you."

My lips feel full, swollen, and my chin is raw from the sandpaper stubble on his. Not that I care, because the burn is a reminder, a feeling of *aliveness* that's been elusive for too many years. His hips are nestled against my hips, his feet tangled with my feet. He's got one hand linked with mine, and the fingers of his other twist and twirl the locks of hair that have escaped my ponytail. He feathers his lips over my throat, my cheeks, my eyelids, kisses like dandelion fluff. He was right...

This *is* good.

Time passes and the light shifts, casting new shadows on the walls. I remember, with urgency, his parents. I check the time and find it's growing late.

No, no, no. I'm not sure when we'll get another afternoon like this.

"I should go," I say to save him the awkwardness of booting me from the cottage.

He pulls away from where he's nuzzling my neck. "Already?"

"Unless you want your parents to find me here . . . with you . . . like this."

He smiles sheepishly and moves away so I can sit up. I let my hair down, combing my fingers through the tangles he made, and gather it into a smooth ponytail. He repositions his hat, watching me, riveted, and then I remember: most of the girls in his country cover their hair. It's no wonder he's always touching mine.

"Can we do this again?" he asks as I finish.

"I'll check my schedule," I tease.

He takes my face in his hands, kisses me again, briefly, fiercely. When he draws back, he says, "Remember when we were on our way to Sacramento? I told you I'm supposed to guard my modesty?"

I blink, my cheeks warming. *This* is what we're going to talk about? After *that*? "Uh, yeah."

"You probably noticed, but . . . I'm not guarding it so carefully anymore."

I'm trying to make sense of what he's saying, where he's going with this line of conversation, but I'm coming up blank. His religion is important to him and I'm important to him, but I'm not sure how we connect—if we *can* connect. "What does that mean, Mati?"

His hands are still bracketing my face, his palms cool against my flushed skin. He says, "Kissing you. Touching you. Being here with you, alone. I've chosen to do these things, even though Allah and the Quran say I shouldn't."

"Because you think I'm a freebie?"

His brows pinch together. He opens his mouth, then closes it, like he's lost.

"Context clues," I say. "A freebie. Like, what you do with me isn't a strike against your morals. We're a window of time that doesn't count, because as soon as you leave, that window will slam shut."

He presses his lips to my forehead, branding my skin with his intensity. "Oh, I think we count. Since we met, I've been trying to reconcile my faith with my wishes, with my dreams, with my desires, and I keep thinking . . . It must be possible to be devoted to Islam while still holding on to my individuality. It must be okay to be Muslim, and *me*. I am a product of Allah. He created me, a person who has fallen for you. I just don't understand how that can be wrong."

I stare at him, struck silent by his honesty and his intelligence and his enormous heart.

We aren't wrong; we *can't* be wrong.

I kiss him, long and slow.

I file the sensation away for later, when kissing him is an impossibility.

I tell him breathlessly, "I love you for saying that."

And then I'm out the door.

My heart swoops-dips-dives in the gray-blue sky.

elise

i love you for saying that.

God, the absolute *worst* time for my filter to malfunction. It slipped—*totally* slipped—because when I'm with Mati, apparently I am at all times compelled to say exactly what's on my mind. I shudder with embarrassment as I walk down the sidewalk toward Audrey's.

Janie proves to be an ideal distraction. We whip up a batch of chocolate-chip cookies (I do the measuring, and she does the mixing), then we sit in front of the oven, watching them soften and puddle, setting into gooey perfection. I tell her a story about her daddy: how, when he was fourteen, he ate an entire batch of cookie dough, raw egg and all, straight from the fridge.

"Nana was so upset," I say, reveling in Janie's wide-eyed amazement.

"Did Daddy get in trouble?"

"Well, sort of, but not because Nana punished him. His tummy got sick and he was miserable for the rest of the day."

She giggles. "Poor Daddy!"

When our cookies are done, I put several on a plate, still warm from the oven. "We should only eat two each," Janie says sagely. "We don't want to have sick tummies."

"That's right," I say, pouring glasses of cold milk for dunking.

We watch *The Little Mermaid* while we snack. Janie sings "Part of Your World" like she feels the lyrics in her little bones; I do, too. When the movie is done, we order pizza.

"Just cheese, Auntie," she says, holding my hand as I make the call.

Later, after a bubble bath and a manicure of sparkly pink polish, we settle on her bed for stories. We make it through *Beauty and the Beast* and half of *Aladdin* before she's out, sucking her thumb, squeezing a plush baby doll to her chest. I wind her music box anyway, then tuck her blankets up to her chin and kiss her squishy cheek.

Her eyes, rimmed in long blond lashes, flutter open. "I love you, Auntie," she whispers.

"I love you, too, girlie."

"Babysit me again soon, okay?"

"You got it."

I leave her room wrapped up in thoughts about how careful I need to be when it comes to spending time with Mati—Audrey can't find out. I can't lose more time with my niece; since my brother died, I've felt a sense of duty to him, and to Janie. It's my job to pass stories of Nick and his childhood antics to his daughter. I can't fail him, and I can't fail her.

I spend the rest of the evening on the sofa, editing images on my laptop. The photo I took of Mati this afternoon is sublime. I see him, all of him, with arresting clarity. It's as if his essence, his aura, his *soul*, swirl in air around him, rendering the colors of the garden in the background bland. I want the world to see him this way: son, brother, writer, dreamer.

When Audrey comes through the door, she's rumpled and weary. She drops her bag on the entryway table and scans the living room, like she expects me to have a troop of Afghan boys hiding behind curtains and inside cabinets.

"Everything go okay?" she asks, collapsing on the sofa.

"Awesome. There's leftover pizza in the fridge, and tons of cookies on a plate in the microwave." I pause, tempted to tell her about Nick and his cookie-dough overindulgence, too—it happened shortly before their time—but she looks so tired. I close my laptop and slide it into my bag, eager, suddenly, to be on my way. "Janie was an angel as usual. We watched *The Little Mermaid*."

Aud slips her swollen feet out of her flats. "She loves that movie."

"I know."

Silence. She's my closest friend, my *sister*, and she'll barely meet my gaze.

"I should go."

She nods, then stands to walk me out. At the door, she takes my hand and says, "Thanks for babysitting. I know things have been rough, but I'm happy to have you back."

Happy in her delusion.

Still, it's a step.

MATI

I love you for saying that
is not
the same
as *I love you.*

This is what I tell myself
as I sit through my parents'
evening conversation.
As I boil water for chai.
As I warm leftovers and eat,
standing alone,
at the kitchen counter.
This is what I tell myself
after I say my final prayer,
as I try, and fail, to sleep.

Because . . .
What if it *is* the same?

I think she could love me,
if circumstances were different.
But for us, love is perilous.

She will be okay if we are friendship.
If we are flirtation.
If we are romance in a fanciful turret,
and long kisses on a cramped sofa.

She will be okay if the
(*bittersweet*) feelings are mine alone.
I love her, I love her, I love her,
but she does not
(*cannot*) love me back.

She will not be okay if her heart is vested.
It will doubtlessly be broken,
and while I can endure the guilt
that comes with courting her,
if I *hurt* her, regret will bury me.

There is so much she will never
(*can never*) know.
The promises I made before her
will seem ill-conceived,
and my commitments
will hold no weight.
Centuries of tribal strife will end
if I fulfill my duty,
but she will not see it that way—
not if she is in love with me.

I leave my bed.
I dress.
I walk, stealthily,
out of the cottage.

I have to know for sure.

elise

i 'm headed down the sidewalk, thinking of Janie and cookies, Mati and kisses, dandelions and shooting stars, when a tall, shadowed figure steps out from behind a stocky tree, right into my path. A shriek escapes my throat, and my hands fly up, curled into fists, a sudden surge of adrenaline demanding *fight!*

"Elise, it's okay!"

Warm hands land on my arms. Draw me forward. Hold me against a solid chest.

Mati.

"I'm sorry," he says, gentle words rustling my ponytail.

My arms loop instinctually around his middle, though my heart's still hammering my ribs in a relentless attempt to escape. I take a shaky breath; his familiar scent eases my nerves enough to let me sputter, "God, Mati, you scared the shit out of me. What are you doing?"

"Waiting for you." He edges back and presses a palm to my chest, just over my heart, letting his heat melt what's left of my panic. "I've been here awhile. I knew Audrey would be coming home, and I didn't want to upset her again."

I look back at her cottage; the front lights are still on, shining through the sheer curtains that cover the arched windows. I reshoulder my bag and slip my hand into his. I lead him down the sidewalk, away from Aud's and town, toward seclusion and safety. We walk to the beach, to the picnic table where, weeks ago, he left the note that changed everything.

We sit on the tabletop, bathed in moonlight, feet propped on the bench. The sky mirrors my ceiling at home, black and sprinkled with stars, like someone tossed a handful of silver glitter into the heavens. I can just make out the ocean's restless waves against the sand below, but otherwise the night is hushed and still. I rest my head on Mati's shoulder. "So why were you sneaking around like a creep?"

He laughs, soft and sonorous. "I didn't mean to scare you. I just—I needed to see you."

"Not that I'm complaining, but why the urgency?"

"You said something before you left earlier. You probably don't remember, but . . ."

Damn it. I've been hoping my declaration went over his head, that he heard it as an offhand comment, just one of those things Americans say. Obviously not.

I giggle, a nervous, giddy, *mortified* sound. "Oh. That."

"Yes. That."

"It just came out, Mati. Because that was nice, what you said—that we count. That we can't be wrong. I was, like, *moved*. I didn't mean to make you uncomfortable."

"I'm not uncomfortable. I'm worried."

"About what?"

"About whether you meant it."

"Oh."

"Elise. Did you mean it?"

"I . . ." Am at a complete loss for words.

Shit, shit, *shit*. I meant it. I love him, and it's possible I have since we met here, at this beach, since that first time my heart reached for his. I've known with certainty since our night in the turret, but I can't tell him—not when he's regarding me with an air of utter terror.

"Either way," he says, "I need to know how serious you were—are. How serious *we* are."

"Mati..." Because, no, we can't be serious, despite how I feel.

He breathes a sigh that sounds suspiciously like relief. "It's okay. It was an expression, one I didn't follow, and that's *good*. Because even though I'm growing to love you with strength that scares me, it's better if you do not fall so hard."

I stare into his bottomless eyes. He stares back, unwavering. I need to say something; I need to respond with comparable compassion. I swallow. "Uh, how is that better?"

His mouth turns up in an endeared smile. God, he is far superior with words, and he knows it. "It is better," he says patiently, "because when I leave, you won't be so hurt."

I feel weird, like I've plummeted into frigid water. My senses are slow, uncooperative, and my reactions are sluggish. My lungs feel heavy, underoxygenated, and the result is a rush of vertigo so powerful, I have to grab the edge of the table to remain upright.

I'll be inconsolable when he goes. How does he not realize?

I forage for words—the right words—to make him understand. "Mati, when you leave, I will *crumble*."

His head drops. "I hoped—"

"What? That I'd kiss you goodbye and go about my day? Do you not see the way I look at you, or feel the way I touch you? Do you not realize that I'm always trying to get as close to you as possible? That I'm constantly adjusting my Mati dial so I can stay tuned in to you through incessant static?"

He's still looking at the ground when he mumbles, "It just—you feeling the way I feel... it seems too good to be real."

"Well, it *is* real. I love you for saying what you said, and I love you."

I lean forward and catch his mouth with mine. I'll kiss the stunned look off his face. I'll drill everything I just said through his thick skull. I'll make him understand how profoundly he's affected me, and how deeply I care.

When I pull away, he gives me a meek smile, his eyes swimming with trepidation.

"Hey," I whisper, tugging his hat from his head so I can run my fingers through his hair. "No doubts, okay? Earlier, you talked about how good we are. Nothing's changed, right?"

He blows out a leaden breath. It takes a second, but he shakes his head. "No. Nothing has changed." He lifts his hat from where it sits on my lap and fits it over my head, ponytail and all. I'm certain it looks ridiculous but, finally, his mouth turns up in a smile.

"We're okay?" I ask.

"I'm not sure we'll ever be okay. Right now, I am two things. *Khoshqháala.*"

He waits, and I repeat: *"Khoshqháala."*

"And *ghamdzhan.*"

"What do they mean?"

His expression is woeful, but his eyes burn flame-hot, the way they do, I've come to realize, when he's thinking about kissing me. He tips his head, pressing his mouth to mine.

"Happy," he whispers against my lips. He kisses me again, lingering. "And so, so sad."

elise

At home, Mom and I maintain a careful cease-fire. We speak to each other when necessary, and with unnatural politeness. She returns my phone, finally, which is the same as reclaiming a limb. Over the weekend, I get another chance to babysit Janie, and Audrey treats me almost normally. I indulge in a milkshake date with Ryan, which, thankfully, is a more cheery meeting than our last conversation in the yard.

Mostly, life feels okay, except for the fact that Mati and I are forced to keep our relationship secret. He still meets me at the beach in the mornings, but we're vigilant now, checking the stretch of sand that used to feel like ours for anyone who might pose a threat. I glance over my shoulder before taking his outstretched hand, and he surveys the picnic area before kissing me goodbye. At night, we sneak off to the dark solitude of the park. When I can't get away, I spend hours on the phone with him. It's a comfort to fall asleep to the timbre of his voice, the melody of his brooding words.

A week before he's due to return to Afghanistan, we spend a

morning at the beach, trudging through the sand, watching my dog scuttle around up ahead without a care in the world. I'm envious. I feel wretched (*seven days until he's gone forever—seven days, seven days, seven days*) and I can tell Mati's mind is working overtime. He pauses to launch Bambi's tennis ball, then watches it soar through the air with a faraway expression.

I touch his arm. "Are you okay?"

He shrugs and starts walking again.

I catch up. "Hey, talk to me."

"I just—I feel . . ." He sighs, drawing a hand slowly over his face. He reappears, looking wrecked.

"I know," I say, weaving my fingers through his. I know, and I don't want to talk about it, acknowledge it, face it, either. I push up on my toes to press my cheek against his. "I know," I say again, my heavy heart dragging my pitch low. "But right now, I want to be here with you— *present*, with you. I want to forget next week, saying goodbye, the future. Mati, help me forget?"

He leaves a trail of kisses on my cheek, a slow journey to my mouth, and then, for a few minutes, I really do forget. Because the beach is ours and he's holding me close and it's impossible to think of anything but the way he kisses . . . as if he cherishes me, as if he's giving himself over to a longing that will never be satiated.

He pulls back, returning briefly to press his lips to my forehead, then starts walking again, with my hand folded into his. He seems lighter, and I *am* lighter. I lean into him, vowing to retain this feeling. To focus on it, the good, every time I start to feel down.

He sidesteps Bambi as she barrels past, sopping wet tennis ball clamped in her jaw. Conversationally, he says, "My baba mentioned you this morning."

"Uh-oh."

He laughs. "The opposite, actually. He really does like you."

"Unlike your mother."

"Mama doesn't *dis*like you."

I roll my eyes. I'm so tired of feeling like the truest part of my life is on display for others to judge, or hidden away so others *won't* judge.

"I mean it," he says. "The truth is, she has very little experience with your culture and because of that, in some ways, from *her* position, you're . . . exotic."

I snort—I can't help myself. I couldn't be less exotic—*more* ordinary—if I tried.

"Think about it," Mati says. "Your life is so different from the life she led as a teenager. By the time she was your age, she was married and managing a household. She didn't have the luxury of exploring the world, of considering colleges, of choosing her husband."

"Like that's my fault?"

"It's not. But it's still a factor. And beyond that, I think she sees you as a threat. She's laid out a narrow path for my sister and brother and me, and when she sees one of us stepping away, her instinct is to look for someone to blame. I've strayed. I've disobeyed Allah and defied the Quran—I've sinned—and she believes that's because of you."

"But that's not fair!"

"I know, and I'm sorry. I'm so sorry you're tangled up in all this, but I promise, the way she acts has more to do with my choices than with you personally."

I fight the impulse to dig my heels in on this, because stubbornness due to hurt feelings is pointless, a complete waste of energy. As we walk, I let Mati's words permeate, making a genuine effort to broaden my point of view. Hala and I lead different lives, but that's not her fault or mine. She loves her son, obviously, and it makes sense that she'd resort to defensiveness when it looks like he might be veering away from his values—especially with a girl she doesn't understand.

Hala deserves grace, even if she doesn't always give it.

"I talked to her about what she saw at the hospital," Mati says, squeezing my hand. "Baba spoke to her as well. She agreed to let it pass."

"That's generous, I guess."

"So generous you'll consider coming by this afternoon?"

I turn to gape at him. Grace or not, that's a terrible idea. But then I think of my own mother, about compassion put into practice, and how she's failing epically. I find myself swayed by Mati's expression, awash in hope. "Oh God . . . I don't know."

"With Bambi. My baba wants to meet her. He asked specifically, and he's feeling well enough to sit out in the yard with her." He loops his arm around my shoulders, tucking me against his side. "Your visit would be good for him, and it would be good for me."

"How's that?"

He leans down to speak into my ear. "I spend my afternoons thinking about you. Wondering about you. Writing about you. Missing you. If you come over, you'll spare me the suffering."

I roll my eyes. "You know you're too good at this, right? It's unfair, really. There's this saying, something like 'he could sell ice to an Eskimo,' and that's totally you. You open your mouth and all these lovely, convincing words spill out, and suddenly I'm nodding, ready and willing to do anything you ask."

He quirks an eyebrow. "Anything?"

I laugh. "In this case, I was referring to bringing my dog to visit your baba. But yeah . . . pretty much anything."

He stops, and I do, too. My breath catches as he presses his hand to my cheek, turning my face up. He's melting me with that heated expression of his, eyes warm and wanting. We stand still, sharing a gaze, sharing a breath. Then he pulls me into him, and I exist in the happiest place I know, Mati's arms, listening to the steady *thrum-thrum-thrum* of his heart.

"You'll come?" he says into my windblown hair.

"Of course I'll come."

elise

*L*ater, Bambi and I walk to Mati's.

He's out on the lawn with his father, who's in a cushioned wicker chair. Rasoul really is looking better. There's color in his cheeks, and the wisps of his beard have filled in a little. He's wearing slacks and a white linen shirt, and when he spots Bambi and me, he grins. He nudges Mati, gesturing to the gate. Mati, chagrined, hops up to open it, his smile like the sun emerging from behind a cloud. He crouches to scratch Bambi behind her ears and she wags her tail like she's forgotten all about how he spent ages throwing her slobbery ball just this morning.

"Thanks for coming," he says as he straightens again.

"Thanks for inviting me." I lower my voice. "Where's your mother?"

"Inside. Remember? She doesn't care for dogs."

"Her loss, I guess." But really, I'm relieved. I'm willing to be decent, to be here for Mati and Rasoul, but standing beneath Hala's depreciating gaze as I try to keep my dog (*dirty*, she said during lunch) from climbing into her husband's lap to lick his face seems insufferable.

I keep a firm grip on Bambi's collar while making introductions.

She's thrilled to be here, and if the way Rasoul beams is any indication, he's just as thrilled to make her acquaintance. He pats her a little awkwardly at first, a flat-palmed tap against her hairy head, but he becomes comfortable quickly. Soon, he's hunched over her, nose-to-wet-nose, murmuring about what a good dog she is. It's beguiling, watching a sick man find comfort in an animal he should, by all counts, treat with indifference.

Mati and I sit in the grass near his chair, watching the display with wonder. I'd bring Bambi here every day, even under the threat of Hala's scorn and my own mother's disapproval, just to see Rasoul so happy.

"Baba," Mati says after a while, "will you keep an eye on Bambi for a few minutes? I have something to show Elise."

Rasoul nods, not bothering to look up from the lovefest he's lavishing on my dog.

Mati gestures toward the path that leads to the backyard, then pushes up out of the grass. He wanders toward the side of the cottage and I follow, curious. When we've rounded the corner, he reaches for my hand and leads me farther into the shade.

"What's this about?" I ask, delighting in the feel of his palm against mine.

His eyes gleam. He points. At the edge of the cottage, just below the slab-stone chimney, sits a patch of dandelions, heads white with fluff. A slow smile spreads across my face: Where any other person would see weeds—a nuisance—Mati and I see wishes.

"This is the coolest," I say, moving toward them.

"I knew you'd think so. When my mama finds them she'll pull them up, but I wanted you to make a wish first. Or many wishes, if you like."

"I have only one wish," I tell him in an undertone.

I bend and carefully pick two dandelions. I extend one to him. He takes it, brushing my fingers with his, sending a wake of tingles up my arm.

He steps closer, crowding me in the most wonderful way. He leans in to whisper, "What is your wish, *shaahazadi*?"

"You," I say, without hesitation. "You, always."

He smiles, part wistful, part sorrowful, and I know what he's thinking, what he's feeling, because my emotions are a reflection of his. This, today, us: perfect, but passing.

We blow our dandelions in tandem, sending their seeds to the breeze. He drops his stem onto the grass, then trails his hand down the inside of my arm, over the sheer skin beneath my elbow and the sensitive interior of my wrist. A succession of shivers ripples through me as he folds my palm into his. We watch our wishes drift away.

It is, without a doubt, the most magical moment of my life.

He uses his hold on my hand to twirl me around, until I'm facing him. He takes a step forward, trapping me between the smooth stones of the chimney and the unyielding wall of his chest. I bite my lip, hovering in that dangerous void between laughter and tears. He dips his head, skimming kisses across my throat, and I grapple for his other hand, until our palms are aligned at our sides. I exhale a tremulous breath.

His mouth on my skin . . .

He makes me boneless.

He finds my ear and murmurs, "*Za ta sara meena kwam*," and even without context clues, his meaning is clear.

"I love you, too," I whisper.

He raises his head, seeks my eyes, lets me sink deep into his. His hands come up to brush my hair back, to cradle my face in their gentle warmth.

Okay, no—*this* is the most magical moment of my life.

I hook my fingers in the belt loops of his jeans, tugging him closer. I lift up on my toes, and we meet in a kiss, a lazy, sultry, smooth-like-velvet kiss.

It's the most extraordinary kiss.

And it's interrupted in the most awful way.

Hala's voice, aghast, *furious*. "Matihullah!"

MATI

She jerks away from me,
covering her heart-shaped mouth
with a cupped hand.
Her eyes are wide, dilated, *horrified*,
as she turns to face Mama.

I do, too.

I have never seen this combination
of emotion on my mama's face.

She is appalled.
She is agonized.
She is apoplectic.

She lets loose a barrage of Pashto,
words that swarm the air like angry wasps.

And then she whirls around
and marches to the front yard,
where Baba sits.

"Stay here," I say to the girl
who stands trembling before me.

I go after Mama.

She stands over Baba,
and her rage is an onslaught.
The poor dog . . .
Bambi shirks beside Baba's chair
as Mama yells, not in Pashto,
but in fragmented English—
so *every*one will hear,
so *every*one will understand.

"Promised! He is *promised* to another."
He brings dishonor to himself,
his people, and Allah.
He brings dishonor to his family. To me! To you!"

For the span of a second, I hate her.

But Mama is not evil,
or even unreasonable.
She is reverent and virtuous,
and I have willfully disregarded
the rules of my faith.
She is bursting with anger,
with disappointment,
and I cannot blame her.

"Hala," Baba says, calm, rational, always.
"He is happy. For now, let him be."

"He is *engaged*!"

My lungs seize.
If there were doubts,
they have been razed.

I imagine her, hearing it all,
realizing I was not forthcoming.
I picture her face, bewildered,
then broken,
and her heart, smashed. . . .

Because of me.

I am yours. Don't give myself back to me.

—Rumi

elise

*e*ngaged.

My back hits the cold, hard stone of the chimney, knocking what's left of my breath away. If I was boneless before, I'm a puddle now.

I strain to listen as his parents have it out.

"He is *not* to see the girl again."

"Hala, it will run its course naturally."

"Always with his head in the clouds. His fantasies will bring trouble—they will bring trouble to us all."

And then Mati: "She is *not* fantasy!"

But I am, and so is he. We aren't real, and we never can be. Not in this town, not in this world. Not that I want to be—not anymore. Hala's words echo in my ears: *Promised! He is promised to another.* I'm trying to summon a rational explanation, mentally arguing against what is becoming agonizingly clear. Not only is he leaving, but he's returning to Afghanistan be with someone else. A Pashtun girl, probably, like Hala wants.

All his talk of his sister's arranged marriage, how unhappy it makes her, and him, and he's going to do the same thing. All his talk of soul mates, of love . . . None of it matters.

Not anymore.

I push off the chimney. Now my spine is stiff with indignation, my features hardened by betrayal. I won't cower—not while they're talking about me like I'm a slab of meat a week past good. Throw me away, or hang on to me awhile longer, just for the adventure of it?

God. I am such an *idiot*.

I throw my shoulders back and march toward the front yard, but just as I make my way around the corner of the cottage, I slam into Mati. He steadies me, two hands that burn my arms like heated steel, then guides me, backward and stumbling, to the shadows of the side yard.

"Elise," he says, rough with distress. "You have to let me explain."

"Don't *touch* me," I say, low, hostile. When he doesn't pull away, I smack my palms against his shoulders and shove with all my strength. He winces—his ribs aren't completely healed—but I don't care if he's hurting, or even if I'm damaging him permanently. I push him again, and again, my vision clouded with rage, until he lifts his hot hands from my skin and holds them in the air, surrendering.

His eyes are bloodshot, desperate. "You have to listen—"

"Don't tell me what to do!"

"Okay," he says. "Okay. I am not telling, I am asking—I am *begging* you to let me speak."

"There's nothing you can say that'll fix this."

I expect a rebuttal, a dispute about how, after all these weeks, after everything that's happened, I owe him a chance to defend himself. But he doesn't argue. He lowers his gaze to the grass and quietly, suppliantly, says, "Please."

I take a step back; his nearness is (always has been) my undoing. I cross my arms over my chest and say cruelly, "Fine. You're engaged? Let's hear about how lovely it all is."

His chin lifts, his gaze drilling into me. "Elise, don't romanticize it."

"Mati, don't *trivialize* it. How could you not tell me?!"

"She means nothing. I don't even know her."

"That's such bullshit. You're going to marry this—this *person*. An engagement matters!"

"It is not an engagement in the way you think. We've talked about this—there's nothing sentimental about it. There is no passion. No love."

Love. The way he pronounces the word traps air in my lungs. I clench my hands into fists, fighting the almost overwhelming urge to punch him. I relish the bite of my fingernails digging into my palms. It's pain, physical pain that's easy to pinpoint. Physical pain that's easy to alleviate. Nothing like what's going on in my chest: the systematic shredding of my heart.

I force a ragged exhale, ensuring that my voice is dangerously calm. "Who is she?"

His face falls, like he was hoping I wouldn't press for details. "Elise—"

"No, tell me. I want to know who she is. You owe me at least that much."

He speaks to the ground. "Her name is Panra. She's a girl from another tribe in Ghazni—a more prominent tribe, one that has feuded with my family's for generations. Her father is its leader, and my baba made the arrangement with him a long time ago, when it became clear that his health was declining and his survival wasn't guaranteed. It is a match that will benefit our people—that's what my baba hopes. A bond that will forge peace between both tribes."

Peace between tribes—that's what I'm up against.

"God, Mati! This is why you're so set on going back? This the *duty* you talk about? I mean, I get it: peace is a big deal. But do you know what's an even bigger deal? The fact that you have a *fiancé* waiting for you in Afghanistan! You didn't think, even once, that this was information I deserved to hear?"

"Yes. *Yes!* I thought about telling you a thousand times, but—"

"But what?" I'm yelling—I'm sure his parents can hear every syllable of my diatribe, just like I heard all of Hala's, and I'm sure Bambi is stressed about my well-being. But in this moment, I couldn't give a shit. "You *knew!*" I cry, jabbing a finger in his stupefied face. "You knew if I found out that you were *promised to someone else*, I'd back away. And, what? You didn't want to say goodbye to your beach buddy? You didn't want to lose your secret girlfriend?"

He whirls around and stalks to the corner of the cottage. He keeps his back to me and even though I want to strangle him, I also want to know what's going on in his head. Because despite what I said all of five seconds ago, my feelings haven't changed. Not enough. I am stupid—so, so stupid. I've fallen in love with a charming boy—a cunning, deceptive, *unavailable* boy.

Audrey's voice runs circles in my head: *A person who can't be trusted.*

The truth of it makes me ache.

He's striding toward me again. He rounds his shoulders and gets right in my face, jaw working, eyes flashing. "I cannot *believe* you would insinuate that my intentions are anything but honorable."

"And I can't believe I've spent my summer with a liar."

"I have never lied to you. Not once."

"Only because I didn't think to ask if you were *engaged!*"

I move to push past him, but he grabs my hand and spins me around. Even as I wrench out of his hold, he's talking, explaining, *pleading*, "Please, Elise. I love *you*. No arbitrary promise will change that."

I stare at him, rubbing away the prickles of recognition—the prickles of *want*—his touch left on my skin. "It's hardly an arbitrary promise when you're going home to her," I say darkly. "Soon, it'll be her hand you're holding. Her lips you're kissing. You'll look into her eyes and spout beautiful, meaningless words. God, Mati! Are you going to write about her?"

His gaze narrows. "Don't diminish what you and I have."

"What you and I *had*. I don't ever want to see you again."

This time, my escape is quick.

He doesn't follow.

I round the cottage to its front yard. Rasoul sits in his wicker chair. He's bent over Bambi, petting her head with slow, methodical strokes as her gaze jumps around the yard. She's panting like she hasn't seen water in weeks. Hala stands on the porch, arms crossed, glaring as I march across the lawn. Just beneath her glare lies the suggestion of satisfaction.

There, I think, aiming a beam of loathing in her direction. *I'm out of his life, like you wanted.*

"Elise," Rasoul says as I retrieve my dog's leash. He gives his throat a rutty clear. "Please don't go. This situation . . . It is not what you think."

I snap Bambi's leash to her collar, then stand to look him square in the face. "It's exactly what I think, and for you to say differently is insulting."

He cringes. "I mean no offense. Mati feels—"

"I don't care about what Mati feels." I realize suddenly, and with acute embarrassment, that I'm crying. I wipe savagely at my face as I bend to meet his gaze. "I appreciate your being hospitable. I appreciate your inviting me over and pretending like I matter. I hope you get better and have a chance to enjoy the peace Mati's marriage will bring, but right now, there's nothing you can say that will make this okay. I just—I want to go."

He nods once, like he understands.

I'm certain he doesn't.

I give Bambi's leash a tug. She hops up and follows me over the path, through the gate, and down the sidewalk.

Far, far away from Mati and the fairy tale he destroyed.

elise

i go to Audrey's.

I knock on the door of her cottage, then wait, and wait, before banging on the wood all over again. Bambi turns circles beside me, whining nervously.

"It's okay, girl," I say, stooping to pet her. A tear rolls down my cheek, then free-falls, landing on her blond head. It's quite possibly the most pathetic display I've ever exhibited—I'm crying with my dog over a boy.

I knew Mati would ruin me, but I never thought it'd be like *this*.

The cottage's door swings open. Audrey stands over me. "God, Elise, what happened?"

She appears blurry, watercolored. I shrug haplessly like, *You were right.*

And then she's wrapping an arm around me, pulling me inside, guiding me to the sofa. She sits beside me, hugs me, smoothing her hand over my hair while I cry into the gauzy fabric of her blouse.

I have never loved her more.

After buckets of tears, I pull away. I feel terrible—hot and wrung out and vaguely nauseated. My throat is sore and my middle hurts, like I've been run over by a truck. Still, I tuck my hair behind my ears and smooth my shirt, feigning composure, pretending I didn't just shatter on my sister-in-law's sofa.

"Where's Janie?" I ask.

Audrey gawks, like, *You come here a sobbing mess, but* Janie's *who you're concerned with?*

She recovers, arranging her features into an expression like tranquility. "Napping."

"I'm sorry to show up like this."

"I'm sorry you're upset." She folds her hands, studying me. "Do you want to tell me what happened?"

I sink back into the cushions, droopy, like a sail that's lost its wind. I take a breath, but . . . I have no idea where to start. I don't even *know* what happened. An hour ago, I loved Mati and he loved me. Despite our imminent end, being with him filled me to bursting.

Now, I'm just . . . *empty.*

"What you said, all of it . . . You were right," I tell Audrey.

Her shoulders fall in a sigh. "The boy."

"*Mati.*" Even now, I can't accept her slighting him.

"I thought you weren't seeing him anymore."

I shrug weakly.

She grimaces. "What'd he do?"

"He lied. Everything . . . It was all a lie."

I told you—now's the perfect time for her say it, and she'd be right. But she doesn't; she pats my hand and says, "Oh, Lissy, I'm sorry."

I tell her everything. Our surreptitious visits, the attack he endured, Hala's disapproval coupled with my mom's, the *I love you*'s we traded, the way he made me feel whole and spirited and special. I tell her about Ghazni and the opposing tribes. The words *feuding*, and *duty*, and *peace* drop from my mouth like stones. I tell her about Panra, the faceless girl who's earned my envy, my fury, my hatred, just by existing. I tell her about the arrangement—the *engagement.*

"He says it doesn't matter," I add, monotone. I blow my nose again with one of the many tissues she's supplied. "He says there are no feelings, that she's just a girl."

Aud arches an eyebrow. "Just a girl? Damn, Lissy. Whoever she is, I feel terrible for her."

I narrow my eyes, tossing my wadded tissue on the coffee table, where it finds a place among its friends. "You should feel terrible for *me*. I'm the scorned mistress in this scenario."

She cracks a smile. "That's something your mom would say. But think about it.... This girl is going to be stuck in a presumably unwanted marriage with a liar who's got feelings for someone else. Sucks to be her."

I lack the emotional capacity required to feel any sort of sympathy for Panra. She's going to gain what I've lost, and anyway, I can't stop thinking of Mati, of the wishes we've made, the endless conversations we've had, the way he's touched my face, the way he's kissed me. He loves me—I don't doubt that—but I doubt his motives. I doubt his integrity.

"I wish I'd never met him," I tell Audrey.

"Me, too," she says softly.

I'll never see him again.

I think, maybe, that's for the best.

Aud collects my tissues, making a neater pile of them on the coffee table, casting worried sidelong glances my way. I watch her handle my snotty mess without flinching, until a question occurs to me, one I can't help but voice. "Audrey, are you glad?"

Her head snaps up. "Am I *glad*? Why would you ask me that?"

"Because you hate Mati."

"Elise, I never, ever want to see you hurt. I could kill him for what he's putting you through."

I shake my head. "It's my fault. I should've listened to you. To my mom."

"Do you think Nick and I always listened to your mom?"

"I mean, basically."

"No. She didn't want him to get serious with me—not at first."

"He told you that?"

"Nicky and I didn't have secrets. Your mom was unwavering on the issues of college and career—priorities, she used to say. She thought I was holding him back."

I recall family dinners, the four of us laughing around the kitchen table. I recall Audrey and Nick wrapped around each other on the couch, watching movies while my mom tapped away at her keyboard in the next room. I recall the two of them closing themselves behind his bedroom door for hours at a time, Mom passing by with a *boys will be boys* raise of her shoulders. She was upset about Nick's enlistment, the quick engagement, and the lackluster City Hall wedding, but when it came to Audrey . . .

"My mom loves you, Aud."

"Now."

"But if you'd run away in the beginning, when she didn't want Nick to get serious, there'd be no Janie."

"Exactly. Your brother and I did what felt right for us. It was hard, but all the challenges, all the pain? Worth it. I guess that's my point: Sometimes you have to trudge through heartache to figure out which path to take. This boy is not the right path for you, Lissy. Now you know for sure."

Before today, in the deepest, darkest cavern of my heart, I nursed a tiny ember of hope. Mati's departure . . . maybe, somehow, it would be postponed. And even if it wasn't, someday, we might find our way back to each other. After Rasoul is healthy, after I earn my degree, after Mati's fulfilled his duties in Afghanistan, we could be together, him and me. But now, with the awareness of Panra and marriage and tribal peace . . .

"Knowing *hurts*," I mumble. "I don't ever want to think about him again." It's the truth—the childish, self-serving, unimaginable truth.

"When Janie wakes up, we'll go to the park," Aud says, smoothing my hair. "Then we'll swing by Van Dough's and get coffees and tons of cookies, a table full of them, and we'll eat and drink and talk and cry until you feel better. Okay?"

The park, Van Dough's, infinite cookies . . . Reminders of Mati. Sacramento, the Cypress Beach Cemetery, the sidewalk outside my cottage, our stretch of sand . . . All colored by memories of him. More than anything, I want to go home and bury myself in bed with my dog and a playlist loaded with angsty torch songs. But I nod.

I'll go to the park and I'll go to Van Dough's, and I'll forget about my splintered heart and the boy who took a mallet to it.

elise

*h*e calls, he calls, and then he calls some more. For the rest of the day, and most of the night. He leaves countless voice mails. I listen to them all, because I'm a masochist.

He texts in the morning. No pretense, no fluff, just . . .

I am so sorry.

For the first time since my visit with Audrey, the urge to cry overwhelms me.

I skip the beach in favor of hanging out in the front yard with Bambi, where I build a wall around my heart, stones and mortar, indestructible. My dog seems to understand my suffering.

Midmorning, Iris comes outside to commence her daily pruning session. I hear her shucking dead buds from her many plants and nestle deeper into the grass, where I've been for a while, staring up at the gray sky, feeling very small and very insignificant in this tremendous world.

From where I sit today, Afghanistan might as well be another planet in a different galaxy, but someday, after the San Francisco Art

Institute, when I'm a photojournalist seeking stories of truth . . . maybe I'll make my way there. I'd like to see the places Mati's described: the Minaret of Jam, the Sultan Masood Palace, Bala Hissar, the Gardens of Babur. The Kabul Zoo, even.

But I won't go looking for him.

Iris says my name, startling me. She's peering over the hedge and I wonder, not for the first time, how often she spies on our yard. She looks at me, supine in the grass, and clucks her tongue. "Are you all right, sweetie?"

I heave myself off the lawn. "I've been better, actually."

She adjusts the sun visor tamping down her salt-and-pepper curls. "You look tired."

"I *am* tired."

"Me, too," she says, lopping a branch from the Japanese maple standing beside her. It's an aggressive cut—unnecessary, from what I can tell—and I wonder if she's paying attention to her task.

"Everything okay?" I ask.

"Last night was rough at the Higgins cottage."

"What happened?"

"Well," she says, severing another branch. "I found out Ryan is in a relationship . . . with Xavier."

"Oh." *Oh.* Poor Ryan. I've been so wrapped up in my own trials, I've hardly thought about him. I fight the compulsion to cross into Iris's yard to find him. But later. It's pretty clear that at the moment, his gram needs to talk.

"Yes, *oh*." She tips her visor up to study me. "You don't seem surprised."

I flush, remembering how I so charitably turned Ryan down shortly after we met. "I've known for a while."

"I don't understand why he'd keep something so important from me."

I fiddle with my ponytail, trying to come up with a suitable answer, one that won't put Ryan on the spot with her later. "You know how boys

can be. They get scared and keep secrets from people they care about."
I'm talking about Mati, obviously, but my rationale applies here, too.

"Hmm...," Iris says. "I suppose that makes sense. But I'm his *gram*."

My skin's itchy with empathy. "Maybe that's why he held back. He wasn't sure how you'd react and didn't want you to be mad, or sad. He loves you."

"I love him, too—that hasn't changed." Her mouth puckers, down-turned, like she's reliving the unpleasantness of what went on last night.

"When you found out, how'd you react?"

Her frown deepens. "Unfavorably, in hindsight. But only because I was surprised. He's disappointed in me. *I'm* disappointed in me." She scales another branch from her tree. "I want him to feel comfortable coming to me, no matter the situation. I want him to trust me."

"You should talk to him."

She eyes me. "Will you speak to the person who's responsible for your stewing in the grass all morning?"

Touché.

"My situation's different, Iris."

"Still," she says, nodding like some sort of guru. "You should talk to him."

———

After dinner, I drag Ryan and Xavier to The Hamlet for milkshakes. We sit at the counter, three instead of two. Xavier asks for vanilla, Ryan orders peanut butter, and I stick with my tested-and-true coconut. When it arrives, I experience an unsettling sense of *déjà vu* at its tropical taste. Except, the last time I had a coconut shake, life was relatively good.

I'm pushing my full glass away, suddenly without appetite when, in a tone unfittingly casual, Ryan says, "Mati called this afternoon."

His name shatters the air like a hammer to glass. "Can we ... not talk about him?"

"He's a mess, Elise."

"*I'm* a mess," I say, too loud. I take a breath and swiftly reinforce my wall.

"He told me what happened. About the"—awkward throat clear—"engagement. He told me about the way his mother acted. She must really hate you, by the way."

Xavier elbows him. "Don't be an ass."

Ryan plows ahead, undeterred. "He *also* told me he's crazy in love with you."

"Did he tell you he lied by omission, over and over? Did he tell you he tried to justify it?"

"He told me he misses you. You're wasting your time with him. Six days and he's gone. I know you're hurt, but come on. You're punishing him for something that's not his fault."

I add stones to my wall, big ones, and bolsters for strength.

Six days. God, it's hard to breathe.

"He's a good guy, Elise."

I won't argue that. He's giving up his future, his *life*, to better his community. Short of my brother's death, I can't fathom a bigger sacrifice.

Ryan leans in, resting his hand on my arm. "He's a *good* guy."

"I know," I whisper.

"Then don't give yourself room for regret."

"Even if this is it with Mati," Xavier says, his tone indicating a fresh perspective. "If you stick to your guns, decide you're done, and that you never want to talk to him again, at least you got to know him. At least you had the experience, right?"

Ryan nods. "Right. But seriously. If you want to give him a call, we wouldn't stop you."

I smile for the first time in too long. "What am I going to do when you guys are gone?"

"Make new friends," Ryan says, like it's easy. He nods at my full glass. "Now, finish your milkshake." Glancing at his own, empty but for a few smears of peanut butter and whipped cream, then Xavier's, practically licked clean, he adds, "Unless you only brought us here to fatten us up?"

"Actually . . . I brought you here because I talked to your gram this morning."

His cheeks go pink. Xavier becomes suddenly fascinated with his straw.

"You hurt her feelings, Ryan."

He draws a hand over his face. "I know."

"What happened? I mean, not *exactly*, but how did she, you know . . . figure it out?"

"She went down the street to Ms. Pinque's after dinner. Xavier came over and I guess we lost track of time. Gram came home and . . . kind of walked in on us."

I wince. "You were . . . ?"

"Kissing," Xavier says with a sheepish, though not entirely repentant shrug. "On the sofa."

"She was shocked, to say the least," Ryan adds.

"She was like, '*Oh!*'" Xavier says, assuming a scandalized falsetto, "And then she dropped the plate of cookies she was holding."

For the first time in what feels like forever, I dissolve into genuine laughter.

They stare at me with nearly identical expressions of disbelief.

"What?" I say, fanning my face. "It's *funny*. I'm envisioning it as it went down: you two, oblivious, and poor Iris, letting a dozen cookies fall to the floor. She's an old lady, you guys. I'm pretty sure she'd be shocked to see her grandson frolicking with *any*one on her floral sofa, but *you*," I say, pointing at Xavier.

He gives me another of his unruffled shrugs, like, *What can I say?*

Ryan's still flushed, but he's flashing his patent grin. "You don't think she's upset about the gay thing?"

"*The gay thing?* I think what riled her is the *intimacy* thing. And the fact that you kept such a big secret from her. Talk to her already. And no more fooling around on her sofa!"

Ryan's beaming and so is Xavier; they're beaming at each other, and I see it in their shared gaze, *love*, sincere and stalwart.

I'm happy for them, really and truly, but I'd be a liar if I said I wasn't envious, too.

elise

*d*ays pass.

I've become sluggish and sloppy, and the thought of food . . . *ugh*. I haven't touched my Nikon; it sits on my desk, jeering, collecting dust. I can't sleep to save my life, though dragging my body out of bed is a task too enormous to attempt.

And then there's the ache. The relentless, carnal ache living deep in my chest: my heart, trying—failing—to reassemble itself.

I should have seen this coming. The day Mati told me he'd be returning to Afghanistan, I should have walked away. Because this brand of misery . . . It's nothing new.

I felt a version of it after Nick died. My mom did, too. We holed up in our San Francisco condo, the two of us, but we might as well have been alone. We barely spoke. Housekeeping was neglected and personal hygiene was optional. We never sat down to meals together. Her writing fell by the wayside, and so did my photography. Sometimes I'd find her in front of the muted TV, and I'd join her, though as far as she knew, I might as well have been an apparition. We'd stare at the screen, worlds apart. It wasn't until Audrey and baby Janie moved into the shrine that was Nicky's bedroom that we pulled out of our mutual depression.

I haven't spoken to Mati since the revelation about his engagement— haven't heard his laugh or felt the calloused touch of his palm or smelled his clean, rosemary scent. He's continued to call, once every evening. I've continued to ignore him, and not even because I'm mad—I lack the energy for anger.

I can't talk to him, because there's nothing left to say.

I understand.

I will never understand.

I forgive you.

It's impossible to forgive a lapse as enormous as his.

I want to see you.

God, what's the point?

I guess I could tell him how much I care—the truth. But even if I *did* understand, even if I *could* forgive, circumstance says reengaging will just make things worse.

It pisses me off that I can't shut my feelings down.

The black walls of my bedroom are *so* grim, and the stars on the ceiling only remind me of thwarted wishes. It's awful, being cooped up in here, where the bed's rumpled and unmade, and a plethora of half-empty coffee mugs sit atop my desk. My vintage cameras stare blankly from their shelves, reminding me of my old life, the life I've forgotten how to lead.

He's leaving in two days.

I'm summoning the energy for a shower when my mom comes bursting through my door, eyes wild. "Please tell me Bambi's in here!"

"No. I thought you let her into the yard?"

She palms her forehead.

"What?" I say, scrambling off my bed. "What happened?"

"I just went out to check on her. The gate was ajar."

"Mom! She got out?!"

"I called for her out front, but I didn't see her anywhere."

I shove my feet into the closest pair of flip-flops and rush out of my room. "I'm going to look for her," I shout over my shoulder.

I dash through the front door and out the gate. I weave through blocks of cottages, hoping Bambi hasn't strayed far. I call her name and clap my hands, keeping an eye out for her blond coat, all the while staving off tears.

She's nowhere.

I head for the beach, thinking she might've made a dash for the surf. My mom's already there. Her cardigan flaps in the wind, and she's shaking a bag of dog treats. I see Iris and Ryan, too, combing the area, talking to strangers, probably asking if they've seen a happy-go-lucky goldendoodle running around. I walk the sand, using my arm to block my eyes from the glare, trying not to panic.

I see dozens of dogs.

I don't see *my* dog.

After an hour, I've lost hope. I turn in the opposite direction, toward where Iris and Ryan are still searching. I'm moving closer to the waves when I spot a familiar form about fifty yards down the beach. Mati, holding a bright yellow tennis ball. The sight of him here, ball in hand, is so normal, so expected, it takes me a moment to wonder what he's doing. I pause, watching him scan the surf, then the shore. His eyes land on me, and he raises the tennis ball with a little shrug.

He's looking for Bambi.

My mom appears at my side. "Ryan called him," she says, nodding toward Mati.

"Oh," I say, detached, as if the sight of him—*here for me*—didn't send a bolt of pain through my heart. "You probably wish he'd go away."

She shrugs. "The more searchers, the better."

That's guilt talking. It's her fault Bambi's missing—benevolence as a way of making up for negligence. I start walking again, recommitted to the search.

"You haven't mentioned him in a while," Mom says, hurrying to match my pace.

I don't know what she expects—it's not like my past mentions of Mati have gone over well.

She's mostly overlooked me in favor of her manuscript the last few days, though she has brought mugs of steaming coffee to my room and given me consoling smiles on the rare occasions our eyes met. For the space of a second, I wonder if Audrey told her about Panra and the engagement—if what I took as an attempt at thoughtfulness is in fact pity—but then, I can't imagine Aud betraying me that way. No matter how intensely she disapproves of Mati, she'd never run to my mom with gossip of my loss.

"You told me to stay away from him, remember?"

Mom takes my hand, pulling me to a stop. "Elise, I don't like seeing you this way. I'm sorry," she says, and for a moment, I think she's talking about Mati, about the way she's treated him. But then she continues: "Bambi's gone because of me. I should have been more careful."

I yank my hand out of hers. "Shit happens," I mutter, blowing past her.

After another hour, Ryan, Iris, Mom, and I convene at the picnic tables. Ryan and Iris are all sad eyes and deep frowns. My mom's full of false optimism. Mati's nowhere to be seen. I'm a heartbeat short of hysterical.

"We'll find her," Mom says. "She's wearing her collar. Someone will call, we'll pick her up, and it'll be as if this afternoon never happened."

I shake my head and take off for town.

elise

udrey and Janie are coming for dinner. Their impending visit forces me off the sidewalks and into the shower. I make my bed, clear my desk of dirty dishes, and run the vacuum across the rug, all in an effort to stop worrying about Bambi, lost and lonely on the streets of Cypress Beach.

I'll be back to looking for her in an hour, soon as dinner's done.

When the bell chimes, I swing the door open. Aud, laden with bags of Chinese takeout, looks me over and says, "She's still missing, huh?"

I nod, biting hard into my lip.

"She'll come home, Auntie," Janie says. She wraps me in a hug, spidery-armed and warm.

My mom emerges from her library to take the food from Aud. They disappear into the kitchen to assess the calendar and dish up dinner while Janie and I head for the living room. I get out a puzzle for her to work on because I'm not feeling all that attentive. As I sit beside her on the couch, staring unseeingly at the pieces scattered across the coffee table, I reach instinctually down to give Bambi a pat. I find empty air, and my stomach turns over.

In the kitchen, I hear Mom and Audrey talking. Someone's turned on the radio, a low-key country station. The smell of Chinese food drifts through the house. God, this night feels bizarrely, infuriatingly normal.

How can everyone just . . . carry on?

I'm working to distract myself, helping Janie fit a corner piece into her puzzle, when I hear distant barking. I freeze, straining to listen, and then I hear it again. Janie hears it, too—she looks at me with eyes like discs.

We leap up and run, holding hands, for the front door. I fling it open to the sight of my dog, stretching to get through the open front gate. Mati's behind her, holding firmly to a length of rope looped through her collar. He lets her go and she gallops for me, jumping up to put her paws on my chest; she nearly knocks me down. I hold tight to her, blinking back joyful tears. Janie giggles as Bambi graces my face with dozens of slobbery kisses.

My mom and Audrey come outside to the commotion. While they give Bambi greetings almost as enthusiastic as mine, I sneak a look at Mati, still standing at the gate, holding the makeshift leash loosely in his hands. He looks satisfied, and at the same time, profoundly sad.

It takes a minute for my mom and Audrey to notice him.

"Where did you find her?" Aud calls across the yard.

Mati scuffs the sole of his shoe against the sidewalk. "She was waiting at our cottage when I returned from the beach."

She misses him, too. Oh, Bambi.

I'm watching Aud because it's too hard to hold Mati's gaze, and her expression confuses me, hovering somewhere between remorse and gratitude. She gives him a tight smile. "Thank you for bringing her home."

"I was happy to," he says.

My mother turns her back and shuffles into the house. Audrey follows, tugging Janie along by the hand.

I'm still stooped over Bambi, running my hand down her silky back, but I feel Mati's attention settle on my shoulders like a physical thing, heavy with penitence. I glance up because it's impossible not to and find him smiling at the sight of my dog and me, reunited.

I mouth, *Thank you.*

He nods once, pivots, and walks away.

I take Bambi into the house, fill her water bowl, and feed her too many treats. My pulse is racing with the adrenaline of reclaiming my dog, combined with the heart-shredding experience of looking Mati in the eye.

Eventually, we sit down to dinner. Mom talks about her manuscript (almost done), Audrey gripes about her job at Camembert (always busy), and Janie chatters about her latest preschool accomplishment (shoe-tying—yay). Aud asks about Ryan and, in an effort to connect— to at least *try*—I tell them about Xavier and Iris and the interrupted make-out session. Aud laughs. Mom cracks a smile.

Nobody mentions Mati, or what just happened in the yard.

After dinner, Janie passes out fortune cookies. Our tradition seems particularly frivolous tonight and my stomach's somersaulting, but I play along for Janie's sake. I put on a smile as she breaks her cookie open, then slides it across the table to Audrey. "What does it say, Mama?"

Aud gives her throat a theatrical clear. " 'Your fortune is as sweet as a cookie.' "

Janie grins. Through a mouthful of crumbs, she says, "What about yours?"

Aud splits her cookie in half, skims her fortune, then laughs. " 'You are the controller of your destiny.' Yeah, right," she says to her bit of paper. "My destiny is so far out of my control it's not even funny. I'm just riding the wave."

"You're doing a good job keeping afloat," my mom tells her.

She smiles. "Read yours, Jocelyn."

I'm thinking about Aud's fortune, about destiny and whether any of us are actually in control, as my mom reads: " 'If you have something worth fighting for, then fight for it.' " She laughs, too, waving her slip of paper like a white flag. "I'm fighting to finish my book, and I hope it'll be worth it."

Cookies and destiny and fighting . . . They're not *my* fortunes, but they're burrowing under my skin. I think of Mati and the way he looked at me earlier, wistfully, entreatingly, regretfully.

I wish . . . I wish I would have spoken to him, thanked him aloud, at the very least.

My chest constricts, and I shift in my seat. Bambi, who's lying under my chair, nudges my ankle with her muzzle, a show of doggy support.

"Your turn, Auntie," Janie prompts, pushing my cookie closer.

I open the cellophane with reluctance, feeling too old, too jaded for this game. Fortunes are malleable; we make of them what we want— what we *need*.

My cookie crumbles as I attempt to halve it, a bad omen. Apprehension skips across my skin. I read silently, the hairs on the back of my neck standing up. My eyes swim with tears as I skim the tiny words again. . . .

Stop wishing. Start doing.

MATI

When the ringing begins,
I am at the park,
in our memory-steeped turret.
The night is alight with stars.

I pull my phone from my pocket,
filled with nerves,
with dread,
with hope.

I miss her like twilight misses the sun.

For a moment,
I can only watch her name
as it blinks tirelessly
against the illuminated screen.

Why now?

She is calling to tell me enough.
Enough calls, enough messages.
Enough wishes of goodwill sent on the breeze.
She is calling to tell me to stay away.

Now, we have a sense of how it will be
when I leave America for Afghanistan.
Something like drowning,
or being buried alive.
Sadness blacking out sensation.
Despair drawing hope away.

I am so scared.

I consider letting her call fade,
unanswered,
into the night.

But I am not that strong.

elise

*t*he eager hum of his voice makes me feel like I've been shaken out of a deep sleep: anxious, alert, *awake.*

It's late. Audrey and Janie went home hours ago, and it's long past my mom's bedtime. Long past the time I should be asleep. Tonight... I couldn't even lie down. I'm jumpy, full of worries, and questions, and doubts. I keep thinking about my fortune. It's just a silly luck-of-the-draw prediction that means nothing, except...

It means everything.

He says my name, softly, almost like he's sleeptalking. Sitting cross-legged at the foot of my bed, Bambi's head resting in my lap, I try to guess his mood based on his tone alone. But it's been too long since our last conversation, when he was frustrated and tense, speaking sharply and imploringly. That's the voice that's tolled in my head over the last few days. Desperate and despairing. Hopeless.

Tonight he sounds... different.

"I'm happy you called," he says, though happy isn't how I'd describe his timbre.

I don't know how to respond. I can't even explain *why* I called—to feel close to him, I guess. I pet Bambi's head, grasping for a calm that keeps slipping away.

"Elise," he says. "Are you there?"

Cautious. Uncertain. Nervous. *That's* how he sounds.

"I'm here," I whisper.

"Are you at home?"

"Where else would I be?"

"On your way to the park? To see me?"

"You're at the park?"

"In our turret."

I lift my hair away from my neck, my skin too warm. Bambi groans, protesting my movement. "Why?"

"Because I couldn't sleep. I didn't know where else to go."

"I can't sleep, either."

I expect him to ask me to join him, and I'm glad when he doesn't. I'm not sure I have the willpower to turn him down. "Thank you again for bringing Bambi home."

"She was sitting in front of our cottage, wagging her tail. I was so glad to see her."

A stretch of silence passes. I wonder if he's been going to the beach the last few days. If he's waited, looking for my dog and me. The image of him standing alone on the sand makes my breath shallow.

"How's your baba?"

"Better. His last scan is tomorrow. Based on his recent progress, his doctors have high hopes."

"That means . . . ?"

"That our time in America is nearly done."

In two days, he'll board a plane. He'll fly halfway around the world. He'll land in Afghanistan and reunite with his siblings. It's so simple, and yet . . . I can't wrap my head around the idea of him not here—not with me.

"I bet you're looking forward to getting home," I say, cringing even as the words leave my mouth. This conversation is forced, falsely polite.

If I'd known I wouldn't have the guts to say what I want to say, I wouldn't have bothered him with my call.

"Elise." His voice, his beautiful storm cloud voice, sounds pained, like he's stretching for something infinitely valuable, yet just out of reach. "I'm happy you called," he says again, as if he's trying to cement the notion in his head, "but *why* did you call?"

Stop wishing. Start doing.

I take a deep breath. It doesn't keep my hands from shaking, but it does make me feel less like I'm going to throw up. "I called because I miss you," I say. It's the truth, but only a fraction of it. "I called because the other day in your yard, things went unsaid. I was shocked, and hurt, and so, *so* mad, and I didn't listen when you tried to explain. I'm sorry for that."

"You should not be the one apologizing."

"It's okay. I needed to get that out."

"Do you feel better?"

"No. I feel terrible."

"I'm sorry, too," he says after a moment's pause.

"Because I found out?"

"No. Because I didn't tell you myself. My reasons for keeping Panra secret were wrong. What you said was true: I knew you'd think differently of me if I told you what waited at home. You, not a part of this summer . . . I couldn't let it happen."

"You were selfish," I say.

He's quiet, and I worry I've pulled the plug on his honesty. Then, softly, he says, "I was."

I fold over to rest my head against Bambi's, comforted by her presence, by Mati's voice. Since he's being so forthcoming, I whisper one of my truths. "I wish I could hate you. Life would be so much easier. I keep wondering . . . Why do I still care?"

"Have you arrived at an answer?"

I breathe through the ache behind my ribs. "Because I know now how it feels to lose you."

"Gutted," he says. "Like a snared fish."

"I was going to go with hollow, like a tree left to rot on the forest floor."

"And you think you're not good with words."

I laugh, tinny and stuttered. "You're better. Have you been writing?"

"Page after page. Lines wrought with angst. I don't think you'd be impressed."

"Oh, I bet I would." It feels good, this lightness after days of dark, but I can't forget what's next: the detailed reality of his future, and the terrifying blankness of mine. "So. Two days?"

"Two days. I'd give anything to spend them with you."

"Two days with your secret girlfriend before you take off to woo your fiancé?"

"Elise." There's conflict in the strained way he says my name, and that old ember of hope sparks to life. "I can't promise she won't be a part of my life, but now, after the last week, I can't tell you that she *will*. If I were thinking only of myself, the decision to return to America one day, to start a new life as a student and a writer, a life with *you*, would be simple. But my choices impact others, and I cannot be careless when so much is at stake."

"Mati, if you come back to America, do it for you. Or, go somewhere else—France or Brazil or, God, Japan. Somewhere that'll make you happy. Be with someone you choose—someone you love. Live the life you want to live."

"Someday, maybe I could."

I want him to say more; I want him to say *I will*. I want to fall asleep knowing his future holds pleasure and contentment, even if I can't be a part of it.

"If I promise to think about it," he says, "can I see you before I go?"

There's a whisper in my ear, quiet, insistent words . . .

Stop wishing. Start doing.

"Meet me tomorrow morning," I say. "At the beach."

MATI

Meet me tomorrow morning. At the beach.

It is all I have wanted to do
since we hung up last night.
But I could not meet her because
this morning was Baba's final scan.

I walk toward the ocean now,
after midday prayer,
while the sun is high in the sky.
I am a patchwork of emotions:
relieved and exhilarated,
anxious and heavyhearted.
My seams are stitched haphazardly,
and I am slowly unraveling.

My time with her has run out,
and I can hardly face the fact of it.

Cowardice urges me to retreat,
but my soul is a compass
whose needle points to her.

She is waiting by the surf,
long hair lashing in the wind.
She is radiant against the steely sky.
I will never love anyone the way I love her—
I know that now.
The trick is in reconciling my feelings,
with my future.

I call her name.
She turns to the sound of my voice.
She walks toward me,
her expression impossible to decipher.
She stops before I can reach for her and,
for an immeasurable moment
we stand,
staring into each other's eyes.

"How's your baba?" she asks.

"Healthy. He has been cleared to go."

She blinks, happy for Baba, sad for *us*.
Her feelings are mine, in duplicate.

"Tell him I'm glad for him," she says.
She paints a smile with careful strokes,
her eyes glittering with tears.
"So, tomorrow . . . ?"

"Tomorrow I fly home."

She takes a step toward me, timid,
as if she is worried I will turn her away.

When I open my arms,
her hesitancy vanishes.
She walks into them,
into me,
and for the first time since we argued . . .

I breathe.

elise

Audrey calls a while after I get home. She tells me she and Janie are coming over, then hangs up quickly, like I might tell her to stay home if given the chance.

I sprawl out on my bed to wait.

Today at the beach . . . All afternoons should be so lovely. Mati and I took a long walk, indulged in a kiss that's forever etched in my memory, and said our goodbyes. He was sensible, and I was realistic. We were more composed than I thought us capable. Tears would have tarnished the good we shared—that's what I tell myself every time sadness threatens to drown me.

My door swings open, and Audrey and Janie barrel in. Janie's dragging bags from the local home-improvement store—they're nearly twice her size—and Aud's lugging gallons of paint.

"What's all this?" I ask, sitting up.

"What do you think?" She looks around my room, nose turned up. "We're going to fix your walls."

"There's nothing wrong with my walls," I say, indignant. But okay, my walls are depressing, and I've known as much for a while. I've been hoping I'd get used to the Obsidian, but here I am, almost ready to start school, and I still feel gloom settle over me every time I set foot in here, which, lately, is often. I eye the cans Audrey's set on the floor. "What color did you choose?"

Janie pipes up. "Mama said no pink."

Audrey smiles. "I didn't think you'd go for it, though I found a gorgeous cotton candy color I might get for Janie's room. For you . . ." She pulls a paint strip from the pocket of her tattered jeans and shows me a blue-green square. "It's called 'Splashy.' Cute, right?"

I study the color. "Reminds me of the ocean."

"Better than a darkroom?"

I shrug, downplaying my enthusiasm. "Do you think it'll cover?"

She taps one of the cans. "Primer. Obviously, I've thought of everything."

Janie grins up at me. "I'll help paint, too, Auntie."

I point at the stars on my ceiling. "They stay."

It takes a while to haul my furniture into the middle of the room and clear the walls of photographs. We're almost done when my mom pokes her head in to ask about the commotion. When she sees paint cans and drop cloths and brushes scattered about the floor, she grimaces. "Are you girls sure you're up for this?" she asks, eyeing me like I might disintegrate at any moment.

"Of course we're up for it," Audrey says. "Want to help?"

Mom smiles, running a hand over my hair as I walk by with a roll of blue painter's tape. She's been particularly nice since Bambi's stint as a runaway. "I'll pass, but let me know when you're ready for refreshments."

She retreats to her library—forty-eight hours until deadline—and not long after, we're ready to crack the cans open. Janie keeps Bambi occupied, holding a bone steady while my dog gnaws. She and Audrey ooh and ahh as I roll tinted primer onto the wall. Their excitement is warranted—even this is an improvement.

Audrey gets busy with the trim. "When's the boy next door heading back to Texas?" she asks, cutting primer along the door molding.

"Tomorrow. I don't know what I'm going to do with myself when he leaves."

"You can visit him."

"Yeah, maybe."

Janie climbs up on my bed, floating in the center of the room like an island, and pages through the picture books her mama brought to keep her busy. I continue rolling, working up a sweat, and Aud makes progress with the edging. I can tell by the way she furrows her brow, concentrating: she's got more than paint on her mind.

Finally, tentatively, she says, "When does Mati leave?"

I cease my work to face her. "Tomorrow. And since when do you call him by his name?"

Her paintbrush hovers idly next to the wall. She opens her mouth to respond, but then Janie pipes up. "Mama hates Mati."

Audrey blinks at her. "I don't hate anybody, baby."

Janie turns the page of the book on her lap, then glances up, all innocence. "Yes you do. I heard you telling Auntie that he can't come over. Too bad, because Mati brings wishes, and he tells silly stories."

Aud glances at the floor, then at me. "I haven't been very nice," she says quietly.

"No. You haven't."

"Have you talked to him?"

I consider lying. To save face, to save this evening, but I can't. I'm tired of feeling disgraceful about a relationship that's anything but. I go back to rolling, but I watch her as I say, "I saw him today at the beach."

"Oh." She dips her brush, wiping off excess paint before taking it to the wall. "Is he going to marry that girl?"

"I don't know. He doesn't know. He's considering alternatives."

"Because of you."

"Not in the way you think. He writes. He's smart, Aud. Maybe he'll come to the US and go to school. Or maybe he'll go to Europe and find a job at a magazine. Maybe he'll return to Kabul and decide he loves it, or maybe he'll go to Ghazni and meet Panra and discover she's exactly the person he wants to spend his life with. I don't care, so long as he's happy."

I want to mean it. I *so* want to mean it.

Audrey props her brush on the lip of the can and crosses the room to loop an arm around me. I let my roller hang at my side and lean into her, trying to smother the sob that's scaling my throat. We stand, silent, staring at the melancholy gray-blue primer, and I feel an overwhelming sense of solidarity; Audrey is intimately familiar with loss. I'm starting to understand what she's known for years: love can't always be enduring—at least not corporeally. But love can be generosity. It can be selflessness. It can be wanting more for the other, even though *more* is currently making me feel like my heart's being pillaged and surrendered for the greater good.

"I'm sorry, Lissy," Audrey says. "I should've trusted your judgment. You deserve that much—*more*, considering everything you've done for Janie and me over the last few years."

I swallow. I will not cry—not now, not anymore. I will not feel sorry for myself, because meeting Mati, getting to know him deeply and completely, has been a gift. I'm going to lose it to circumstance, but I've held it in my hands, and delighted in the perfect weight of it.

That has to be enough.

Later, after we've pried open the can of Splashy paint and rolled two coats onto the walls, we lie on my bed with Janie, who's shaken herself awake from a snooze. We admire our efforts and I admit, only a little begrudgingly, that Audrey was right: The black was dreadful, and this new color, cool and cheerful, is a vast improvement. I feel better than I have in days, and I say as much. Audrey takes my hand and gives it an affectionate squeeze. I take Janie's and pass the gesture along.

Even knowing that tomorrow will be the worst, I feel lucky.

elise

i love Audrey for being so damn pushy about paint colors. Her chosen blue-green is equal parts tranquil and buoyant, and my ceiling of
silver stars is kind of beautiful suspended above it.

My furniture is back in place, and my photos are back on the
walls. Early this morning, I processed the one I took of Mati in front
of his cottage, printed it out, and tacked it over my desk. A reminder
of this summer, of my first love.

He's leaving, he's leaving, he's leaving.

The air in my bedroom smells chemically, of pigment and hard
work. I've got my window open in an attempt to flush out the fumes
while I sit on my bed with my computer, sorting through the digital
images I took of Janie yesterday, paintbrush clasped in her little hand.
As always, she's an ideal distraction. I'm cleaning up a picture of her
almost touching the tip of her brush to Bambi's nose when I hear voices
out front.

I leave my laptop on the quilt and move to the window, looking out
toward the street where Xavier's Jeep is parked. He and Ryan are
standing beside it.

Ryan's leaving for the airport soon, and they're obviously saying their goodbyes. I'm blatantly spying, but I can't help myself. Watching them, I suffer their emotions like they're my own. Xavier's shoulders are slumped, and Ryan's crying like a big baby, fogging up his glasses. But as painful as it appears, there's something hopeful about their goodbye, something honeyed and full of promise. Because, of course, Ryan and Xavier will see each other again.

I think about what Xavier said at the diner last week, his advice regarding my argument with Mati. How, even if he and I move into our individual futures without further contact, I'm better for knowing him. Xavier is right, and he and Ryan are living that sentiment now. I see it in the way Ryan hugs him, laughing through his tears. I see it in the way he touches Ryan's hand before climbing into his Jeep.

I hurry down the hall and out the front door of our cottage, calling out just before he shifts into gear. "You were going to take off without saying goodbye to me?" I say through the Jeep's open window.

He reaches out to tug my ponytail. "I'll still see you," he says. "You're stuck with me until I'm done at the MLI, until I ditch Cypress Beach for bigger, better assignments."

"Want to meet at The Hamlet this weekend? We can drink milkshakes while feeling sorry for ourselves."

He smiles. "You got it." He looks at Ryan. "Call me when you get in?"

Ryan nods, sniffling. I link my arm through his and we stand together, waving until the Jeep disappears around the corner.

"Well," Ryan says. "That sucked."

"I bet. And to think, you still have to say goodbye to me."

"About that. I was thinking that we just . . . don't."

"What do you mean?"

"You better believe I'll be imposing myself on your life even after I get back to Texas. So what's the point of a drawn-out goodbye when it'll just make us feel shitty?"

"There is no point. Especially since I barely survived my goodbye with Mati."

Ryan shakes his head. "I can't believe you're not going to see him today."

"Am I awful?"

"I don't know. Maybe you're smart—smarter than me, anyway. Because it's pretty terrible, watching someone you care about drive away."

"Being smart has nothing to do with it," I admit, doubting my decision to cut off contact a day early. But, no—I'm surviving. I look at the cracked sidewalk, avoiding Ryan's gaze. "My heart physically cannot handle another encounter with him."

He slips his hand into mine. "I don't want you to be sorry later."

"I won't. Yesterday at the beach . . . He knows how I feel."

But does he? Did I tell him how deeply he's affected me? Did I tell him I don't want him to go? A thousand times I talked about how we'll never work, but did I ever tell him how often I wish we could?

He's leaving, he's leaving, he's leaving.

Oh God, this is agonizing.

Iris pokes her head out the door, jingling her keys. "Ready to head for the airport?"

Ryan juts his lower lip out in a pouty face so ridiculous I can't help but smile. I throw my arms around him. "You're going to have a blast at A&M, and you're going to come back to stay with Iris the first chance you get. Xavier and I will come to Texas and kidnap you if you don't."

He laughs, weepy-sounding. "I'll miss you, neighbor. Make some friends at that new school of yours, but don't forget about me."

"Never."

He gives me one last hug. He draws back and removes his glasses, then uses his T-shirt to polish them. "Go inside," he says with a valorous smile, "or I'll never get out of here."

I back slowly toward our gate. "Good thing we skipped the drawn-out goodbye."

He smiles his golden Ryan smile. "See you soon, Elise."

elise

My mom's waiting in the foyer. She sees my face, my tears, and sweeps me up in a hug.

It's been a long time since she's held me this way, a long time since she's shown affection that wasn't motivated by panic or guilt. I hug her back, an instinctual reaction because she's *Mom*, but my head's spinning.

She must sense my internal chaos, because she eases back and blots my face with the sleeve of her blouse. "You'll see Ryan again."

"I know," I say, leaning in to her, trying to counteract the weightlessness I'm experiencing. After a summer characterized by bests and worsts, I'm back where I started—a loner in a rented cottage, and I have no idea what to do with myself.

She takes my hand and leads me to the kitchen. She sits me down at the table, where I lean over to stroke Bambi's head. I watch Mom fill the coffeemaker with water and scoop ground beans into a paper filter. She finds the perfectly imperfect mug Nick made and spoons sugar into its bottom, humming as the kitchen fills with the aroma of coffee.

After a few minutes, she brings my mug and one for herself, then sits down with me. "Rough day."

It's not a question, but I nod.

"Things will improve. Summers are funny that way. They're days unaccounted for, a time-out from real life. As soon as school starts, you'll be yourself again."

She's trying to help, but she's only succeeding in making me want to cry all over again. I don't know who I am anymore—I'm not the girl who pulled a stranger out of the surf, who left him sitting alone at a picnic table. I'm not the girl who took him to cemeteries and kissed him in turrets. I'm not the girl who opened her heart because her soul told her she should.

That girl who used to make wishes and count on them to come true—where did she go?

My mom has no clue what happened to me this summer, during those days unaccounted for, and I so desperately want my brother. He was always better with emotions—better with *life*. If he were alive, here in Cypress Beach today, he'd be beside me, acknowledging my feelings instead of attempting to wave them away.

"School's not going to make me feel better," I tell my mom.

She sips her coffee, then changes the subject. "I sent my manuscript to my editor today."

I dig up the wherewithal to smile. "Congratulations."

She puts down her mug, then straightens the pile of napkins in the center of the table. She's focused on her task when she says, "I want us to spend more time together, Lissy. I want to come to the beach with you and Bambi. I want you to show me more of your photographs. I want to hear about the classes you'll take this fall. And I'd like for us to go to Sacramento together, to see Nick. I've been thinking about what you said, how I haven't been present, and you're right. Since your brother . . . I haven't been myself."

"Mom, neither of us has."

"But you've managed your grief better than me."

"He was your son. There's no right way to cope with his death."

She shrugs, allowing this, then reaches for my hand. Her palm is cool and dry. "I hate that I've disappointed you this summer, but my feelings regarding that boy haven't changed. I'm relieved he's leaving— look how miserable he's made you. He's not good for you, Elise. He will *never* be good for you."

"Because he's Muslim."

She looks at me, unflinching in her bigotry. "You'll understand, one day. You'll meet a nice boy, the *right* boy. You'll have children of your own, children you're desperate to protect, and you'll see that what I've been saying is true. You'll see that I've had your best interests in mind. When you're older, when you've gained some life experience, this summer will become nothing but a distant memory."

She's wrong—she's *so* wrong. This summer may amount to a memory, but that doesn't make my feelings less real. That doesn't excuse her intolerance, her refusal to see Mati for who he is rather than where he's from. It's unbelievably audacious, her assertion that I'm the one who needs to acquire life experience. She's so stuck in her head, in her *racism*, she can't see good when it's right in front of her.

She purses her lips. "I know it's hard now, but trust me—his going back to where he came from? You'll be better off in the long run."

I rear back, shocked that she'd say such a thing, today of all days, while I sit empty, desolate as a dried up lake bed. I think of that afternoon with my brother, when he gave money to the homeless veteran in San Francisco. *Don't walk through life blind,* he told me.

I have never understood a directive so clearly.

Our mother is blind; Nicky was not.

I want to be just like him.

I rise from my chair. "I won't be better off when Mati goes back to Afghanistan, Mom. Whenever I think of him, for the rest of my life, my heart will hurt. Neither time nor distance will change that. You won't, either. I love him, and I don't care if you approve. I will *never* care if you approve."

I turn on my heels and walk out of the kitchen. I don't have strength left for arguing or spite or bitterness; I'm sapped just trying to keep it together. Besides, my mom's the loser in all this—she missed out on Mati.

And so I make my way out the front door, into the fresh air of the yard. I march all the way to the sidewalk, where I continue to move west, toward the beach, because there's nowhere else I'd rather be while I'm so consumed with thinking of him.

I'll never see him again, I think, my feet dragging.

I should have told him. I should have said it outright....

Mati, I don't want you to go.

MATI

I walk to the beach in a fog,
driven by a desire to see the horizon,
that elusive place where water meets sky.
This beach, after all,
is where she swept me to sea.

My bags are packed.
Our cottage is tidy.
It is nearly time to go,
to fly, fly, fly home.
But first . . .

I reach the cluster of picnic tables,
where the air smells of salt and cypress,
and is haunted by conversations past.
I run a hand over the smooth tabletop
where I once left her a message,
then make my way to the stairs.

I find the beach empty,
with the exception of a lone figure—
a figure so familiar, my stomach dives,
seagull-like,
before soaring skyward again.

She is sitting on a driftwood log,
knees pulled to her chest,
wearing the sweatshirt her brother gave her.
I move closer,
studying her as the space between us shrinks.
Her caramel hair hangs loose around her shoulders.
Her eyes are bright, her cheeks rosy-red.
She is biting her lip, distorting her heart-shaped mouth.

Even now,
as an overwhelming sense of loss thickens the air,
as my ears buzz
and my eyes burn
and my knees quake . . .

She dazzles me.

Since we said goodbye yesterday,
I have been a dandelion seed adrift,
snagged by an errant breeze.
Now, I am rooted.

Rooted in her.

She is not surprised to see me,
and so,
I think it is meant to be.
I sit beside her,
take her in my arms,

murmur against her ear,
"Za ta sara meena kwam."
I speak to her in Pashto;
my voice is sure to break
if I attempt English.

She fists my shirt in her hands,
pulling me closer,
her long hair whipping in the wind.
She exhales, shaky, and says,
"Mati, please. I don't want you to go."

"I have to. You know I do.
I cannot forsake my family. . . .
Not yet."

My parents and I
have spoken about the future.
Baba is unhappy,
but says he will try to smooth things over
with Panra and her family.
I think, perhaps,
he is envious of my autonomy.
Mama thinks I am selfish, foolish, idealistic.
She cannot look at me without disdain.

My parents' displeasure
will never be enough
to keep me from her.

I take her face in my hands.
Her cheeks are hot, damp with tears.
I look into her eyes,
and make the only promise that will ever matter.

"Elise, I will come back to you."

Close your eyes. Fall in love. Stay there.

—Rumi

elise

My senior year passes with surprising speed.

Somewhere between my part-time job at The Hamlet, work on my photography portfolio, and monthly trips to Sacramento to visit my brother, I get to know the girl I spent the summer becoming.

In September, I join Cypress Valley High's yearbook staff. Quickly, I become a lead photographer. I make friends. Maybe not forever friends, but I think that's okay. I find myself laughing again, and anticipating school days with something not unlike enthusiasm. I log countless hours on the phone with Ryan, and video chat with Mati every chance I get. Luckily, connectivity in Kabul is decent.

In November, Audrey and I sign up for a painting class. We're the youngest students by decades. She thinks it's lame, but I become kind of obsessed. I cover canvases with smears of paint: of my dog, San Francisco's skyline, Cypress Beach's horizon.

I still love photography best.

I spend the early months of winter hanging out with Bambi, meeting up with Xavier for milkshakes, and baking cookies with Janie. Ryan comes to visit at Christmastime, bunking at his gram's, so I get to spend tons of time with him. Mati and I continue to email daily—hourly, sometimes. I send him snapshots of our beach, our park, any dandelion I happen upon. He sends me poems about nothing, and poems about everything.

In January, after a painting class I attend on my own (because Audrey gave up brushes and acrylics weeks ago), I treat myself to a slice of pie at The Hamlet. I have a table to myself, only my thoughts for company, and it feels good, being alone but not lonely; it's a sense of peace, a strengthening of character thanks to new people and new experiences.

I realize I like this girl I've become. I think my brother would, too.

It's there at that table, halfway through my wedge of cherry pie, that I make myself a promise: I will continue to funnel energy into myself, but I will try to reestablish a relationship with my mom, too. It will have to be a new relationship—a *different* relationship—because while her opinions regarding Afghans and Muslims and *Mati* haven't changed, I think it's possible to love her despite her prejudices.

On a chilly Saturday morning in February, as I'm getting ready to drive to Sacramento to see Nick, she walks into my room. "I'd like to come along," she says, voice quavering.

I turn away from my mirror to face her. She's dressed in a pair of khakis and a cable-knit sweater, and she's holding two travel mugs. "I'd like that," I tell her. "Nicky would, too."

She drives, slow and cautious. Halfway to the cemetery, she broaches the topic that's been tabled since August: Mati. "You're still in contact with him?"

"Every day."

"What's going to happen?"

"I don't know, Mom. Hopefully, I'll see him again—we're working on it."

"It's not good for you, pining for that boy."

"I'm not pining for him—I'm carrying on. I'm staying busy. I'm making a life for myself. But I love him, and nothing you say will change that."

"I wish you'd never met him," she murmurs, almost to herself.

I pat her arm, sorry for her obstinacy, and sad about the good she misses because of it. But my sympathy only stretches so far, and my voice is ironclad when I tell her, "I'm so glad I did."

This is what I've learned: While my mom might continue to dig her heels in regarding Mati, his culture, and his religion, I don't have to stop modeling acceptance. I don't have to stop believing that someday, she'll come around.

In March, Xavier moves to San Antonio. He's been stationed at Lackland Air Force Base, less than three hours from Texas A&M. I'm bummed to see him go but thrilled for him and Ryan. I use my surplus of free time to do more reading on Islam. I learn about its doctrine and its customs. I come to appreciate its history and its values.

In April, I find out that I've been accepted into the San Francisco Art Institute. Mom cries, and I do, too. I'm happy—so, so happy—but I'm going to miss Cypress Beach. I start to spend more time on the sand, more time on the quiet sidewalks, more time in the overpriced boutiques. I soak it up, this town I thought I'd hate.

In June, I graduate from Cypress Valley High. I ask my manager at The Hamlet to up my hours. I squirrel away every cent I earn. Living in San Francisco is costly, and even though my mom has agreed to help me with rent (I found a furnished studio apartment in a safe neighborhood, close to campus), there will be plenty of other expenses.

In August, I begin to pack my things. I spend every spare minute with Bambi, because she has to stay in Cypress Beach while I'm away at school. I hope she'll keep my mom in check.

A week before the semester is to begin, I walk my dog next door, where Iris will keep watch over her while my family and I head for San Francisco. Then I climb into the loaded-down BMW with Mom, Audrey, and Janie, and we drive north to the city.

They help me unpack. Audrey paints the wall next to my bed the same blue-green she picked for my room back home. I hang some of my photographs and paintings, sporadic, like a little gallery. My mom stocks my cabinets with cereal and bread and cans of tuna, new dishes, a toaster, and a rice cooker. Janie draws a picture of the four Parker girls on a stray sheet of packing paper, then tapes it to the fridge.

When they leave, a piece of my heart trails behind them.

At the same time, though, *finally*, I am free. Free to make choices that are right for me, to love the soul handpicked for mine.

Two days later, I hail a cab for a ride to the San Francisco International Airport.

Mati has been granted a student visa and accepted at San Francisco State.

I am *joyful*.

Like me, he's renting a studio apartment. I checked it out for him yesterday; it's only a few blocks from where I'm living. It's full of light and there's a built-in writing desk next to a big bay window. It's perfect.

I arrive at the airport early and loiter near the baggage carousels. The place is full of people: families returning from tropical vacations, smartly dressed men and women traveling for business, plus lots of greeters, like me. I long to pace the floor, but it's too crowded and I'm reluctant to appear as eager as I feel. I snag a miraculously empty chair and people-watch, fidgeting, until . . .

Oh God.

Until I see him walking toward me, long and lean and beautiful. He's wearing jeans and a black T-shirt, and there's a sweatshirt draped across his arm. He's got a backpack slung over one shoulder. His hair is shorter than it was the last time we video chatted, like he's recently had it trimmed.

His eyes are the same—bright, blazing.

They settle on me, and his face opens in a grin, and before I register moving, I'm out of my seat, running toward him. I leap into his arms, wrap myself around him, bury my face in his neck. We're a spectacle.

He's laughing and I'm laughing and finally, *finally*, I pull myself together enough to call up the sentiment I've written at the end of every email, every letter I've sent him over the last year.

Only now, I get to use it while holding his hands, while losing myself to his wildfire gaze.

"Za ta sara meena kwam."

He grins, misty-eyed, and kisses me.

Minutes, hours, *days* pass. I'd forgotten this—how his kisses feel, and how they make me feel. When it's over, I'm warm, malleable, practically purring. He grins, knowing, and weaves his fingers through mine. Hand in hand, we walk to the baggage carousel, where we'll wait for his luggage.

"So," he says, pulling me into his chest, touching my hair, my cheeks, my neck, his eyes skimming my face like centuries have passed and all he cares to do is relearn my features. "This is San Francisco."

I smile up at him. "This is San Francisco. We've been waiting for you."

"No more waiting," he says. "No more distance. Never again."

This time I kiss him, and it's the *best* kiss, because I'm certain now. A million more will follow.

ACKNOWLEDGMENTS

I am so fortunate to be part of the Swoon Reads family, where I feel at all times supported and celebrated. Jean Feiwel and Lauren Scobell, thank you for cultivating this incredible community. Kat Brzozowski, working with you has been a dream. Your insight, wisdom, and warmth have taught me so much. Because of you, *The Impossibility of Us* is a book I am truly proud of.

Kelsey Marrujo, thank you for rocking all things publicity. Emily Settle, thank you for your helpfulness and eternal patience. Ashley Woodfolk, thank you for championing this book, and for your brilliant title suggestion—it's so much better than mine was! Lauren Forte, thank you for lending your copyediting expertise to this story. Liz Dresner and Becca Syracuse, thank you for the beautiful, beautiful cover; I still can't stop staring at it! And to the authors known affectionately as the Swoon Squad, um . . . wow. What an amazing group of people to walk this road with.

Victoria Marini, I can't imagine doing this publication thing without you. Your guidance, expertise, and humor are invaluable. Thank you, thank you, thank you for everything.

Arvin Ahmadi, Rania, and Silanur, thank you for imparting your knowledge of Islam on this story, and me. Your thoughtful feedback and generously shared personal experiences have made Mati, Rasoul, and Hala stronger and more complex characters. Khalid Ahmad, thank you so much for your assistance with the Pashto translations in this book. Any inaccuracies in story or text are mine alone.

Alison Miller, Temre Beltz, Riley Edgewood, and Elodie Nowodazkij, you are far and away the best critique partners a girl could ask for. Your combined intelligence, compassion, and generosity are awe-inspiring. I am a better writer thanks to the four of you. Additional thanks to Rachel Simon, Jaime Morrow, and Lola Sharp for the beta reads. Your early enthusiasm was exactly the encouragement I needed.

Tracey Neithercott, Karole Cozzo, Mandie Baxter, Liz Parker, Christina June, Jessica Love, Christa Desir, Sara Biren, and Erin Bowman, thank you for the reassurances, the much needed moments of commiseration, and the celebrations. How lucky I am to have you all in my life. And to the many 2017 Debuts who've become wonderful friends, thank you for sharing this journey with me.

Mom and Dad, thank you for your boundless support and infinite love, and for hand-selling my books to your friends. Mike and Zach, while you might not be fans of young adult romance, I know you're fans of *me* and really, isn't that all that matters? ☺

Bev and Phil, thank you for making me feel like part of the family from day one. Andy, Danielle, Grant, Reid, Caroline, Sam, Kacie, Grandpa, Michele, Gabe, Teddy, and Thomas, your continued cheerleading means the world to me.

Claire, you inspire me every day. I look forward to putting this book in your hands; I hope you love it as much as the Judy Blume novels you're constantly devouring. Lizzie, you are a source of endless smiles, and I'm eternally grateful for your presence in our lives. Girls, you bring me indescribable joy. Love you forever.

Matt, this book wouldn't exist without you. Thank you for the nudge, and for your help with the story's mentions of the military and Afghanistan. Your genuine excitement over my successes, both big and small, make me feel unstoppable, and very loved. You are an amazing friend, father, and husband, and you are *still* my happily ever after.

Check out more books chosen for publication by readers like you.

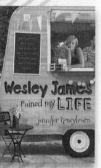   

DID YOU KNOW...

readers like you
helped to get this
book published?

Join our book-obsessed community and help us
discover awesome new writing talent.

1

Write it.

Share your original YA manuscript.

2

Read it.

Discover bright new bookish talent.

3

Share it.

Discuss, rate, and share your faves.

4

Love it.

Help us publish the books you love.

Share your own manuscript or dive between the pages
at **swoonreads.com** or by downloading the **Swoon Reads app**.